STORM

*For Arthur, John and Mavis
who were storytellers*

STORM

ALEX HUBBARD

Seren is the book imprint of
Poetry Wales Press Ltd
Suite 6, 4 Derwen Road, Bridgend,
Wales, CF31 1LH

www.serenbooks.com
Follow us on social media @SerenBooks

© Alex Hubbard, 2025.

The right of Alex Hubbard to be identified as
the author of this work has been asserted in accordance
with the Copyright, Designs and Patents Act, 1988.

ISBN: 978-1-91175-205-9
eBook: 978-1-91175-209-7

A CIP record for this title is available from the British Library.

All rights reserved. No part of this publication may be reproduced,
stored in a retrieval system, or transmitted at any time or by any means,
electronic, mechanical, photocopying, recording or otherwise without
the prior permission of the copyright holder.

The publisher acknowledges the financial assistance of the
Books Council of Wales.

EU GPSR Authorised Representative
Logos Europe, 9 rue Nicolas Poussin, 17000,
La Rochelle, France
E-mail: Contact@logoseurope.eu

No part of this book may be used or reproduced in any manner
for the purpose of training artificial intelligence technologies or systems.

Cover artwork: Clock tower adapted from original,
photograph © Jaggery (cc-by-sa/2.0)
Bowl adapted from original, photograph by Mae Mu
Walking figure adapted from original, photograph by Leon Seibert
Open book adapted from original, photograph by Pixabay

Printed by 4Edge Ltd, Hockley.

This is a work of fiction. All of the characters, organisations,
and events portrayed in this novel are either products of the
author's imagination or are used fictitiously.

Ar Galfaria yr ymrwygodd
Holl ffynonau'r dyfnder mawr.
Torrodd holl argaeau'r nefoedd
Oeddynt gytfain hyd yn awr:
Gras a chariad megis dylif
Yn ymdywallt yma'nghyd,
A chyfiawnder pur a heddwch
Yn cusanu euog fyd

[On the mount of crucifixion
fountains opened deep and wide.
through the floodgates of God's mercy
flowed a vast and gracious tide.
Grace and love, like mighty rivers,
poured incessant from above,
and heav'n's peace and perfect justice
kissed a guilty world in love]

'Dyma Gariad Fel y Moroedd' by Gwilym Hiraethog

FIRST DAY

CHAPTER ONE

I like to believe the last moment of your life is the longest one. That final breath, when the tired lungs balloon to become a little larger than they were before, a limp memory of more oxygened days, with the body itself now a tired and out-dated mechanism, must feel like eons.

Yes, as we age, time moves quickly, but only because we are tired of it. We know it too well. We do not know death, so it must feel endless. I have always been very afraid of endings. This makes my job very difficult.

But picture it: they are dying. The fire is low, and from their bed it is a blurry, diminished haze of red embers and, below, a low black cloud of coal. On the television, an actor hands a small, four-pointed medal to a man in a fluffy black hat.

'It's just not for me,' he says, with some sadness.

In the time it takes for him to finish the sentence, they will be dead. They are alone. All those who loved them are away from here. Some are making arrangements: phone calls in a hushed voice arranging childcare, morbid innuendos with doctors and nurses, lukewarm lunches in the hospital canteen. Others have sent flowers, letters, and prayers, and now can only hope. Dying in bed, they wonder – where is Josephine?

A name. Our first. A daughter, born both before and after this death. Lost, like Caine in the wilderness. Come home, little lamb. Let us forgive you. Let us love you. I cannot die without a last kiss.

No, I am being selfish again. Forgive me. I hurt you. I should have loved you with all of myself. I did not. Now, you'll wander, away from it all. But I am wandering, too. I will wander from death and across time. I still have my last breath, and there are so many ways to find you.

I confess, not every voice you will hear is my own. But we are coming, now – coming to the beginning. Bring your book closer to the light and see the words before you. Close your eyes and feel me. Do not worry. I am no one.

We are looking for her.

I'm sure all of this will seem quite unbelievable to you. But time and place are not what you think they are. Let me show you our story. It will be utterly true, I promise.

*

Before the beginning, a student said he could swim in the sea during a storm. Then he went swimming: having stripped to his briefs, his skin pimpled, his member shrivelling, his breath shortening. He ran towards the water which gathered itself into a steely coloured wall, and leapt. He told his friends that he would complete six strokes out and six strokes back. Water slipped through the slight gap between his lips and began to fill. It went under and over. Backwards and forwards. Three strokes in, the student started to cough. Water spluttered out. Over the wind, his friends shouted *come back*. He heard soft sounds, muffled by water's harsher conditions, but kept on. His arm came down. The current caught it. Ashore, they saw him dip beneath the surface. They saw him again four days later, bloated and seaweed strangled.

The world assaulted itself. Along the streets, sewage swilled over from gutters, mixing with rain. Water from above and below. Water from the west. In the town square, a clock tower chimed. Umbrellas took flight up from hands and out to sea. Inside, people made tea. The pier trembled and groaned, steel bending to the will of wind and water. It bowed to the world and fell into the below. Starlings huddled under what was left standing shook their little wings, mourning those that nested too far out.

When it was over, there was a lazy dawn of new light and spent clouds. Life went on. People forgot.

*

But what is happening now? Look into the almost-darkness of the deep sea and the star-scarred sky. Bursts of foam signal the breaking of waves. Creatures swim, crawl, and breathe. Spools of gas burn years ago. We move. We move like a wave, like an unmanned ship, towards the shore which, at this point, is like a constellation covered by cloud: unreachable, unseen, undeniable.

There it is!

Yellow lights, bright and burning. The wind is hard and fast, cutting at your ears and the bones beneath your skin. The waves marshal. Now, there are the shapes of buildings. Hulking above everything, hiding in shadows like the silhouette of a half-moon, is the Old College: yellow brick and high towers and etchings of leaders from long ago. There is the curve of the coast, upon which a lone car moves. A great swell whirls, dashing against the sea wall, rising over railings and onto the pavement as the car turns away.

On land, people are walking. They look out at the sea, eat kebabs, stumble, sing and shout. There are people in the bedrooms of houses and flats trying to sleep.

Where is she?

STORM

*

Josephine is coming out of Yoko's. A streetlamp across the square illuminates falling drops of rain. Long stretches of water stream down the streets. A rivulet leads to the pier and the chirping of nesting starlings and the sea. Another runs down the high street and towards her flat. Josephine, standing under the awning and watching the rain, puts on her coat and zips until metal presses throat. The club logo and the adverts for cheap drinks and deals plastered all over her t-shirt are hidden. The high street is empty. The revellers have gone home, and the takeaways have closed. The early-morning workers have not yet woken. She walks down the middle of the empty road. The hours of touchy hands and hoarse, insistent voices are finished. No one current wants or needs her. She is, for now, no one.

Josephine imagines herself as a drop of rain splashing on and running down tarmac. She thinks of evaporating, whistling steamily into the air, but hunger and thirst make her feel like a balloon: big and bloated with absence. The wind blows against her, whipping her curls back towards the club. Josephine thinks again of drifting, of being lifted. She feels water run down her face. After the heat of the club, it is cooling. The rain pushes down on her like something great from the big up above. Josephine wonders if there is a force strong enough to push her all the way down. Is it too much to want both? To dream simultaneously of flattening and flying?

She imagines the details of this fantasy; caught between the power of sky and the immovability of earth, skin pressed and stretched, bones cracked and ground, blood mixing with water sluicing down gutters, pouring out to the Irish Sea. Her whole self disintegrated, before the first shop has stretched its awning.

Josephine lives above a barber's shop. During the day, the shop is all boys waiting to be sheared and the shop floor is covered in hair so greasy you could fry chips with it. George's haircuts, like the flat above his shop, are cheap and cheerful. Josephine moves past the shop quickly when it is busy. Now, though, the shop is dark and empty, George having swept the floor of yesterday's business. Josephine likes it this way. She wonders if it is possible to keep the shop like this. To keep Aberystwyth like this: quiet, in darkness. Still. She imagines a deep frost rushing through the woods, the hills and the houses. Sometimes, when Josephine is drifting, she thinks of secret, frozen mammoths. She imagines them out in the arctic somewhere, undisturbed and unchanging until someone comes along with a pickaxe, cracks the ice, and with their pencils and pictures, records. And the world has hold of you again.

As Josephine walks upstairs, she smells the cheap thickness of strong instant coffee. The scent wakes her. Robbie is at the table, rolling a cigarette. Steam drifts from his mug.

'Morning,' he says, looking out at the dark window and then back at her. 'Where've you come back from?'

'Work,' says Josephine.

'Really, at this time?' His lips play into a smirk, his words thick with suggestion.

She feels an urge to force every perverse fantasy and wondering from his mind and out of his mouth.

'Yes, really,' she says.

He is quiet. Josephine hangs up her coat and hopes he will let her go.

'What's it like working there?' he asks. 'You must get quite the show every night.'

'I suppose,' says Josephine.

'You ever recognise anybody there? Ever see them doing things they shouldn't?'

Josephine has seen plenty. She's seen Robbie at work, too. How he forces girls into corners, whispers in their ears, hands them VKs. How he riles up the big lads with short tempers. Once, she saw a man hit him. She heard a crack and a crowd of gasps. Saw a rush of people. Then, Robbie dragged to the exit by Fred. He was bleeding and laughing, as if that were all he'd ever wanted.

'I don't see much, to be honest,' says Josephine. 'It's busy.'

'Shame.' He finishes rolling his cigarette and stands up. He stretches his arms and lets out a long yawn. 'I'm going for a smoke.'

He picks up his mug and moves downstairs. Josephine waits until she hears the door shut. She listens to the silence. Her stomach rumbles, interrupting the peace. Josephine puts a slice of bread in the toaster. She fills the kettle with water and flicks its switch. There's no sign of Vic, likely still asleep. Josephine feels safer with Vic.

After eating, she goes to her bedroom, thankful to be away from Robbie. She hears the front door lock turning. Her bedroom is small and narrow with barely enough space to walk around the bed which takes up half the room, a single mattress with several loose springs. The rusted coils dig into her back and the wooden frame sounds as if the boards might break at any moment. She lies down on her bed and sips from her mug. She feels the steam and the flavour revive her senses, finally away from the black paint, bright lights, and booming sounds of Yoko's.

She tries not to think so much. She feels immensely tired, the kind where eyelids will only shut. As if against a clock, she puts her tea on the narrow edge of floor between the bed and the wardrobe. She takes off her jeans and gets under the covers. Josephine is so tired she does not even fear sleep, like she does most nights. She forgets what she will find in her dreams. Soon, she is drifting away, and then, she is falling into what has been waiting for her.

*

The dream of Mother, half rotting flesh, yellow teeth and grey skin, half naked skeleton so white it burns, grinning like she is stuck in a joke that has not reached the punchline. When it begins, Mother's hair is trimmed short across her whole skull, like it was when the treatment started. She tears tufts out, slowly at first, then ferocious and rapid, as if she is digging for something. Josephine tries to look away – wants to escape – but she can't. Her eyes will not shut, her head will not turn, her legs will not run. Mother makes no sound as she tears the last locks of hair from her scalp. For a moment, there is silence. Josephine feels the pain that comes before crying but the tears do not arrive. She contemplates a life trapped under the gaze of this rotting vision. She prays for something to save her. Then, there is the sound. Water on a rusted tin roof. Slow drips, building and hastening. The pops of many different fires all crackling at once. Many voices saying words she can't make out, sounds she doesn't comprehend. Then, starkly, and only briefly, everything. She needs and knows all of something and thinks it will kill her. She kneels.

She wakes. The room is empty. She turns around, moves her feet towards the floor. The dinking of porcelain against wood. Wetness at the bottom of her left foot. In the darkness, she searches for the mug, picks it up and moves it down to beyond the foot of the bed. Thinks about kitchen roll.

There is the grunt of a chair in the kitchen. Robbie is still awake. Not wanting to see him, she takes a dirty top from her wash basket and mops the tea with that. Throws it back in the basket like something shameful. She lies down on the bed, Breathes till her heart slows, till the banging on her ribcage softens. She closes her eyes. Why can't she forget?

*

Six months before, on the anniversary of her mother's death, Josephine went to the beach, took a pill, drank two bottles of wine and climbed a hill. Often, she said this phrase to herself, liking its nursery rhyme quality, how it blunted the sharpness of the day.

Before any of that, she spoke to her dad. She had to explain why she was not coming home. It felt cruel to admit the truth: she did not want to look at old photographs and squeeze his arm as he wept. She said something else instead.

'It's just, emotionally, I'm not sure I feel ready to be in that space at this time,' she said. 'Exams are soon, and I'd hate to lose my stability. But I'm thinking of you. Of course, I am.'

On the other end of the phone, he let out a deep sigh, one of many which drifted down the line. They sounded like coastal winds. 'I understand, darling, of course, I do, though I can't pretend I'm not disappointed. But don't let that affect you, God, no. Look after yourself. That's number one. You and your degree. It's what your mum would have wanted and it's also what I want. Alright?'

'Alright, Dad,' she said. She set the phone to speaker and placed it on the windowsill. Josephine washed a pizza-stained plate from the previous night. The water was hot and made her skin feel sharp.

'Right then, I'd better leave you to it,' said her dad. 'I'll be thinking of you. You know where I am. Just give us a call when you next get a chance.'

Josephine said she would.

'Well, I suppose I should go,' he said, before adding, 'she would be very proud, if she were here now, of you, you know.'

'Thanks,' she said. Neither of them knew what to say, so they said goodbye. Once she was off the line, Josephine stopped cleaning and looked at her reflection in the window. She liked her life more, now. She was happier, if more alone, here. It was easier to see her own lightly dark skin now her mother was dead. How could you try to say such things to the only person that really loved you enough to raise you? She went back to cleaning.

Vic came into the kitchen as Josephine put her plate on the drying rack, holding a copy of a book called *Austerlitz*. She went to the fridge, opened the door and took a white paper bag from the top shelf. She sat at the kitchen table, facing towards the sunlight through the window and Josephine.

'Who was that?' she said. 'Anyone interesting?'

'No,' said Josephine. No one here knew what today was.

Vic opened the bag and pulled out a battered chicken ball, softened from its time in the fridge. She took a bite.

'It's missing something,' she said. 'The sweet and sour sauce. No need to reheat, you're in for a treat, if you have sweet and sour sauce.'

Three nights ago, Vic had watched *Lost in Translation*. Since then, she'd been trying to turn everything into a slogan. Josephine turned around and humoured Vic with a smile. She could feel sunlight through the window. 'Leave some for me,' she said. 'I need some salt and grease.'

Vic got up from the table, opened the fridge again and picked up a polystyrene container. The book and the chicken balls were left on the table, next to each other.

'You can have some,' said Vic. Sitting back down, she pushed the book away and removed the lid from the container. 'I'll eat too many if I'm left alone with them, anyway.'

Josephine sat down and took a ball from the bag. It squished under the pinch of her fingers. She dipped it deep into the sweet and sour sauce. When it emerged, it was covered in sticky red. She took a bite and savoured tender flesh, fat, salt and sugar.

'I thought you were vegetarian?' said Vic as she dipped.

Josephine chewed, nodded and swallowed. 'Mostly. But sometimes you just want to swallow a dead thing, you know?'

Vic stared at her own chicken ball, wondering.

'Do you know what I mean?' Josephine asked.

'Don't get me wrong,' said Vic. 'I love chicken balls. But no, I don't know what you mean.' She took the ball in her mouth and chewed, still wondering.

Josephine looked at the Sebald book and thought about asking how it was. She had not attempted to read a book in two months and had not finished one in five. She did not like the boy on the front cover, the way he stared with a pompous half grin. She took another chicken ball, dipped it in sweet and sour sauce, and devoured.

*

At midday, Vic and Josephine laid towels down on their chosen spot of beach, some coarse sand between the bandstand and the pier. Vic had a Bluetooth speaker in her bag which she connected to her phone. As Josephine laid on her towel, feeling the cheap material scratch at her elbows, the song began. A soft breeze came off the ocean and onto her skin. The song was jaunty and bustling and featured a harmonica. It was 'Pastures of Plenty.' Josephine liked the way it sounded. She liked to think she could come with the dust and go with the wind, too. That was what brought her here. No one could claim her, here, and she did not have to struggle so desperately against her dad, who wanted to remember what she wanted to forget and forget what she had no choice but to remember. The waves went in and out, in and out, forever. Somewhere else, a child was screaming and the sound stretched beneath the wails of harmonica.

'Do you want an ice cream?' said Vic. 'I fancy ice cream.'

'It's the sun,' said Josephine. 'And I want banoffee. And a Coca Cola. I'll pay you back later.'

Vic nodded and moved towards the kiosk. Josephine stretched and let the light sink in. She closed her eyes, enjoying the darkness and the gleaming balls of light at their centre. It reminded her of stars, how they burnt in deep darkness. Then, she thought about how they reminded her of stars because they were lights from a star. Josephine felt dumb and liked it.

An unwelcome coolness descended, and the globes extinguished. Josephine opened her eyes to see Robbie standing over her in an unbuttoned orange and floral Hawaiian shirt, showing a tight body and red skin. His beard was sandy and his hair seemed to gleam. He was grinning, and in the right corner of his grin hung a hand-rolled cigarette. He stood as if at any moment he might drop down and feast on her. Josephine smiled. She pushed herself back so that her feet were directly below him.

'Enjoying the weather?' he said, smoke puffing from his mouth and the end of cigarette glowing amber. 'You look like you are. It's lovely.'

Josephine nodded, barely. She and Vic had moved into the flat Robbie rented above George's about a month ago, and since then he had been trying to sleep with them both. They'd agreed the best way to deal with him was quiet refutation.

'You're blocking my view,' said Josephine. 'And your shadow is cold.'

Robbie shrugged and moved to the side. As he did so, a little ash fell from the cigarette and drifted down to settle on Josephine's forearm. It burnt quickly and brightly with a hiss. Seeing that Robbie had not noticed, she kept quiet.

Robbie let himself fall onto Vic's towel, crossed his legs and stared out to the sea. He sighed deeply, then threw his cigarette butt at a seagull. It hawked before flying away. The butt stuck up in the sand like a sword from a stone. Robbie put his sunglasses on, looked up at the sky, then back at the sea. Then he sighed again.

'What are you doing?' Josephine said, trying to make him go away.

Robbie turned his head deliberately towards her. 'I'm thinking of summer. I'm thinking of what I'll make this town do for me.'

Josephine rolled her eyes and looked at her hand, half buried beneath the sand. She was not going to be in Aberystwyth for much longer. She was going to travel. There were work-aways booked in Prague, Paris and Edinburgh at hostels and bars. Something to do. A way of not keeping to one place for too long. That was the key: to keep moving.

The sharp crunch of shoe on sand signalled the return of Vic. She was holding two ice creams in one hand, and two bottles of coca cola in the other.

'Robbie,' she said, her voice flattening. 'I didn't know you were here.'

He took a bottle of coke from her hand and opened it. It let out a fizz that reminded Josephine of the foam left over by waves on the shore.

'I am everywhere,' he said. 'Always expect me.'

Vic snorted. 'Funny,' she said, sarcastically.

Robbie took an ice cream from her and passed the Coke to Josephine. She drank from it and tried to keep thoughts of Robbie's spittle away. Vic licked her own ice cream, then saw Robbie licking the one meant for Josephine.

'That's not yours,' she said. 'Get your own.'

Robbie grinned and passed the ice cream over. Josephine could see the imprint his tongue had left.

'Sorry,' he said, laying down in the patch of sand between the two girls. 'Heat like this. It makes you do crazy things. Not that it's that hot here. But the sun's out. And that brings something, doesn't it?'

Vic and Josephine looked at each other. They couldn't stand how he flooded their conversations with his boasting, as if you couldn't even grab the air to speak around him. Robbie stretched his smirk wide and spoke again.

'Anyway, who wants to bury me?'

STORM

*

A thick line of pale yellow stretched across the horizon, the last echo of orange glimmering. Josephine sat by a fire, drinking from a bottle of beer. The fire was large, made from lots of logs bought at a petrol station. The discarded green netting had blown off in the direction of the bandstand and disappeared into the dusk. The wood was doused with lighter fluid so that the flames were yellow and large and licking, but she could still feel the cold on her back. Music was playing loudly from somebody's Bluetooth speaker. Not Vic's; Vic had gone home. There was something playing that sounded new and beachy, like it wanted you to move to it. People were, their darkened silhouettes appearing like apparitions through the flames, arms moving luxuriously, almost as if in slow-motion, coming together then falling away again.

Josephine took another swig from the beer which was warm and tasted of washing-up liquid. To her right, two boys talked, one with a shaved head facing away from her. The other boy had short black hair and a long navy coat. He was nodding intensely to every word the other said.

'So, Glyndŵr was like this guerrilla fighter,' said the first one. 'Like medieval Cymru Viet Cong. And he basically spent his whole life fighting in forests, ambushing his enemies. Never beaten, never captured, and never killed. It's interesting, right?'

'Right,' said the second.

'And he had bases. One right here, in fact. He kept men in that very castle ruin on the corner of the coast. But really, he was a man for an ambush, for an attack. And maybe that was his downfall in the end. He was more about vengeance than independence.'

The boy with the shaved head shifted thoughtfully as he said this, so Josephine could see the outline of his nose and lips. The boy with the black hair and the navy coat simply nodded now.

'Yes,' he said. 'Yes that makes sense.'

'And his last battle,' said the boy with the shaved head. 'His last battle deserves at least something worthier than what it has got, in terms of legacy. An ambush on an old rival. A victory. A capture. A ransom. Then, a final disappearance. He left us waiting for him to appear again.'

'Yes,' said the boy with the black hair. 'Yes, incredible!'

Josephine drained the last of the bottle, got up and walked away. Stories like that, with all their grandeur and glory, all their nostalgia and wistfulness, bored her.

*

Up in the sky the many stars burned brightly and whitely, dying as they did so. The moon was yellow like a sick man under-fed. Josephine stood next to the Pen Dinas monument, looking at how it stretched towards the sky, one long stone tube with nothing but its upwardness. She had climbed the hill to find somewhere quiet. She had climbed the hill to think about her mum. She had done that thinking and now wanted to stop. She read the plaque mounted at the foot of the Pen Dinas monument, using the torch on her phone as a light. She read that it was built to honour the Duke of Wellington. The name rung gently in Josephine's ears. Something to do with the Battle of Waterloo. *Couldn't escape if I wanted to.* But she had escaped, and everything was as far away as it could be. She looked out over the sea, seeing waves dimly in the distant dark coming, hearing their low ushering. The storm, she thought, was finally over.

*

But let her rest, now. We must get back to the storm. Run across the darkened, lamp-lit town. Watch the man in the hooded jumper and the shorts run through the rain by the marina. Is he running from something? Or running something off? Perhaps last night's take-away. He certainly looks as if he is purging. The way he puffs and mumbles to himself, his body pushing along like a bike up a hill. And in the rain, too. Up goes the right arm and down comes the left leg. He is soaking all the way through to his fast-beating heart. Up comes the left arm and down goes the right leg, sweat rolling down his cheeks. Bits of sea spray flick at him, mixing with sweat and rain. He is not particularly fast, just mechanical, like the early morning train just firing up now at the station.

He pushes down the incline and past the boats towards his house. He shares it with three people, and there are often others kipping on the sofa, discarded takeaway boxes spread over their chests. He turns left onto another road and then he is home, pushing the door as he twists his key in the lock. The house is drafty, but after the rain and the wind it is shelter. Low snoring rumbles from the living room. He flicks a switch and dull yellow lights the narrow corridor. Glynn adds his trainers to the pile in the corner, throws his jacket over the banister and lays down on the bare staircase. The rough wood scratches his skin, the steps pressing into his spine. His muscles pulse, aches that move in comfortable circles.

In the kitchen, he cracks two eggs into a jug and mixes them with milk, adding a little salt and a lot of pepper. He's been cutting down over the last year, watching the fat around his belly thin. As he inserts two slices of bread into the toaster, Glynn hears a stirring in the deep darkness of the living room. Just as the butter has melted into the pan and the eggy mix is turning thick and rubbery, he hears the door creak open, like dawn breaking on a grey day.

'Alllriiiight?' comes a yawning voice.

'Hey, man,' says Glynn, keeping his eyes on the pan as the mix becomes fluffy and pale and yellow.

'What are you cooking?'

Glynn recognises the softness in Jake's Carolina tone now, knows he will have the faded cream dressing gown with all the tobacco and food stains draped over his thin body.

'Eggs,' he says. 'Want some?'

He is leaning on the door, arms stretched towards the ceiling, eyes closed and face scrunched.

'I'm ok,' he says. 'I think I've got some kebab somewhere.'

Glynn nods and, though he says nothing, feels a pang of resentment at Jake's ability to eat takeaways and drink so regularly without having to worry about his figure as he does.

'Fun night?' he asks.

'I don't really remember,' Jake says. 'We were in Yoko's for a bit. That was good. Anna bought a bottle of Prosecco and gave us all some. There was one guy that kept coming up to her, though. Kept trying to get her to dance with him. Would never happen with Bill around. She told him I was with her just to shake him off, like that would of scared him. He wouldn't listen, so in the end I shook up the prosecco bottle and fired it at his face. He went crying to the bouncers and we had to leave after that. Fair enough I suppose, but this bloke got away completely scot-free and that doesn't seem right to me.'

'It's not,' says Glynn. He butters his toast.

'Right? Then we were just walking around the seafront, looking at all the stars and stuff, which turned out quite nice in the end, especially 'cos of the rain that's starting now. They reckon it'll stay for a few days. And I still had the bottle of Prosecco, so we drank that. Then Bill met us, we came back here, smoked for a bit and fell asleep.'

Glynn lays his toast on a plate. He pours the scrambled eggs. 'Sounds good.'

Jake shrugs. 'I don't know. Do you ever sometimes feel like you're living the same thing over and over?'

Glynn remembers things from before. 'It can get like that.'

'I mean, most of the night was alright. But when I was dancing, I don't know, it was one of those mixes they always play, and not just in there but in every bloody bar. And I'm dancing to it, and I just feel like every move I'm making is a move I've made before. It's like I'm on repeat or something.' Jake looks out the window. A clouded morning gathers outside, the beginnings of a slow shift from dark to grey.

'Maybe you need a break,' says Glynn, sitting down at the little table near Jake. He cuts at his scrambled eggs with his knife and fork. 'Maybe take some time off going out.'

There's squishing and crunching between Glynn's teeth. The eggs are fluffy and good.

'And do what?' says Jake. 'There's nothing to fucking do around here.'

'Go for a walk?'

Jake takes a glass from the cupboard and gets some water from the tap. He takes a sip. 'I've been thinking about that,' he says, wistfully. 'I'd love to see more of this place, get out of town.'

'It's not hard,' says Glynn. 'You just do it. Put on some boots and get out there.'

'Really?' Jake looks at him. 'When was the last time you left, then?'

Glynn thinks back proudly on his walk to Borth, his conquering of the cliffs and hills and wind. He realises that was seven weeks ago now. He chews shamefully.

'I guess it's been a while.'

'You get trapped in here,' Jake says. 'Don't beat yourself up about it. It's hills and hangovers.'

Glynn eats. Jake yawns. He takes his phone from his pocket and stares into its electric blue light.

'Think I'm going to sleep upstairs,' he says. 'I've got a lecture later. Might try and make it. Maybe I'll take that walk, beforehand.'

'You could try Tan-y-Bwlch,' says Glynn. 'It's just over the bridge. Not too far.'

Jake pauses. Nods. 'Maybe I will,' he says.

He drifts away and Glynn is alone, scraping at crusts and the last squidgy blobs of egg. Glynn looks out the window and waits for morning to come.

CHAPTER TWO

The rain is still coming down and the black clouds block out any light that tries to shine on this little town. Day still somehow comes. It does not come quickly, but as this spot on the planet shifts back towards the sun, the clouds turn from black to grey. The sea is green like a giant's snot, each wave sneezing up over the promenade and drenching the streets. Time moves.

People are leaving their houses, yawning, flasks in hand, layers topped up, big coats with fluffy hoods, swearing under their breath at the weather. On Iorweth Avenue, amongst the detached red brick houses, there is a mother ushering her twins into the car. Can you see the bags under her eyes? Her boys are not much past four years old. They were kept up all the previous night by the wailing of the wind, convinced it was some creature lying dormant under their beds.

On Chalybeate Street, a baker unlocks the door to his shop. He feels the wind cut into him. He looks down to where the road curves onto the high street. Just out of his sight is the Greggs, staffed by students and the semi-retired, stocked with neat rows of pastries and sandwiches. It has been like this since their first delivery truck skirted around that corner, passing his shop like a haunt. They will outsell him, as they do every day. He goes inside to begin his work.

On the promenade, away from the pier where the chirping starlings swirl and shift in the sky there is an old wooden shelter with dirty windows and faded colours. Many people have sought its protection while eating chips, smoking cigarettes or sleeping. Now, it is empty except for a lone seagull pecking at some scraps. He catches his reflection in the window.

'Harwrk!' he shouts. The other does not move.

'Harwrk!' he repeats, to no acknowledgement.

'Harwrk!'

The seagull bashes its beak against the glass. It is thrown back. That did not feel like feather and flesh and bone. It felt hard and cold. The supernatural seagull is still there, staring back, unmoved, offering no resistance and refusing to submit. The gull goes again, butting at the glass. He tries once more, falls back, his webbed feet unsteady. Looking at the figure staring back at him he lets out a hawrk of defeat and flies into the wind. A gust catches his wings and sends him back into a nearby lamppost. He drops to the concrete, the first casualty of the storm. Maybe it is time to move elsewhere.

The dog-walkers walk their dogs, as always and ever. This one is an older lady, quite small, particularly next to that vast, angry ocean. She is dressed in thermals and a woolly hat; her joints are stiff as she moves along the sand and stone of Tan-y-Bwlch, south of the dead seagull, as far from town as one can get without encountering some mighty hill. Her big mastiff pulls her along, and barks at the gulls. He sniffs at rocks, working out where the dead used to be and where they might be still. Soon, the tide will come in to spit up stones and old things.

*

Knocks sound like bells on Josephine's door. It is eleven but it feels like six. The wind gurgles against the windows and the crash of waves booms so that even here Josephine can hear them. She awakes bleary eyed into the world to the familiar feelings of her quilt's warmth against the cold of the room, the mattress's loose springs digging into her back and neck.

'Hey!' says Vic from the other side of the door. 'Are you coming up?'

Josephine never expected to be the kind of student whose attendance at any given lecture was uncertain. It would have seemed shameful to her just months ago. Outside, the winds howl a warning to stay inside. She wants to heed it.

'I'm cosy,' she says. 'Do we have to?'

Vic has played the motivator so many times with Josephine. She is growing tired of it. But in that same howling wind which Josephine takes as a warning, Vic hears a rallying cry.

'Come on, Jose.' She leans her arm on the door, presses her head against her palm, as if trying to sink through the wood. The words reverberate against the oak surface. Vic wonders why she even said them.

But on the other side of the door, something changes. Watch: if you pay attention, you can see it happen. Josephine's grip over the quilt covers loosens. She opens her eyes and looks out the window. She notices that while the wind is still hard and strong, the rain has taken a brief reprieve, the last droplets running down her window. Now she is sitting up, looking out at the grey sky. There are cracks in the clouds where pale light bursts through. It is not that she takes it as a sign – Josephine is far too grown up for signs – but it does something.

'I'll make tea,' says Vic in her last attempt.

'Ok, I'm moving.'

And she does. She puts on some jeans, a t-shirt, a jumper, a hoodie and a jacket. She has learnt to wear layers in Wales. The flat is cold. All the heat built up in between eight and nine the night before when the radiators burned has fled through single glazing and old walls. When she comes into the kitchen, there is a mug waiting for her on the table next to a crumb-covered plate.

Vic nods at it. 'Yours?'

'Robbie's, I think.'

'Should've known.' Vic motions to the bits of tobacco left next to the plate. 'It'd be nice if he cleaned up after himself for once.'

'It's not that bad.'

They have talked about this before. Before they moved, they'd taken too long to find a flat for the next year. They saw the ad on Facebook: *hilarious history student seeks two flatmates to save him from eviction*. It was characteristically egotistical, but funny enough that they thought he might just be a little overly eager. Since then, Josephine and Vic had near weekly conversations about his sexism, narcissism, insensitivity, and, as if representative in its shallowness of it all, his messiness. But this morning, Josephine just didn't have the energy for it. 'I know we keep going over this,' says Vic, 'but he seems to get creepier and creepier.'

Josephine sips from her mug and feels warmth trickle down her throat. She rubs sleep from her eyes and hears the wind stretching down the street.

'Maybe he knows its bothering us,' she says. 'We just have to learn to ignore him.'

Vic leaves the room and comes back with a bright pink rucksack. She is a better student than Josephine; often taking notes, at least attempting the required reading, watching public lectures from John Mullan on YouTube. Josephine still sips at her tea and stares out the window at the darkening sky and its rifts of light.

'I think sometimes that's the worst thing you can do,' says Vic. 'I mean, if his behaviour just continues then who knows what it could lead to. I've heard of people who've ended up doing awful things, all getting the benefit of the doubt in the lead up because they're a friend or family or co-worker or even just someone living in proximity and then they end up really hurting someone.'

Josephine pours the last of her tea, too hot to down, into the sink. 'Maybe you're right,' she says. 'But what are we meant to do? It's not like he's actually done anything.'

Vic sighs. 'I know,' she says. She checks her phone 'Are you ready to go yet?'

Josephine nods. She goes to her room and picks up her bag, feeling for the notebook inside it. They walk downstairs. Josephine runs her hands along the walls of chipped green paint. Pieces come away on the tips of some of her fingers. Opening the door, wind rushes to greet them. The rain has resumed and is spinning in circles. They enter the storm together, walking up the road, preparing for the push of the hill. Josephine regrets her change of mind, wants the storm to push her all the way back into bed. Vic is undeterred, her face scrunched against the wind, her legs moving like the mechanics of the clock tower in the town square. It has been a while since Josephine has walked up the hill and, even though she gets a pretty good workout from her shifts at Yoko's, her lungs wheeze and her legs ache. The rain calms to a steady spit. They pass Bronglais Hospital. There is a woman cradling the large bump protruding from her stomach with one hand and smoking a cigarette with the other. Vic glances over and tuts.

'Can you believe people do that?' she says, her arms and legs moving furiously. 'You have a fucking baby. It's just crazy.'

Josephine imagines a child inhaling and exhaling the smoke within the trusting warmth of its womb. Then, she thinks of a design on a cigarette box where a mother smokes, with a see-through stomach showing the baby smoking, too, the mother holding the very same cigarette packet, so the image goes on and on. She looks at Vic and thinks about explaining this little image which makes her want to giggle.

'Yeah,' she says, deciding against it. 'It is.'

Vic nods but her mind is somewhere else now. Her eyes are fixed on the bridge at the hill's summit. Josephine points at the green shelter across the road where an old lady and her dog wait. Her hair feels almost matted under the hood of her jumper.

'Shall we get the bus up the rest of the way? It's nasty out here.'

Vic shakes her head. 'We're nearly there now! We'll feel better for the journey.'

They keep going, passing the old lady and her dog, up towards Pantycelyn. Josephine looks down the road leading to the National Library. It looks very grand from far away – like the headquarters of a Bond villain. She wonders what it is like inside. Books, probably. She's heard mention of paintings before. Probably lots of things she desperately does not want to learn.

The bus hurtles by. Josephine sees a flash of faces pressed against the glass. She knows that the warmth in there will be uncomfortable, the result of too many bodies wrapped in damp coats pressed against each other, but at this moment, wind-battered and rain-beaten, it is inviting. They at last turn onto the street leading to the concourse of grey brutalist buildings, seeking refuge in the long rectangular newbuild.

*

The lecture hall is bright and warm. From the high ceiling, lights burn their way down, making Josephine's sleep-blinking eyes ache and squint. Even the heat is uncomfortable, after the whipping cold. It makes her skin itch in splotches: to the right of her stomach, her left arm, her neck.

As she moves with Vic towards their usual spot in the third row from the back, she sees some of the other students in the half-filled hall have brought coffees or energy drinks. One even has a bottle of water. Her throat feels so incredibly dry. She summons up some spit to swallow.

Arla is stood at the lectern. The lectern is a big desk which stretches wide and high. Arla is short, blond, and pretty, with fine features. She's confident, too, one of the sharp ones, but with the lectern in front of her, she looks as if she is taking cover. She is looking at the computer screen in front of her, frowning, biting her bottom lip, while the large projector screen above shows a picture of Aberystwyth University, a group of students laughing on the grass, the sun, and, in the top left corner, the Microsoft explorer shortcut icon.

Down the hill, Glynn wakes up with a start. He looks at his phone, then up at the ceiling. He groans. Last week he had seen a video about waking up early to be more productive. Since then, he has woken up at five in the morning four times. Each time, after his jog, he has fallen asleep, literally unable to keep his eyes open. He'd been certain that the presence of the nine o'clock lecture would force him to stay awake. Whipping his towel off, he pulls on some clothes and runs out the door.

Just as the clock ticks towards ten past the hour, a PowerPoint slide appears on the screen. On it, there is a picture of a large man with improbably big hands holding a series of stapled together pieces of paper. One set of papers hangs limply down towards the image's shadowy end. The man's mouth is slightly open, as if he is going to say something.

Arla looks up from the screen and steps back from the lectern. 'Well, I have to say, given everything,' and she raises a hand up above her head, bending her fingers as if grasping a small sphere, as if she might hold within it the very world, 'everything being the weather, the time, and the writer we are studying today, this turnout isn't half bad.'

There is a little mutter of laughter from the students. Arla walks around the lectern. She is the reason people have shown up, thinks Josephine. Vic is always talking about Arla, how well she explains things, how cooly she deals with the small number of over-confident men that seem to dominate classroom discussions, how nicely she dresses. And she does look nice, in her corduroy trousers and delicately baggy brown jumper. Her skin is clear and white, her teeth bright, her voice soft, yet forceful. Everything about her was made for a job like this.

'B.S. Johnson,' says Arla, and as she speaks Glynn is waiting at the taxi rank, soaking and trembling in the heavy sheets of rain, waiting for a car to come, 'was a man who never really knew what he wanted to be. His life was a bit of a storm, full of sound and fury, but very little light.'

Vic is already scribbling things in her green Pukka Pad. Josephine sinks back into her seat. She is never quite sure what she can pull from these lectures for her own assignments. They are at least better than the seminars, where awkward painful silences are punctuated by occasional desperate questions.

'He was at his happiest, and this may be of some interest to you, when he came to Wales. Stuffed away in Gregynog Hall, practicing Cymraeg in his cockneyed voice. But he was at his worst, too. He wrote little of consequence, then.'

Josephine looks at the man again, his half-open mouth and his soft eyes. To be of little consequence, away from things. Maybe it was what he wanted.

'He was at his best when he was brutal, when he spoke what he saw as the eternal truth: that life is painful and then it ends. This is what he learnt from where he mostly lived and died, in London, though he grew up on its unfashionable edges.'

Like her. No one here knew of Cheam, Sutton or Carshalton. When they thought of London, they thought of its brighter places, its Hackneys and Sohos and Shoreditchs. They saw its sparkling hybridity. Her London was one of endless rows of houses, construction works and petrol stations. And mothers so infected by blogs on the dark web that they thought... No, not that, not now. Still, it was London, that was her point. The red buses barrelled through all the same, and she'd always had an Oyster card. Maybe Josephine understood this London Arla had summoned up.

This lecture, Arla posits, will look to use B.S. Johnson to consider the very joint which pulls together fiction's seemingly oppositional purposes: to represent the real, and to imagine something other. I wouldn't read too much into that.

Back in town, Glynn hails down a taxi and gives the driver the building's name. He runs a hand through his hair and when he pulls it away, it is briefly shining.

Arla says that Johnson weighed a compulsion to fit in with everything around him with a desire to break everything apart. How his very sentences grapple with this. To be or not to be, for Johnson, is to play the game, or cheat.

Often, she says, he chose to cheat. 'Fuck all this lying,' he declares in one novel. Even *The Unfortunates* – and now she takes the book from the table, a strange box reminding Josephine of those video cases people had back when they also had video players – is a novel unsure of whether it wants to be. 'Why else,' Arla asks, 'would he make us shuffle its order each time?'

Josephine has not done the reading. Looking at the picture of Johnson and his collection of stapled papers, and Arla and her box-shaped book, she puts two and two together.

'So, you have to shuffle the chapters?' she whispers to Vic.

'Yes,' Vic hisses back, flicking her gaze between her notes and Arla.

Arla goes on. Johnson regurgitates the past like it's a sickness. In another novel to this one, a man bedridden in the hull of a ship continually goes on deck to throw up over the side, and throws up his memories, too. Out they come, glaring back at him in odd, disordered chunks. There, Arla reckons, lies the rub. Johnson wants to tell the truth, but he believes that fiction, by being constructed, is like a lie. But truth is just a thing trying to cover an absence.

There is a bang and the door swings open. All in black, dripping wet, like Heathcliff or Lockwood come in from the moors, is Glynn. Arla pauses and looks at him.

'Hello,' she says.

He pants as he speaks. 'Hi,' he says. 'Sorry I'm late.'

'Quite alright,' Arla replies. 'Wet out there?'

He pauses, not quite sure what she's said, until he hears the little ripple of laughter and catches her quiet half smile. 'Yeah,' he says. 'Sorry.'

'It's quite alright,' she repeats. 'Take a seat.'

Glynn moves quickly to a seat in the front row. He unzips his bag, conscious of the accompanying fizz echoing across the hall.

Looking down, Josephine recognises him from somewhere, but can't quite place where. He was talkative, she thinks, perhaps too much. Not like he is now, so awkward, gangly and shy.

Arla comes back. Johnson, she says, is a shammy fortune teller who has fallen for his own yarns, just like Orson Welles. He's gone too far, way out at sea, drowning, and he did drown, in the end. Suicide, in a bathtub, over-powered by his own self-torturous practice. Glynn puts his pad in front of him and unclicks his pen. Her last lecture he did not make many notes. He found she went on a bit, even if he did feel bad for thinking it.

Josephine is drifting, again – thinking of home. Remembering when she would meet up with friends underneath the bridge and drink. Only two years suddenly feels so long ago. When mum was ill and hurting her, those hours felt like the only ones where she was really alive. The other times, she tried her best to make herself nothing.

Then, she feels it. Something burning into the back of her neck. Mother. Without even looking, she can the white bone and the rotting skin, can almost hear the awful shriek. She turns around, slowly, taking a breath.

Just a boy slumped in front of his Red Bull. Vic looks over.

'You ok?' she asks.

Josephine stretches her arms and moves her head back and forth. 'Fine,' she whispers.

'Question?' says Arla, stopping and pointing in Josephine's direction.

'No, no question!' shouts Josephine, so loudly it makes Arla's eyes widen, and she jumps back with a little start.

Vic lets out a giggle under her breath. Josephine feels heat in her cheeks.

'Shut the fuck up,' she says.

Arla carries on. There are others who learn that birth can be transcended, that identity is not solid, but Johnson liked solidity and stillness even as his bending, reaching sentences suggest flux and disintegration. He doesn't make sense. But nor does life. That, she concedes, is narrative's lie. But we should not resist it. Let it take you over and twist you. Let it take control. Forget what you think you know. Don't try to fight it, because you'll drive yourself mad.

It's possible she doesn't say all of that.

What she does this say is this: 'if you were to write about here, for instance,' and she gestures with that same world-holding hand to all that is around here, 'you would have to spice it up a little bit.'

There is another murmur of laughter from the lecture's more caffeinated attendees. Josephine nods. One thing that drew her to the place when she'd seen the pictures on results day was its remoteness, the way it seemed like a blank piece of paper upon which she could write whatever she wanted.

'Why?' says Glynn. He does not mean to. The word slips out his mouth before he can even think, and his voice is louder, too.

Arla looks up. 'Well,' she says, still smirking, 'it's only Aber.'

Another chuckle. Glynn looks down shily, then back up.

'There was a Celtic fortress here, once,' he says. 'Owain Glyndwr besieged and captured a castle. There were ships that sailed to America, one to Africa. Cymdeithas yr Iaith Gymraeg and the language protests. I mean,' and he pauses now, getting stuck, 'there's the elephants!'

More laughter. Everybody knows about the elephants. There are black and white photographs of them all around the town. He gives a good-natured grin, as if conceding something.

Arla holds up her hands. 'Sounds like *you* might be able to write a wonderful story about here,' she says, smiling. 'But in between those moments were days, weeks, months and years where people did nothing but live and die. There are things we have to forget, so that we can remember.'

Josephine nods at that. She wants to forget, like the rest of the world. But she remembers everything.

*

'That's me, thank you, the seminars are later this week. Make sure you've done the reading,' says Arla. 'Stay safe and stay out of the storm. Goodbye.'

Everyone rises. The roar from outside demands that coats are zipped and hoods will flap. Glynn joins the sea of students leaving through the entrance by the lecture stage and Josephine exits at the back of the room. For now, they are still separate, with separate fragments of the lecture swirling around their half-attentive brains. But we are getting closer.

Josephine waits outside for Vic and they follow the curve of the campus towards the steps leading down to Pantycelyn. Glynn follows the road the other way up slope towards the sports centre. Vic is talking about the lecture, running breathlessly through thoughts on emotions and the human condition. Josephine is nodding, feeling a vague regret for not having read the book, and looking over the heads of the groups and the roofs of the buildings in front of her under the cast of grey clouds to the green sea. They are fattening and darkening. The wind blows cold and hard at their faces, whipping their hair back. The rain, though, has stopped, though rivulets still stream down the hill and leaves and roofs still drip with water. It all looks as if it is waiting for something. Glynn keeps his eyes on the ground, watching for puddles from the rain which has momentarily stopped. He is walking around the National Library, looking at the same horizon just half a minute after Josephine.

Ssqqquiilllkk!

Glynn feels water soak through the rips in his trainers. He imagines the dirt seeping into his feet. Shoes he needs to buy for himself now. No one around to transfer cash or scheme a birthday present back in Blaenau. Just slate and memories gathered up in piles and graves. He looks down at his foot, sunken into the mud.

*

'What did you think?' says Vic.

Josephine is walking along the main road, lines of traffic stretching down towards the shore.

'It was good,' she says. 'It's interesting. All that stuff. All those struggles. You assume they didn't have them then.'

'Did you read the book?'

It had turned up yesterday, a square box containing stapled piles of paper. She had joked about it at work.

'I started it,' she says, by which she means she added it to her online shopping cart two weeks ago. 'I just never find the time.'

'I think you'd have liked this one,' says Vic. 'It's kind of gloomy.'

'And what about gloom makes you think of me?' Josephine laughs.

'No, in a cool way,' says Vic. 'Chic gloom.'

They discuss the phrase chic gloom as they walke past the entrance to Bronglais Hospital, where the smoking pregnant woman was before. They wait at the turning to the car park as a Ford Focus moves slowly down the left lane. By the time they have crossed, Vic is back talking about B.S. Johnson.

'Well, he's incredible. It's like reading the thoughts in your head. He just carries you along, and it's like you don't even realise, but you're drifting with this character's thoughts…'

Glynn is on the main road, about a hundred metres and two groups of walkers behind Vic and Josephine. Now he has joined the rest of them, he wishes he'd carried on down the longer, quieter way, through the housing estate, up Llanbadarn road towards the high street. But he wants to get to the sea, wants to watch the waves come in.

Vic and Josephine reach George's.

'I'm hungry,' says Vic as Josephine is reaching for her key. 'Let's get some chicken wings.'

She walks purposefully onwards and Josephine follows her haplessly. They walk up the street. Josephine used to go to the chicken shop with Taylor back home. They'd spend hours there, at the place in Green Wrythe Lane, with boxes of chips and meat and cans of coke, tucked up in a corner by the muted TV, talking.

Suddenly, Josephine realises the thought of fried chicken makes her want to gag.

'Vic,' she says. 'You had chicken balls yesterday.'

'Yeah.'

'And the day before you had fried chicken,' says Josephine.

'Your point?' says Vic, smirking.

'I mean,' Josephine pauses. 'Like, are you ok?'

Vic laughs. 'Alright,' she says, turning back towards the flat.

Glynn is browsing packets of bacon in the SPAR almost directly across the road from George's. He picks a packet of smoked organic and takes a loaf of brown Hovis. He pays at the counter with a twenty-pound note. He recognises the girl behind as a course-mate from his first first year, two years ago.

'You decided to come back?'

'Yeah, well, I'm a glutton for punishment.'

'I think that's amazing. I mean, brave.'

He looks at her. She is pretty. He remembers thinking so when they were sat next to each other in class. Long blond hair, delicate features, pale skin. A Brummie accent.

'Thanks,' he says. 'Bravery's not got much to do with it. I had to.'

Vic and Josephine are walking back towards George's. Cloud cover is stretching further across the sky and turning darker. The winds are picking up. The lights on in the nearby buildings look warm and welcoming.

Glynn is walking up the high street on the other side of the road. He needs to cross, but he won't do it unless the traffic lights he is approaching turn red. He is coming up to them as they turn amber. The cars come to a slow halt. Glynn crosses over.

Josephine and Vic are talking about their plans for the upcoming night. They are wondering where to go and who to invite. They think about how to hide their plans from Robbie. Josephine says she does not feel social but is tempted. She has a night off from the club.

Glynn does not want to see the sea, anymore. He wants only to cook up a bacon sandwich for lunch. He does not notice Josephine.

And now they are walking past each other, shoulders almost brushing, one moving west and the other moving east. Let us disturb things.

Glynn will drop the shopping bag. The contents will spill out onto the pavement. The plastic bag, relieved of the grip on its handles and free of the weight inside it, will be blown by the wind. It will hit Josephine on the head, wrap itself around her. She will turn in the confusion, and momentarily her vision will be nothing but the lime green colour of the plastic. Then, the bag will break away from her, flying down the road and up the hill. She will be left looking at Glynn, and Glynn will be looking at her. And we will have ourselves a point of contact.

Watch. Thft! There slips the grip. Kalnt! Out go the groceries. Fowuuu! The bag flies away. Shkt! It wraps itself around Josephine's head.

'Blwargh!' she cries.

She spins around. The bag is off. She sees Glynn kneeling on the pavement, making sure his precious packet of bacon is not damaged by the fall.

'Are you ok?' Vic says, trying to stop her shaky laughter.

'Yeah, I'm fine.' Josephine pulls loose strands of hair back behind her shoulders, giggling and looking at Vic. 'You fucking love this,' she says to her.

'I do.' Vic nods and carries on laughing. 'You actually said blwargh!'

Josephine puts her hands on her knees, looks up at the sky and then down at the ground. There is a low rumble up from above.

Glynn looks up at her, bacon in one hand and bread in the other. And he sees her. He sees her brown skin, her green eyes, her long, curly hair. And how lovely she looks when she laughs. Something moves in him, just as, again, the rain starts to fall.

'I'm so sorry. I didn't...'

'No, it's ok! It...'

'Just lost my grip. Didn't even realise anyone was...'

'It's such a strong wind out! Who'd even...'

'I feel like such an idiot.'

'No. Don't.' She laughs.

Those last two words she says hang in the air as if held by a string. Glynn smiles. Josephine smiles. Glynn stands up, the loaf of bread tucked under one arm, the packet of bacon in his other hand. They nod to each other and go their opposite ways.

'Cute,' says Vic.

And there we have it. Just a chance encounter. But now the ball is really rolling.

CHAPTER THREE

Glynn comes into the house just as the rain begins to pick up. From the doorway he watches the heavens burst, listens to the trickling of streams down small hills towards gutters. *Awish*. It is enough to induce jealousy, that free-flowing sound. *Awish*. The air feels heavy in Glynn's lungs. He looks up at the clouds. They seem, despite their unleashing, as if something else is building in them, stretching across town like a big bubble of greyness, except for a few cracks and rifts where blueness shines brightly. Glynn wonders what might be beyond them. He thinks better of this and turns back to what is around him. A neighbour runs by, a bag over their head as makeshift umbrella.

As wind gusts, Glynn can hear the chimes of the marina sounding softly. Warnings. He looks over at the derelict boats on dry land, those past sailing, and behind them the strange mix of boats, yachts and trawlers. Glynn likes to look at the old fishing vessels. They are large and bright and rusted. It feels like seeing medieval armour, an elephant's skeleton or a fallen tree. Turning away, Glynn closes the door and takes his shoes off. The warmth of the nearby radiator wraps around him.

'Hello.' It's Anna, sitting on the stairs, watching him. 'How was the lecture?'

'Ok,' says Glynn. 'I don't know. I found it kind of difficult.'

Anna nods absently. 'Do you fancy going back out?' she says. 'I could do with a coffee. Kick this hangover. Maybe some food, too.'

Glynn holds up his SPAR bag. 'I've got my lunch here.'

'Please?' says Anna, cocking her head and widening her eyes like a sad hamster. 'It's cold and I don't want to go on my own. We can be miserable together.'

Glynn's breath sharpens and his stomach feels watery. He has never been much good at saying no to her. 'Do I have to?'

Anna smiles. 'You'd make me really happy if you did.'

'Ok. You owe me.'

Glynn puts his food in the fridge and slides back into his coat and shoes. The rain is falling straight and hard. As soon as they leave, it hits Glynn's skin with small, stinging slaps.

Anna turns to him, zipping up her coat and throwing the hood up. 'Thanks for coming. Bill's too shattered to move right now.'

They turn left and see the Castle Pub looming over them. It's early, but Glynn catches a glimpse of a figure moving towards the bar through the windows. The Castle is not a place students go, but Anna occasionally works shifts there. He visits her on Sundays when they have the bands on, but he wonders what it would be like on a day like this, probably just a few quiet and aged patrons served by a bored, tired student. He read somewhere that it used to be the customs house, back when there were all those ships. All those people from all across the world. This was a different place, then.

They walk up the street, turn right, and see roads crossing into each other. They turn again and are walking by the Angel, its dark windows staring out at them, its door closed. No music or chatter. There is only the sign moving back and forth in the wind, squeaking incessantly, like some sort of cry. It depicts a winged figure emerging from the sun, a choppy sea beneath her. Across the road is the Academy, a bulking church of grey stone converted years ago into a pub. The stained-glass windows are still there, offering divine views of pool tables and a long, well-stocked bar. The blare of football commentary escapes from an open window.

'It's quite beautiful,' says Glynn, pointing to the Angel's sign. 'Something radical about these pubs. You know this town used to have campaigns for temperance?'

'For what?'

'It means not drinking.'

'Oh yeah, you've told me before,' says Anna. 'They didn't work.'

Anna goes into the Starbucks and Glynn, unsure of what she expects of him, waits outside. He sees her chatting and giggling with the boy behind the counter and feels the familiar shoot of jealousy. He walks over to the plaque on the clock tower to distance him. The plaque stares back at him. The name of the man who gave himself to that failed cause. Glynn feels a kind of remorse for him, and guilt too. He is part of that sinful desecration the man fought against. Even now he desires, as he looks away from the plaque and back through the window. It is a curse, he can confess that, how easily he falls in love. It makes him ache in his shoulders.

When she comes back, she is holding her coffee and smiling. They walk without speaking, feeling the weight of things. It is cold and Glynn's hands are shivering. He tucks them into his pockets and tries to fold in on himself.

'He's sweet,' says Anna, looking back at the coffee shop.

He wants to tell her he wishes she would flirt again with him. 'Bill wouldn't be pleased,' he says instead.

Anna sighs and glares at him. 'Oh, it's just chat, Glynn. Can you not think about everything all the time?'

'Sorry,' says Glynn. 'I was just joking.'

'But you weren't. That's the thing. You're always watching and judging and working things out. It's this incessant need to just mention, to think. It's exhausting.'

Glynn looks at the Academy, how it hulks over them, and for a moment he thinks he sees something in its windows. It's a nice distraction from all this. He stops and looks for a little while, sure there is something behind the water running down the glass. Then he sees her, looking at him.

'I'm not trying to do anything, Anna,' he says. 'I just came to keep you company because you asked.'

Anna sips her coffee. 'Yeah and why are you doing that? It's awful out. I'm drenched through.'

'I thought you might get me one, too,' he says, nodding at the coffee.

She laughs. Water trickles down to gutters. They carry on moving.

'You did hurt me,' says Glynn. 'I can't help but be bitter.'

'I know,' says Anna. 'I really am sorry. But it worries me. This isn't right. We're near each other so much and it drives us both mad.'

He did not know he drove her to anything. The idea he might cause something like madness warms him. He didn't know she thought of him like that.

'What's your solution?' he says. 'I don't want to not know you.'

They are moving down the street now. Glynn can hear the rigging ringing against the metal masts again, and the waves crashing. He imagines them splashing over the prom.

'There isn't one, I think,' she says. 'Everything fucking stagnates here.'

A guttural droning sound falls onto them. It beaches itself onto their ears, all huge and unmovable, like something dying and washed up. Within it are other sounds; a high-pitched, ascending squeal and a middling, mundane hum. Anna looks fearful for a moment.

'A jet,' says Glynn. 'From the military base.'

They look up at the low gloom. It is somewhere above all that, swerving its way around the storm. Some pilot bragging about risky manoeuvres pulled off. The sound goes on. Anna presses the back of her hands to her ears. They have both stopped and are looking up for the source. Glynn saw one that flew so low once he was certain its hull would be ripped by the pointing figure of the memorial angel on South Beach. The droning goes on and Glynn can hear the wind sieving itself through the plane's wings. Some seagulls by the beach flap and try to escape but are trapped by the opposing gust. Glynn looks at a drain overflowing with water and thinks this must be how it feels to lay at the bottom of all that, to have everything above tip over you.

'I don't like this,' says Anna. 'Can we go in?'

'It would be good to see it,' says Glynn.

'It hurts,' says Anna. 'And I'm cold.'

Glynn looks up at the sky. There are no longer any of the rifts through which he might have earlier spotted something. 'Yeah. Me too. Ok.'

They move quickly back to their house. He puts an arm around Anna, and she folds into him for a little while, shivering. He remembers she has a fear of loud noises, something to do with when she worked in a shop before she came here.

'Sorry,' he says.

'It's ok,' she says, moving towards the coat rack. 'Just try to be a bit more considerate.'

Glynn watches Anna as she takes her coat off, the perfect shape of her back, remembers how he would watch it shift, admiring the twist of her spine. From the living room they can hear the blare of video games, the occasional shouts of Bill ordering someone what to do.

'I guess he's not so shattered anymore,' says Glynn. 'Not too shattered to play video games, anyway.'

She hangs the coat up and leans back against the wall while he takes off his. Staring into the darkness of the many coats, he says what he has searched for.

'I know you're hurting,' says Anna. 'But you can't let losing her stop the rest of your life. It's not the same as forgetting, moving on.'

Memories. Nan had texted him that morning. He was so upset about Anna, he didn't reply. Then, she was gone, and he was truly alone.

'Things changed because you slept with someone else, Anna,' he says. 'Let's not dress it up as anything but that.'

'It's not like we were married, Glynn,' says Anna. 'We weren't even together. It was one night. You never said you wanted anything more.'

They look at each other for a while, feeling the past re-emerge. It is huge and long. Anna stands still. She sips her coffee.

'Thanks for coming out with me,' she says. Then she turns away, back to the living room, where the other living start to stir.

*

I'll let you in on a little secret. Everything is always living, even when it's dead. You can hear the past, if you listen. It is speaking, now:

'Imagine your skin stripped away, peel by peel. Your bones pulling from each other. Your organs left unarmoured and useless. Imagine yourself stripped bare like this. Your soul, unencumbered by form and feel. Would you be as clean as Adam first was? Can you conceive what that could mean? Or would you find yourself worn from all the sin and sickness? I know only that I could stand before God and say I was not tempted, that I urged others not to be tempted, also. Some listened, many did not.

'When I spoke, I told them – my congregation, my masses, my flock – that I could only point them in the direction they had to go. I could only hold the lamp up and gesture the few feet of road it illuminated, promising they would find their way past the darkness if they only kept faith. Alive, I was loved well enough. But I understood love of me was really love of God; that my own successes from the pulpit were God's, just as my nation's beauty is a fraction of His made manifest. When I died, I knew that too was part of His pattern, that I was dying as every man must, following what was expected of me. When I came to in this square of stone, staring down Great Darkgate Street, the clock tower ticking over me, I kept faith that this was also some sequence of spiritual significance I had to complete. I have waited, watching as my town and my country have disrobed virtue and instead wear sin. My own plaque has become an irony, my call for abstinence a monument from some failed and forgotten fool's errand.

'I have watched those that stagger and slip and sing in the evening time. How I miss the clear as water voices of my congregation, undefiled by spirits and sex. When I watch the lost couples kiss upon my stone, I pray Judgement Day might come and I might be lifted, and they sent down. I try to remember, Judas kissed Jesus. Wrongness exists so we might forgive it.

'There was a boy in my congregation I watched grow into a man. Wyn. His hair was bright blond and his laugh was beautiful. His wits were sharp. Children do not always understand the severity of service, and regularly he did not. I still believed in him. His father was a shepherd, but Wynn grew to be a sailor. Then he stopped coming to service. I saw him through the windows of dimly lit pubs, drunkenly slurping over beer and women. It is painful to have one's failure announce itself so loudly. I could see it in front of me then, like God saw Cain and the absence of Abel.

'It was not long after that I led the parade. Seven hundred strong, all for God. I converted sailors, stopped them spending in the taverns and gave them sober shelter in my chapel. I had the children make banners. I wrote hymns. We stormed through the town, up towards the castle. Some, mostly sailors, came and jeered us, waving mugs of beer, laughing, and pointing. But we were many and undeterred. I remembered to love those lost souls then, to remember that they were of God as much as I was, and I shouted this to my followers, who heeded. I saw the castle ruins ahead of us, thought of Owain Glyndŵr. To my left was St. Paul's Chapel, one of our own dear victories, a chapel built in place of a tavern. I believe in a process that leads to divine blessing, not in the finite squabbling of mortal men, but even I was grateful for the symbolic resonances of that victory. On my right were the sinners, mocking us with their blaspheming sign and their loud jeering. Emerging from the door was Wyn. He saw me and looked away. I could not help myself. I called his name. I asked him to come and join us. I said it was not too late for him to see himself, to see God in himself, to see God everywhere, to save his soul again. I ran after him, grabbed his shoulder. He pushed my arm away and I saw the blond-haired young boy in his dark locks and his stony features and the way his face scowled like a fork of lightning. I saw a thing fallen away from the beauty that it was God-given. And I said that he would find himself lonely and too late for saving if he carried on this way. He pushed me away again, cursed me and cursed God, cursed those that marched. We went on, undeterred, but it burned in me and does still.

'Wyn died. There was a storm that lasted eight days. Rain drops came down with all the heft of little oceans. He was drunk and he took shelter in an alleyway. They found his body cold and drenched and covered in sick. His mother had to take his clothes and wash them. Such a beautiful boy, and he made himself ungodly.

'I have heard what those who in this new age think themselves wiser have said. I know what they see me as, and I know what I am. I have always believed that there is more than the vice and pleasure of this world. I fought for my people to learn to lead good lives. We gave them education, we helped them realise the possibility for beauty and glory and divinity within their imperfect, brittle bodies. Belief, it seems, has become a much-maligned thing. But though it pains me to wait and watch, I do so. When the sign comes, I will go walking again. Till then, I spend my time in prayer, believing. When the fornicating sinners sit upon my cold stone, I imagine kissing them, loving them, forgiving them.'

*

Josephine and Vic walk into the kitchen to find Robbie sitting at his chair with a girl on his lap. She is shorter and wider than him, with red curling hair and fake purple lashes. There is a can of San Miguel on the table where his black coffee usually is. The girl is laughing at something Robbie has said.

'Ellen.' Vic blinks. 'How are you?'

'Hiya Vic,' says Ellen, elongating her syllables, stretching her arms out.

Ellen sits in the front row of most classes, asking the lecturers questions and patronising her classmates. Josephine thinks she is the kind of person who has been told they are a go-getter one too many times.

Vic hangs up her coat and leans on the wall. Josephine stays where she is. Rain batters the window over the sink.

'Do I not get a greeting?' says Robbie, his mouth forming a thick and wide O-shape. 'Me, the one who brought about this class reunion?'

'It's not a reunion, Robbie.' Vic shakes her head. 'We were in the same lecture together, like, twenty minutes ago.'

'Fucking wank, wasn't it?' said Ellen. 'I mean, I just think her style is a bit airy, you know? Like, give me actual concepts, content, knowledge I can better myself with. I don't need your passion.'

Josephine nods at Robbie's can. 'Bit early?'

'No, no, a drink in the morning, it's nice. You've just got societal expectations and conventions in your head. I mean, I've had my coffee, I've had my toast, it's not like I've not eaten. And now I'm having a beer. And it's nice. Refreshing. Crisp. I don't need it. I'm not an alcoholic.' He pauses and looks around at his audience. His grin grows so wide it threatens to split his face. 'Well, mostly.'

Ellen lets off a giggle that starts high and falls lower, while Robbie makes an ape-like laugh made up of repetitive O sounds. She puts a hand over his cheek.

Josephine and Vic look at each other. These are the kinds of things Robbie likes to say to spark worry. To get attention.

'Robbie,' says Josephine, dryly, picking the skin of her left index finger with her right thumb. 'You are just not interesting enough to be an alcoholic.'

Vic laughs. 'You are literally just another dude drinking larger.'

Robbie's eyebrows crease as if this has hurt him. Then he takes another sip.

Ellen looks confusedly at Vic and Josephine before turning back to Robbie. 'You can't drink in the mornings,' she says. 'It sets a bad precedent.' She looks back at Vic and Josephine. 'He doesn't listen.'

Vic looks at her feet. Josephine wonders how long Ellen has been able to tell Robbie anything.

'Of course, I don't,' says Robbie. 'It's all just conventions. Meaningless social obligations that we get told are the way to live.'

'Who tells us?' says Josephine.

'You know, them, the government, the parents, the teachers. Everyone who holds all the power. And they tell us to eat a proper breakfast and to not do drugs and to only drink at the times everyone else drinks. And it's all bullshit, you know?'

This is the way Robbie operates in conversations with women; like they are unworthy receivers of his gospel. He gestures to the window and the rain clattering against the glass.

'I want to be like that storm there. Totally of my own will, desire and demand. Total control. Everything bending to me and my wants.'

'How many of those have you had?' says Ellen, giggling with a touch less comfort now. She squeezes Robbie. He slips her arms off from his head, so she is sat on his knee, her limbs limply over her lap, like an over-sized, out-of-action puppet.

'I'm not drunk. Come on. This is my first. I'm speaking properly here. Keep up,' Robbie shakes his head, stares at the can and turns his face away. 'I'm my own fucking animal.'

Josephine goes over to the counter and pours herself a glass of water.

'Let's go out tonight,' says Robbie. 'It'll be good. Storm's raging. Pubs will be full. Packed. Sweating. Something's bound to spark.'

Ellen's eyes spark up like car headlights in the night. 'Yes! Let's go out! The four of us! It'll be fun! A laugh!'

Vic and Josephine look at each other, thinking of the miserable time they will have.

'I don't know,' says Josephine.

'If you go, I'll come,' says Vic, before turning to Ellen and Robbie. 'Wouldn't want to be an intrusion.'

Ellen smiles and stretches her arms back over Robbie.

'You wouldn't be,' says Robbie. Ellen's arms go limp around him. He smiles to himself.

Vic and Josephine look at each other, uncertainly. Somehow, Robbie always seems to worm himself into their plans. The town is so small, they're bound to see him if they go out, as well.

'Yeah, alright,' says Josephine, heavily, hoping they can lose him after a couple of pubs. 'We'll go.'

Ellen squeals and claps. 'Oh, fantastic. It'll be so fun.'

Josephine blinks, and for just a second in the darkness of her eyelids she sees Mother pointing a finger and silently weeping. When she opens them, it is Ellen and Robbie smirking.

'Yeah,' says Josephine, looking at Vic.

Robbie elbows Ellen and nods to Josephine. 'You think I drink, you should see her. She gets fucked up.'

'Josie?,' Ellen opens her mouth wide. 'I had no idea!'

Josie was what her mum had called her. The half-skeleton face burns inside of her. She needs to rid herself of it.

'That's not true,' says Vic. 'Stop making shit up.'

Josephine closes her eyes and when she opens them, Ellen looks different. She is paler, stiffer.

'Now why do something like that to yourself?' says Ellen, laughing. 'Don't you want to remember anything?'

Mother's voice seems to sliver out of Ellen's tongue, mocking and haunting. Josephine keeps her breathing steady and her body still.

'I don't know,' she says. 'It makes me feel good.'

And she imagines it would make her feel good, or at least, make her feel not empty, literally filled, no longer totally under the domination of Mother. And when she is sober, all she wants is to hide.

Robbie smirks. 'She has the right idea.'

Ellen slaps him playfully on the arm. Josephine feels Vic's eyes on her. Vic is the only one she has told about the dreaming and the pain, and after she told her, under the influence of four lines of coke and six double vodkas, she decided never to mention it again.

*

Glynn is sitting on the blue sofa in his living room. Its loose spring is digging into his left buttock but he is so accustomed to this mild pain that it has become familiarly, almost comfortable. It fits with the ache of his muscles from his run and the press-ups and sit-ups. Glynn does not trust total comfort anyway. Anna is next to him, her legs over his lap, sucking on a cigarette. Jake is on the floor, watching a television screen, playing on his console, focusing on virtual gunfire and making pixelated bodies of the various violent henchman coming after him. Bill is sat on an armchair, staring at the wall like he is trying to get somewhere beyond everything.

'I want to go out tonight,' he says. 'I want to get pissed and feel the storm wrap itself around me.'

Anna shakes her head. 'I'm crashed, love. Can't we stay in? I'll just end up missing lectures and slumming around all over again. And it'll be fucking freezing and wet.'

'Exactly.' Bill carries on staring at the same spot of wall. 'It's part of it. Get nice and soaked. Get shivering. Feel like we're living. It's what we're supposed to do.'

'Yeah. Drinking and debauchery at all costs. I've seen it said so on the news,' Jake contributes, still focused on his game.

'Can't we just do what we want to do?' says Anna.

Bill grins and keeps looking at the wall. 'I want to do what's expected of me.'

'Robbie will be out tonight,' says Jake, wistfully American. 'He asked me to meet him and his new bird.'

'Might finally get a chance to deck the cunt.'

Robbie likes to be the boy who gets hit and Bill is the man who does the hitting. It's clear just looking at him. He stares at walls, clenches his fists and grinds his teeth as if in preparation for some future slight he will have to get worked up about. They know each other well. Robbie used to make a habit of rubbing Bill's head, joking that it was a bowling ball. That was all good fun, but since Robbie made another move on Anna, the joking had ceased and there was a sense that some sort of dramatic and final confrontation was required.

'You don't need to do that, man,' says Glynn, hesitation in his voice. 'He's more trouble than he's worth. You know this.'

Bill turns and fixes Glynn with his gaze. His eyes burn blue like naked flames.

'Why are you standing up for him? He fucked her when she was your girl, didn't he?'

Anna's legs stiffen over Glynn. She puts a hand on his shoulder and pulls herself up with the elbow of her other arm.

'Why are you saying stuff like that? She's not anybody's girl, she's not a possession. And everyone else has put it behind them.'

They'd never been anything serious, he and Anna. They had never had the talk where parameters were agreed, so when he came out and found her kissing Robbie good morning he had no right to say anything other than 'oh,' which he said with much pain and shock – enough for Anna to realise she'd hurt someone she cared deeply about by getting with someone she found slightly repulsive. They had talked it out, taken sex off the table as an avenue for their relationship.

'I just don't get why the guy has to be such a pacifier all the time,' says Bill, looking at Jake and snorting.

'I'm not being a pacifier, Bill,' says Glynn. 'I just think you'll be giving him what he wants if you go and hit him.'

Bill shakes his head with disgust. 'Who gives a shit? If the cunt deserves a punch, punch the cunt. It's as simple as that.'

Glynn is quiet and wonders what would have happened if he had punched Robbie rather than silently watched him from the staircase. Perhaps he and Anna would be together, properly together, and he wouldn't feel this strange little pain in his stomach every time the two of them shared a laugh, every time they silently confirmed that their relationship would never again be anything more than it now was.

'You shouldn't have fucking said that, Bill,' says Anna.

Anna often feels a need to react particularly severely to the less pleasant aspects of Bill's character, like she is apologising for something. She keeps her legs on Glynn's lap.

Bill turns his head back to the wall and hangs a hand in Glynn's direction. 'Sorry, pal. No hard feelings, yeah?'

Glynn presses his hand against Bill's and briefly wants to expunge himself. He detests everyone in this room, even Anna. They are proof that he is not with the right people, that, somewhere in his life, he has failed terribly.

*

Josephine finds herself smoking a cigarette outside the flat with Ellen, who is nattering incessantly in her ear about Robbie. She is certain that Robbie did not come out with them so he could find some respite from Ellen. But Ellen seems to have not noticed.

'It's just crazy you know because I am like just not a commitment girl, not at all, and neither is he, really – commitment guy that is – oh my God, but you know we both just like to flow through things – you know we are only young after all – but there's something about what happens when we are together you know, and I just think – and I know he thinks too – that it would just be crazy not to follow that, you know what I mean?'

'Yes,' says Josephine, taking a drag, not knowing at all. 'I think I know what you mean.'

Ellen takes a small puff of her cigarette and looks at Josephine with a little smirk on her face. 'Does he bring a lot of girls back, Robbie?'

Josephine watches the smoke go up as the rain comes down. 'Yes,' she says. 'Quite a few.'

This stops Ellen, who grimaces, her lips quivering, Josephine not seeing, silence briefly descending.

'That's it though, isn't it,' says Ellen. 'History. It happens. I don't mind. I have loads of it…'

While Ellen goes on, a young man stands under the doorway of the pub up the road, watching the rain fall, wondering where he just emerged from. He is breathing fresh air for the first time in a very long time. He looks out at the streets, at the water running down them. He knows, at least, that he is home. He steps out from the doorway, sees Josephine and Ellen standing and smoking, remembers what he is looking for. He walks over to them, finds a cigarette is already in his hand.

'Got a match?' he asks.

Josephine raises her eyebrow, holds up a lighter. 'Will this do you?' she says.

He stares at it for a very long time. 'What is that?' he says.

Pressing down, Josephine ignites a flame from the lighter and sees the man jump back in shock. 'Yes, funny, now light your fag,' she says.

The man puts his cigarette to the flame, takes a breath from it. 'Thanks,' he says, moving away quickly.

Ellen and Josephine watch him walk away in the rain, just a blazer and a pair of corduroy trousers on, somehow not shivering.

'What a fucking awful line,' says Josephine. 'I hate it when boys try to be cute like that.'

'He is cute, though,' says Ellen. 'Red hair. Those eyes. Lovely. I wouldn't say no.'

Josephine looks at her.

'Well obviously I would now, because of Robbie. Oh my God. Don't tell him, will you? He'll get so jealous. I can tell he's the jealous type. You know how with some people you can just tell? I can just tell with Robbie. I know! I know! I know! It's so obvious…'

*

Reviving rain keeps falling upon the town as Glynn stands at his front door, shivering a little already from the cold, holding two black bin bags full of empty takeaway boxes and ready meal containers. He looks up at the gulls and sees them circling, searching for scraps. He looks again at the bin bags, and he worries. Plenty of times already he has woken to find rubbish littered across the street and torn bags fluttering in the wind, but the rubbish piles up if it is not put out. Glynn remembers last week, when the stench was so bad you couldn't escape it, no matter where you went in the house. You have to leave it out and hope for the best, is what he has concluded. He steps off the doorway, squinting against the harsh coldness of water and wind.

On the other side of the street by the marina, where the boats rustle and bells sound, a piece of piping on an old house drips water down from above to the concrete. Each makes a splash on the pavement, spreading over the smaller droplets falling from the sky. Slowly, without witness, the drops – each falling onto the same spot – begin to build into something. First, just a layer of still water, somehow suspended from running down to the drain next to where Glynn is placing the bin bags. More drops fall, and the water thickens, grows, into something like skin, something like a body, until a woman is standing there, dressed in strange finery and utterly drenched.

Glynn spots a few stones by the wall and places them over the bags. As he places the last one onto the last bag, he is, for the second time that morning, struck by the sight of someone. This time, it is their strangeness rather than their beauty which catches him. She is wearing a white gown that glitters, a delicate necklace from which a single pendant hangs. She is walking towards him along the path, looking around at all the houses, her eyes wide, as if everything is as new as the day itself. He wonders why she is dressed like that, and if she is unwell.

'Hello,' he calls out to her, waving his hand. 'Are you alright? You're not lost are you? Do you need an umbrella? Or a coat?'

She looks up at him and stares for a while. Then she smiles. 'No, no,' she says. Her accent is more than English – it's posh. Very posh. 'Or at least, not at this moment. Just before you spoke, I had no idea what I was doing, but you've reminded me, somehow. Thank you.'

Glynn blinks. 'You should get out of the rain,' he says. 'If you're not going to borrow an umbrella or a coat.'

She laughs. 'I think I should be quite alright. But thank you.'

He thinks about insisting but is not quite sure how he could. She's obviously not well, he's certain. But he's just not sure what to say or do. In the end, he simply nods. 'Alright. Stay safe,' he says.

'Yes,' she says. 'Thank you.'

That seems the end of things as she moves past the house and up the street. Then, she looks around again for a final word.

'You haven't seen a boy have you?' she says. 'With red hair and fine green eyes? The baker's boy?'

Glynn pauses and pretends to think about it. It irks him to hear someone describe a voice. 'No, sorry,' he says.

She nods and smiles and moves further along up the street. The wind picks up again and Glynn moves back towards the warm yellow glow of the house, shivering like there is something on his back he cannot quite get off.

CHAPTER FOUR

Anna has decided to stay in. Glynn is walking with Bill and Jake, two people he does not like, through the wind and the water, feeling miserable, longing for the warmth of the pub and the cool of lager and the kind of conversation with these two he can enjoy after his sobriety and his sanity have been sacrificed. Port Trefechan glows in the distance, all wrought iron and Victorian-white lamps. Last night, he watched a documentary on S4C about Saunders Lewis and the language protests. All that battling, and what do they have? Bilingualism, devolution, and their own television channel. It seems like so much and not enough at the same time. Glynn thinks about sharing this with the boys, but knows they do not care. He listens to the sea coming in hard enough that the sound rises over the rushing of the Rheidol River.

'I want to get so drunk I can't see,' says Bill. 'I want to be found snoring into a pizza tonight, snorting cheese into my nostrils.'

Jake laughs and nods. 'Yeah. You'll be gone. I want to wake up in a puddle on the side of the road with chips and mayonnaise all over my face.'

'You'll freeze to death,' says Glynn, smiling and trying manically to join in, to fit with them just briefly. 'The storm is so harsh you'll freeze to death.'

Bill looks at Glynn like he is working something out. 'You can never quite hit the right notes, can you, mate?'

They carry on walking, Bill and Jake proposing more hypothetical situations of debauchery. Glynn wishes Anna was here so she could link arms with him and talk about something. There is nothing, he has realised now after some thinking, particularly interesting about what she says. Maybe he really does only want her because he can't have her, because he feels strange that she could go with people like Bill and Robbie and not, anymore, him. But he knows she wanted him too, once.

They move down a set of stone steps leading to the Rummers pub. Glynn read it used to be a barn. It is hundreds of years old. There is something about the agedness of things which Glynn can't get his head around. He thinks it might be wrong, somehow, to hear the loud, pulsing pop music and smell the cheap vodka which define the place now, defying some sense of the building's purpose, perhaps. But people have always got drunk.

Next to the door, Robbie is smoking a cigarette, his foot against the wall, his head nodding up and down in time with the music. When he sees them approaching, he smirks in that way you have surely become familiar with, by now. Bill's hands scrunch into brick-hard fists. Jake looks at Bill and then at Robbie as if waiting for something to happen. Robbie opens his arms.

'Hello boys! What a miracle. How are you feeling?' he says.

'Like an onlooker in a western,' says Jake.

'Witty as ever, bud. Bill, you look tense. And Glynn! The three of us are missing someone here. We should form some kind of appreciation club.'

Glynn stays quiet but his cheeks redden. He feels a heat inside that burns against the cold.

Bill steps forward. He is close enough to headbutt Robbie, or kiss him. 'Don't talk like that, mate.'

Robbie takes a drag of his cigarette and blows the smoke over

Bill's head. 'I'm doing what I'm meant to do, Bill.'

There is a long quiet. Jake stands in front and puts a hand on each of them.

'Fellas,' he says, with a jazzish grandeur, 'neither of you are really drunk enough to be doing this.'

Bill nods and moves past Robbie wordlessly. Jake follows. Glynn stays.

'You got a spare fag?' he says.

'Didn't know you smoked,' says Robbie, handing over a cigarette and a lighter.

'Only occasionally.' Glynn lights it and takes a puff. He remembers what Robbie is and steels himself. 'I'm only going to say this once, Robbie. Stop trying to make trouble. This stuff with Anna, it doesn't need to be anything. You know Bill. It's for your sake as much as anything.'

Robbie chuckles softly. He pats Glynn on the shoulder. 'Looking out for me, are you?' he says. 'When are you going to stop trying to be like everybody else and start showing us what you actually are?'

Glynn steps away from Robbie's hand. 'You don't know a thing about anybody, Robbie.'

'I know that you're not like them. You're not some stoner-come-bruiser. Or maybe you are, but you're not like Bill. If I wanted a fight, you'd be last person I'd fight, the absolute last. You're shy.'

Glynn stifles a cough. It has been longer than he realised since he last had a cigarette. He thinks about stepping forward but keeps still. 'Just don't throw all that stuff in my face. I don't want to think about it.'

Robbie flicks the butt of his cigarette over the staircase. 'Oh, that doesn't bother you as much as you pretend it does. Get out of your grief.'

'What are you on about?'

'I've seen you! All gloomy walking around town, glaring at me from the corner of every pub and place that we happen to both be in at the same time. Jesus, Glynn, if it bothered you as much as you act like it does, you would've hit me by now. You just want to ruminate about something.'

'I don't need your advice,' says Glynn, stung. 'Or your analysis.'

'Fair enough,' says Robbie, shrugging. 'Makes no difference to me.'

He opens the pub door, yellow light framing his dark silhouette like some divine iconography, briefly. Then he is gone, and Glynn is left alone, smoking a cigarette he doesn't particularly want, preparing to go into a place he does not particularly like.

*

Josephine waits at the bar to be served. She can feel the stick of the counter suckering the arm of her shirt. A group gather their drinks and move away. At the other end of the bar, he is revealed. His clothes are dark colours, all emerald and pitch. His stare is lost, sunken eyes with deep colours. The stubble on his head and his face reminds her of the outline of a skull. The boy with the bacon packet. She recognises his face from somewhere else, perhaps a house party or one of the bonfires in the summer. There is something in him this time that has not been there before, something deep and dark and sad. At this moment she cannot make it out, but the knowing that it is there, whatever it is, makes her want to know him more. Josephine turns her gaze to focus on getting the attention of the barman, who is down the other end, pouring pints of lager into glasses. She stares at the right cheek of his face, as if her gaze on its own might cause him to turn. It does not.

Glynn does not see her look at him, but he does watch her stare at the barman, marvelling at the harshness of her gaze and the coldness of her posture. The girl with the plastic bag. Her hands push against the bar, the muscles of her arms tensed, her thin body stretched across the wood like she is protecting something precious. He remembers her, more than she remembers him, but he never caught her name. Robbie took her to one of the summer beach fires, back when he was friendly with Bill. It was dark and Josephine kept her distance from the fire, so she was just a silhouette sipping on a can, staring out at the sea and the moonlight. It was only when she approached the glare of the flames to tell Robbie she was bored and going home that Glynn caught sight of her. And now he thinks of it, his heart did softly speed its beating when he glimpsed those curls, how they cascaded softly around a face that seemed suited to scowling, how that scowl in the fire showed sharp cheekbones and lily pad green eyes.

She catches the attention of the barman and waits for the drinks to be served. Allowing herself a brief look around the pub, she sees groups of students huddled over wooden tables, the flashing blue lights of the mixing desk, her own group chattering and then, briefly, him looking at her before he turns his gaze back to his pale hands. He glooms on the edge of the bar. She keeps her gaze and hopes for him to look back up at her.

And he feels her gaze on him. He looks up and to his right, and they are looking at each other now. Gently, he grins. There is still the possibility somewhere that she might glare back, might send him back to where he was before this moment, back when he was hopeless and loveless and whirling misery. But instead, she smiles, with closed lips and those eyes that seem to refuse softness.

She nods at the glasses in front of her. 'Sorry, I beat you to it.'

'That's alright,' says Glynn, and a little pulse in his stomach says he would like to keep forgiving her for things. 'I like standing at the bar. You've done me a favour, really.'

Josephine takes a couple of steps away from the glasses and towards him. 'And why is that?'

'I like standing at the bar, trying to look brooding. It feels very movie-like.' The words are coming out too fast and Glynn almost winces as they do. But she laughs, and her eyes widen.

'Yeah? Are you the leading man with the missing girl?'

They both laugh. There is something in the comfort between them that seems new and frightening. Each can feel the sharpness of their breaths.

'I saw you earlier,' says Glynn, before realising his only follow-up is to acknowledge the embarrassing incident. 'I hit you with my plastic bag.'

'Yes,' says Josephine. There is a pause before she continues. 'Thanks for being sweet, though.'

'Yeah, well,' Glynn repeats. 'It's Glynn, by the way. I think we'd met before that.'

'Josephine. Yeah, you looked familiar,' she says.

The barman places the last of Josephine's drinks on the bar. She pays and gives Glynn a smile.

'You out tonight?'

'Yeah,' says Glynn. 'ok.'

She pauses.

'You were asking not inviting,' Glynn laughs awkwardly, 'weren't you?'

Josephine nods, beaming. She lets out a little trill of a giggle.

'Do you want some help with those glasses?' says Glynn, holding out his hands. 'I mean, not to be patronising, it's just there's a lot of them, and…'

'Yes, please,' says Josephine, and she allows herself a small laugh.

From the table behind them, Vic is pointing out to Robbie and Ellen that Josephine seems to be getting particularly close to the boy with the shaved head. She recounts the tale of the bacon packet and the plastic bag.

'I recognise him from some seminars,' she says. 'He's quite

chirpy. One of those ones who seems to know everything.'

'I hate those people,' says Ellen, wetly. 'Acting like the whole room's for them.'

Vic shrugs her shoulders. 'He's always seemed alright to me.'

Robbie puts his arm round Ellen and smirks. 'I know him. Lived with him two years ago. He's a fucking freak, man. Spent three days straight in his room staring at the ceiling. Dropped out and had to get his nan to come and pick him up. We've had a few encounters since. He's a fucking sap.'

Ellen puts her head on Robbie's shoulder. 'I knew there was something weird.'

Robbie shrugs and shifts away from Ellen, so her head dips into the space suddenly between them. Quickly, she sits straight and forward.

'People like that just seem to keep going no matter how much you wished they disappeared,' she said.

And as she speaks there is a clap of thunder like the flash of dynamite, a hard gush of wind which cries in opposition and a renewed, hard clattering of rain thudding down on the roof. The people shriek too, briefly little howls of excitement and laughter at the drama of the storm. In fright, Josephine puts her hand over Glynn's.

'Fucking hell,' she says, not moving her hand away.

Glynn stays still. 'You scared of storms?' he says.

Josephine laughs nervously. 'Who isn't?'

*

They pour into the Yoko's night club, seven of them now, briefly together, briefly in détente, briefly forgetting every tension and crease to dance and drink and waste away some time, to give themselves some form of blurry half-memory to look back on in later ages. In the queue their voices felt loud and boisterous, unworried by the storm's bellows and stomps, but beneath the booms of bass and the crashes of drums and the shriek of synths they can only shout in vain, half-hearing, squinting to see the faces they could see clearly under the outside's bright streetlamps. Josephine and Glynn have not left each other's side since their meeting in the pub, their fingers interlocking and moving around each other's hands, as if trying to uncover the multitude of ways they fit together.

They move along the throughway and into the expanse of dancefloor. There is a platform at the back with some sofas, where a couple are snogging while their lonelier friends chatter. In front of them is a man in a Hawaiian shirt and aviator sunglasses, dancing slowly with his arms stretching out wide like a soaked butterfly trying to get back in the air.

'I want some shots!' says Bill, elongating his final word so it seems to blow through all of them like the wind outside. 'Stay right fucking there.'

The bar is on the opposite side of the room to the platform. Bill points to it with his right arm. He points his left to the ceiling and starts flicking it back and forth in motion to the music. Then he charges, entering the throng of people jostling to get a drink and cutting through them effortlessly, like a jousting knight.

'Look at him,' says Robbie, to no one in particular. 'I wish he didn't hate me so much because I fucking love him.'

Then he goes too, Ellen reaching after him, going to grab his hand and missing it, leaving her alone with the rest of the group. Vic gives her a smile.

'He can be like that sometimes,' she says, feeling a burst of sympathy in the pit of her stomach. 'You shouldn't take it personally.'

Amidst all the loudness, Ellen's voice sounds screeching and small. 'He's not like anything! He likes his own space and I also like mine! Do you want to dance?'

'Yes,' says Vic. She can't help but feel sorry for this girl, and that makes her strangely want to befriend her.

They move onto the first square of the dancefloor. The DJ and his decks stare over them behind clubbers who move like a tide. Josephine and Glynn part from them and settle by the tables near the drinks queue, not moving, talking, laughing and holding each other in their very small way.

A little glance up those steps shows us a group of three sitting on a sticky black sofa, left over leaflets on their laps, drinks at their sides. They are the Aberystwyth University Christian Society. They have spent the evening passing leaflets around, advertising a lunch-time lecture complete with complimentary food for the next day. Now, they have left the leaflets on an alcohol-soaked table and are talking about God as the bass thuds.

Hope chatters excitedly about the Lord and night clubs, about how the two are, truly, intertwined. Her Texan accent lodges itself insistently into nearby ears. 'You see, it's people congregating, praising,' she says. 'It's a space of love and joy. It's everything you would want from the most beautiful of services. It's there to be emulated. We need to emulate this.'

Jake walks by, holding a bottle of yellow VK, bobbing his head. He looks at the four of them and nods. They nod back at him. He burps, loudly enough that the sound flies over the drones of the bass. 'Bless me,' he says and moves on.

He sees Glynn and Josephine and sidles up to them. All the time he has lived with Glynn, they have never really connected. Now, he sees a chance.

'You know, I really feel this is a wonderful place to study the arts,' he shouts at them. 'The place is art. It seems to speak back, you know?'

'Yeah,' says Glynn, nudging Josephine playfully, pretending he would never be so pretentious.

'You ever looked at the clock tower outside? The plaque, it's to some old pro-abstinence firebrand preacher. Now everybody's getting off on it and throwing up over it. This place is layers upon layers. I'm going to walk to the secret beach tomorrow. I want to see what I can take from every part of this town.'

'The secret beach?' says Glynn, straining to hear him. 'Do you mean Tan-y-Bwlch?'

'Yeah, it's like a hidden place. There's magic there, I know it.'

Glynn laughs. 'Jake, you can see it everywhere.'

'Well I think it's a great idea,' says Josephine, leaning her head to the left and swaying, her mouth open and giggling, her arm around Glynn's body, like he is a lamppost she's swinging around.

'What are you reading at the moment?' shouts Jake, looking expectantly at the two of them.

Josephine laughs again and looks up at Glynn, who grimaces, feeling caught between two worlds.

'*Dark Philosophers*,' he says. 'You read it?'

'Yeah, bits,' says Jake, lying. 'That's a Williams something, right? From round here, yeah?'

Glynn raises an eyebrow. 'Thomas. Gwyn Thomas. And no. Just Welsh.'

Jake nods as if faced with something genuinely and particularly thought-provoking. Like a saviour, Bill sails back from the bar with seven small plastic cups in his hands, each filled with tequila. The smell rises. Jake sees Bill and shifts.

'Drink!' he bellows. 'I would like one of those drinks, yes please.'

Bill passes the drinks around. A boy in a sports jacket bumps into him and liquid jumps up in the cups.

'Fuck off,' says Bill as if sneezing to dispel a bit of dust stuck up his nostril. 'Blazer boy. Who the fuck wears a blazer?'

The boy moves away quickly. Glynn and Josephine take the shots and Bill moves forward, searching for the others. Jake has disappeared.

'That guy can talk,' says Josephine.

Glynn shrugs. 'He's alright, really.'

They knock back the shots, pull faces at each other, agree Bill bought the cheap stuff.

Robbie, it turns out, is talking to an underdressed Anna, who has arrived in her jeans and a baggy t-shirt looking for Bill, who texted her telling her to come out and see Glynn pull. Sure enough, she sees him talking to the beautiful girl who usually works behind the bar. Anna feels a little bitterness and pain in her stomach watching Glynn laugh with her. Seeing Robbie, she takes the chance to engage in a conversation that might distract her. And he, seeing an old flame and wondering if he could stoke it, is open arms and large smiles, pulling her into a big hug and kissing the top of her head.

'How are you, beautiful?' he says. 'Good, yeah? Getting treated good by Bill, yeah? We're alright now, you know, he was just here, he bought me a shot. He's disappeared somewhere. Probably beating some bloke's brains in, the Neanderthal. Anyways, your little sad lover boy has game. Chatting up Josephine. She's not easily impressed but she's talking to this one.'

'Right,' says Anna. 'I should find Bill, actually. See you later.'

She puts an arm on Robbie's shoulder in farewell, who grabs her wrist. They stop for a moment. Then they hear him.

'What the fuck!' says Bill, appearing in front of them from the throng, his body shaking, and his fists clenched.

*

Jake is making the face where he looks really disgusted by the beat to communicate his deep enjoyment of it. His elbows are at his hips and his shoulders are popping up and down. Jake is enjoying dancing on his own. It is hot and the sweat on his skin feels freeing. The DJ and his decks are next to Jake's right ear, and he feels like his brain is going to sweat out his forehead. The feeling is very exciting. Across the room, a scuffle is going on; Jake can see people scramble and the bouncers move in. It's Bill, he realises, swinging for Robbie, who has dodged every strike while smirk smirk smirking. The bouncers are dragging Bill towards the exit. Anna is shouting and running after them. Robbie is by the doorway clapping. Jake feels beautifully disconnected from the whole thing. Vic and Ellen were in front of him, but Ellen has gone running after Robbie and Vic has gone running after her. He will later buy chips, go home, and tell Bill he saw nothing and wondered where he'd gone. The taste of salty fried potatoes excites him more than any fight or romance ever could. For now, he carries on moving, like everything else. He thinks more about chips. Then he stops dancing and moves towards the door.

*

'Things went dark, first. A darkness like you've never seen. A darkness I cannot adequately describe. The pitch of silence. A piano without its ivory. Not just a sight but something to wade through, something thick with sludge. I do not know what I felt with. Sensation surrounded my soul. And then I saw Him, and this I shall not attempt to describe.

'You need only know that briefly I saw the Earth and the galaxies in all their glory, and fullness. Every secret unveiled itself to me. Every soul stretched its song towards me. Like some ship that sees dry land after too long, I knew in a way I could never have known that my whole life and everything around it was in the hands of something so large and surrounding. And yes, He was there, standing above it all. I had no body to kneel or bow with, but I did my best. Surely as my new knowledge had come, I knew it would have to leave me again. There was need of me still in the mortal realm.

'When I awoke, I knew not even my name. There was only that view of Bridge Street running a long descent in the direction of the hill and its woods. I could sense the castle behind me, could feel the ruin of its many souls. I stayed still and began my wait. Over a century in stone, memories made their return to the dried rivers of my mind. When English royalty invited itself thrice to this town, I remembered that I was once a shepherd of its people, that I once fought for this land to rid itself of false idols. Watching those that carried eggs and banners, I was heartened to see many had not given up the fight. I saw the drunkards and the drugged stumble and slip on rainy nights towards homes and taxis, and I remembered how I tried to save them. I wept in what way an entombed soul could. And I remembered kissing a sin-filled cheek when I saw her walk away from me, she whose name I have learnt is Josephine, and I longed to do it again. That name, which once held up an Emperor, which promises the Lord's victory. She betrays it all. The stench of sin is on her, working and drinking in that darkest and direst of public houses behind me. I have watched her holding hands and kissing various figures who mean as much to her as seaweed to a fisherman. Over time, I have come to realise she will be the thing that sends me walking again. Her soul is the one I must save, the one I must forgive, and in my love she might turn towards the light, or someone might. Her, trying to press in so much her own soul might be crushed. What our contact will bring is not my concern, that is the Lord's purview alone.

'The moment of my moving has not yet come. I know this. I do not know when it will arrive, but it shall. I know it is close. Just now she touched my cold casing for the first time. I heard her voice, the way her laugh rose up from her into the rainy night like something divine. I cannot feel the rain, but like a parched man I wanted to, then. It seemed the droplets were her voice coming back down, showering us. His voice followed, like earth and mud and hills and all the things I have known. I could feel my own blood in him. It gave me hope till I heard that he was using his preacher's gifts to mock me.

"And it's ridiculous, right?' he said. 'This big monument to someone who failed so abjectly. I mean, like, the most abject of failures. I mean, the kind of failure people commemorate by making him fail again and again and again. It's incredible. Sort of glorious.'

"Can't say I'd noticed it before,' she said.

'It meant something that she did not mock, but the pain of his cruel words burned in me. Anger rose for the first time in a long time, and I did not fight it because I knew it was righteous, willed by God, one that was a matter of faith. His retribution would beckon soon. I could feel something like a body begin to form around me. For the first time I noticed the coldness of the stone around me.

'She took the v shape of his shirt from which his neck emerged and pulled it towards her. She pressed his forehead against hers, keeping their mouths apart so that water trickled down between them.

"I'm tired of noticing things,' she said, and she smiled wide, showed teeth.

'They kissed, his cheeks all red and his hands shaking from the cold winds that swept through the town and from something else. I felt my bones and realised I could move but also that now was not the moment. I stayed still like a lecher for the Lord and let them take liberty of their souls on me. They moved away, holding hands, and I knew they would sin that night and that it might be too late to redeem them. I remembered Wyn and shut my eyes. It was then I learnt I had eyes to shut.

'It was also then I learnt that what was to come required more than just my own soul or shade or whatever this essence of me is. I knew what great labours I would once again have to undertake. I knew that there would be a greater pain and difficulty than parts like this had ever seen before. And I knew they would be gone almost as quickly as they begun. The castle called to me, and I knew its spirits and I would meet soon enough. My body forming, I waited for the trumpet to send me walking.'

*

'I am thinking as the things are happening. I am thinking as he is holding my hand and taking me back to his flat. He keeps calling it a flat, but it's a house, albeit a dingy one. The landlords here don't care about the conditions of things. They just want spaces for people to move into and move out of. It's ok because in three years we're all going to get jobs and move to the city and forget we ever slept in those damp, mouldy bedrooms.

'I am scared because I have only ever been with Taylor. Taylor was my friend in secondary school. By the time we got to sixth form, I was in love with her. She liked to play games with people. Often, she'd play me against our other friends, Beth and Tanya. I don't think that either of them was in love with Taylor, but they certainly wanted her to like them. Maybe I'm not giving them enough credit. Tanya always seemed to talk to Taylor with mild disdain, and Beth was sort of pushed away because of how rarely she would do what Taylor wanted. Maybe I give myself too much credit, and the truth was that I was a weak little lap dog that followed Taylor Yates's every move, desperate for her to give me attention. But one night she did. If she hadn't, maybe I wouldn't still be so desperate to think about her, but one night she did, and I am thinking about that night even now, as Glynn takes off my coat and kisses the back of my neck, making the hairs stand on edge. I like the way his hands feel around my waist, all firm and eager to please, the slightest tremor in his fingers. He makes my body feel lithe, he makes me feel sexy. I move into him, and he lets out a little moan.

'With Taylor, I had put my hands on her, first. It was after the news broke about Beth, and around about the time Mum was in the first stages of chemotherapy. She had grown more violent than usual. After she threw a glass and it just missed my shoulder and smashed into the wall, Dad had suggested I stay with a friend till things calmed down. This was a regular occurrence. Something would happen, and I would need to go away while it was sorted. I never really knew what the things were, though in this case it was obviously the treatment, but I always felt like they were my fault. Mum was always convinced Dad and I were plotting against her. Often, I think I had to be discarded in the same way an officer would have to drop his weapon before he entered negotiations with a kidnapper.

'I was at Taylor's, and four days before, we had been at a house party. At the house party, Taylor had made fun of Beth for being too scared to try weed. She had called Beth a lot of things that played on her insecurities, because she knew what those were and how to really push the knife in. Beth left the party crying, and we carried on for the rest of the night. At one point, Taylor danced with me by putting a hand on my shoulder and swaying against my body. She looked into my eyes, and I almost kissed her then, but I got the sense she might pull back and laugh at me, as if the whole thing were some practical jokes. She could really hurt you like that.

'We are moving up the stairs and I can feel my want for him. I can feel his want for me, too. It is exciting to want someone. We get to his room, and he opens the door. When I was with Taylor, we were already in bed. But before that, her dad had come in and told us that Beth had tried to kill herself by swallowing bleach. He stressed that she was going to be alright. He understood we were shocked. He had spoken to my parents. Everyone agreed it was best to keep things as they were for now, unless I was desperate to go home. I said I wanted to be with Taylor, and he said he thought I would. We talked a while and he left. Once the lights were out, Taylor started to weep, and I held her to my chest. I could feel her mouth and her tears on my skin. I felt wonderful and guilty.

'He is taking off my shirt and gasping at the sight of my body. I take his face and press it against my breasts and feel his mouth and look up at the ceiling. I tell him his touch feels so good because it does. I surprise myself.

'When Taylor looked up at me, her eyes were full of want. It was the first time she had ever looked at me like that. She asked me to kiss her, and I did. We kissed for a long time. That was all we did, then. We kissed and we felt each other's bodies, and we kept crying. We were crying for our own reasons, and we were crying from how much we needed each other. I didn't want to let her go. I knew that the moment I did, she would hurt me, and, after some time, she did.'

THE SECOND DAY

CHAPTER FIVE

On the outskirts of town, something is about to happen. Now, the fields are empty. Cows have been ushered to their sheds. An old manor looks down from the hillside. The Ystwyth River pours. Dawn is still a while to come. and clouds have snuffed out the shine of the stars and the moon. There is only the burning of distant light from the town, hazily lighting the falling, furious rain. The black sea pushes and pulls; waves meet each other as they bounce from rocks and stone. Something is emerging from its depths. Something that fell deep, but not deep enough to touch the ocean floor. Think of that which slips and surprises. As the water grows shallower, an emerging, bulking body tastes air and is cut by wind and stone. There, out in the nothing, advancing towards the stony beach, is a sperm whale, scars across its skin scratched-in by squids, half its mouth still submerged, breathing shallow breaths of spluttering water. Say, welcome! to our strange little miracle. It scrapes and heaves and is upon the shore now, water pushing at the end of its tail. A squawk sounds out into the near dawn. A seagull lands upon the beast's back. It begins to peck. The whale's eyes parallactically perceive the cool darkness of stone and the re-forming, glooming cloud. Rain falls. The whale's vast lungs deflate. The seagull pecks, trying to tear a piece of flesh. It hawks a summoning call to the clouds. And the rest of the scavengers come like little sharks at the bottom of the ocean, they pick and pull but the whale's skin is tough. The birds slip and struggle. The whale heaves a final breath, its tail floating limply, gently swaying back and forth in the salty foam.

This is not the first time an old leviathan has washed up here to die. Centuries past, a sperm whale haunted these parts, taking fish that men on boats thought was theirs. The fishermen were no fools. They knew of ships broken in half, of men swallowed whole or in part. For a while, the boats stayed docked in the harbour and the whole shore belonged to one whale. For a while, it seemed to the men that the world belonged to the whale. But the shallow sea is no place for giants of the deep. Soon it beached upon pebbles and grit. Then, as now, it died on Tan-y-Bwlch. Then, it was the farmer's son who'd gone and told the fishermen. He found them sitting outside the Angel, drinking their beers and cursing their fortunes, and they went and saw the sight themselves. It brought smiles to their faces and laughter to their voices. The sea was theirs again. They shooed away the scavengers, kept watch for red kites and crows, cut up the whale as best they could. A new venture in the familiar business of harvesting the water's dead. Some of the meat they kept and cooked, most they sold. Once it was at its end, they each took aimlessly selected remnants of its skeleton as trophies, keeping them in chests and drawers and on mantelpieces. When they first went back out to the water, it felt like coming home. But with time, every unexpected splash and sound reminded them of the beast. They would squirm and start at the sight of every dolphin and seal that burst through the sea's surface. In the evenings, they were certain they heard a long, piercing call. They took to drink to kill it. They drank till they never came out again. Dial y morfil.

Now, a whale lies here again. As the gulls gather and find themselves unable to feast, dawn quietly breaks behind the clouds. Soon the kites will come, too. But even then, the whale's body will stay tight and slippery. Those who look for a while will notice that its skin is impossible to break. For now, it remains unperceived, save for the eyes of the chip-fattened and sea-drenched seagulls, and unrecorded. The farmer occupying the nearby field is too focused on his land to see what the sea may have washed up. Someone will spot it soon enough, and then the bureaucracy will set in: the yellow tape and the men in orange jackets and the signs asking people to keep well back. But for now, stare down at the scene, at the birds and the sand and the storm and this creature that should not, by any means, be here.

*

'I waited until grey light rose over the darkness. I pressed my hands against the stone and pushed, and yes, I had hands to push with. I pushed not to move the clock tower, not to split foundations, but to emerge myself from my prison like a whale bursting from the water. I felt the cold of the rock and the cold of sea winds. Then the rain, like liquid stone, dribbling down my trembling fingers. I smelt the sick of the previous evening and the salt of the sea. When my eyes emerged, I allowed myself to flick them back and forth; taking in, for the first time in so long, the sight of Pier Street and of the castle behind me. With my mouth I breathed in air and my lungs bloomed like maguey. I sighed and was still for a moment, halfway towards being whole again. I watched a gull struggle against the elements, screeching its sorrow, the gust propelling it from a roof where its chicks called out. Summoning my faith, gathering my beliefs like sticks for a nest, I pushed hard against the rock. And then I was whole, lying on the concrete amidst the desolation: polystyrene packages, metal cans and the rest. My left cheek was wet, and I realised I had landed in sick. Lifting myself up from the ground, I shivered and saw that I was naked. In the next instance I was clothed and cleaned and warmed by something beyond earthly fires. I began to move again, knowing already where to go.'

*

Grey sunlight breaks again. The rain thuds, fat droplets that splatter like squashed bloated flies, and make heavy puddles. Over by the marina, they are in bed together, Josephine's arm across Glynn's chest. Leave them alone.

Jake is walking to Tan-y-Bwlch. Finally, he is walking out of this town, as he has wanted to for so long. Under the warm quilt, such desires felt soft and quiet, but outdoors they are as strong as the wind itself. The wind makes his coat billow. He opens his arms and welcomes it, blowing back his long hair, slick with grease, making the furry scratches of stubble on his face tremble. As he reaches the harbour light, free of the town and the eyes and ears of others, he begins to hum. He wishes he could hum something clever and fitting, but nothing comes to mind. So instead, he hums little tuneless noises, looking at the big waves, feeling wonderful sensations. At the bottom of them is something richly fishy, and yet ever so slightly reminiscent of off milk.

Jake looks at the steep hill on the other side of the beach. It is not one he has ever thought of climbing before. In fact, he has barely even acknowledged its existence, it being on the edge of the borders of what he considers to be his lands to roam. But he can picture himself now standing on its peak which rises to the sky like the finger of a reptile's claw, as if he were one of those old-fashioned poets. He is so focused on the hill, in fact, that he misses the whale, walking along the path above the beach, his eyes so set on its steepness. He catches the stench, and its thickness makes him scrunch up his mouth and nose. It is like salt and shit, mixed up and spread across the stones. He follows the path, pinching his nostrils, fixated on that mighty peak and his need to conquer it. When he reaches the foot of the hill, he sees its steepness, mud and difficulty. He looks at his trainers, battered and without much grip, and changes his mind. He decides instead on a walk along the shoreline where he looks ponderingly over the Irish Sea. The smell is stronger on the sand, and he stifles a gag from deep in his stomach. Something is dead. Jake wonders if there is a seal or a dolphin nearby. He raises a hand to his mouth before a loose grain of sand flung forward in the wind hits his eye. Letting out a small cry, he turns and falls with the gust. Just then, before his lids close over his pupil and his hands cover his eyes, he catches it. The grey stretch like a large rock looming over the waves. He jumps back in fright, loses his balance and stumbles. He and it lie like that for some time, the rain and undulating tide drenching their exposed skin, both pairs of eyes closed. Jake pulls himself to his knees, his left eye watering the sand away, and looks up in front of him.

'That's a fucking whale,' he says. 'An actual fucking whale.'

The force of the tide pushes the carcass back and forth gently. Iced air pushes itself between them, Jake's fringe hangs over his vision. Pushing it to one side, he rises so that he is standing over the dead beast, the smell no longer so off-putting.

'Where the hell did you come from?' he says, almost expecting an answer.

There is no whale song in response, just the low bellows of wind and wave. He walks towards the body. Sea spittle foams along its grey skin, and he can hear the rattling pebbles trapped beneath. Freezing water sinks through his trainers. He winces. He steps forward. The sea is up to his ankles and the whale lies in front of him. Jake stretches out his shivering hand, feels the smooth sheen of its skin. The stench is enough to make him bring his hands to his nose, but he doesn't. He cannot help but breath the wet rot in. If there was anything that could give him a poem, this would surely be it. Yet he cannot think of any lines or words. There are just the hard gusts, the cold sea, and the dead beast.

'What brought you here?' says Jake, running his hand down the whale's snout.

And then something happens. Another wave comes in, and Jake feels movement from inside the beast. Before he can tell himself it is the tide playing tricks, he hears the deep guttural huff of the sperm whale's breath, feels its body shake. A gust of stench arrives with it and Jake feels momentarily certain he is going to vomit. He sees the whale's eyes flicker and focus on him. A dribble of water spurts from the body and rolls down. Jake steps away slowly, his face contorted by the smell. He begins to walk quickly back towards town, scared and uncertain. The dog comes up and sniffs at his shoes. Then, catching the scent of its source, runs off in the same direction. The woman waves to him.

'Not quite right for a dip, eh?' she says, before catching the scent. She wrinkles her nose and looks away.

'No,' says Jake, striding past her.

'Suit yourself,' she mutters, seeing the blurry shape of her dog sniff at something large among the waves. She calls for him to get away.

It is the woman who later reports the whale. But by then, it has stopped breathing, again.

*

Nathan wants to live his life as if it were gospel. The circumstances of his birth, the trials of his youth: all of it has led purposefully to this moment, which will in turn lead purposefully to other moments, which will lead finally to the great moment of eternal purpose. But what is this current moment, this point somewhere between the instant of birth and eternity? He is under the concrete overhang of the Hugh Owen building, watching the rain lash onto the road, the hill, the trees, and the houses. He is holding a thick bunch of leaflets and he is waiting. The leaflets are for a talk on God in the social media age. The talk includes a free lunch. The speaker is a vicar coming from Shrewsbury. This time, they have agreed to put the food on the other side of the room to the doors, to stop people taking food and leaving.

He sees a hooded figure over there, coming up the concrete steps leading to the concourse He rushes over, steps clattering, puddles splashing. There is someone he can speak to. It is Jake, still hurrying away from the whale towards the library, seeking shelter from the storm and feeling very awed.

Nathan holds out his hand and speaks. He tries to keep his voice strong and hardy, like an old ship refusing to sink. 'Good morning.' The cracks and creaks are coming already. 'Would you like a free lunch?'

That stops Jake. His current account's balance has been tipping into his overdraft, and he won't get money from his parents till the next month. 'Always,' he says.

Nathan smiles and hands Jake a flyer. Splodges of rain make the ink run but the title is still legible. 'We're having a talk later today. And there will be plenty of sandwiches. We're a friendly bunch.'

But Nathan can already feel his failure in the whiny pitch of his own voice. He is falling again from orator to annoyance. Jake stares at the poster as if considering.

'No, thank you,' he says. 'I'm not Christian.'

'Are you sure? I promise, we're not intense about it. We're not a cult.' Nathan shouts an awkward laugh. He can feel the words are all wrong. 'Why don't you take a flyer just in case?'

But Jake simply puts his hands up, shakes his head and moves along. Nathan watches him go. He must remind himself that these failures are what faith is built from. He touches the promise ring, attached to a pendant round his neck and stuffed down his shirt. He remembers love. Love like light. Necessary to avoid darkness, chaos and confusion. The storm is cruel, but without the sun it would be tyrannical. As it is, the sun tempers it, and will be here long after the clouds have lifted. He thinks then of those planets where storms rage for years. That future where light swallows itself. Nathan swallows the lump forming in his throat. Those things are not for him to explain. They are beyond. They are God's. God has given him a simpler task.

He hears the slapping of feet on wet concrete. Hope is coming down the walkway. She smiles and, despite her being in a raincoat and jeans, that is enough for him to feel watery in his stomach and twiddle with his fingers behind his back. Leaflets flap at her side like troublesome kittens under a mother's paw. He walks towards her. Behind the windows of the library are students typing at computers, staring at books, scribbling on paper. Their whole lives, Nathan thinks, are emptier than this one moment of meaning. He takes Hope in his arms and kisses her. The kiss is slow and long. He faintly enjoys the prospect of all those unsaved souls looking out, seeing the two of them, realising this is what faith and love look like. She pulls away, smiling, then frowning.

'She's coming,' Hope whispers.

They detach from each other and take a few steps back. Sarah walks towards them, wearing the same beam she always does: the one that looks twenty years too old. There is a moment of quiet beneath the weather's arguments where Nathan worries that he may have been found out. And with all those witnesses. It would only take one word.

'Someone took a flyer,' says Sarah, still smiling. 'I think they'll come. They said they'd see.'

'That's great,' says Hope, her syllables stretching. 'I haven't been able to get anyone. I guess an American talking about Jesus Christ is a little too predictable.'

Nathan remembers the advice given to him at the summer conference. 'Our best bet is not to talk about the man himself too directly,' he says. 'That will put people off in the early stages.'

Sarah and Hope grin at each other.

'I'm sure nobody's being too loud,' says Sarah.

Hope puts her hands up as if confessing. 'No, no, I've been told. I'll go back to my post and stop screeching hallelujah. I'll try hello instead.'

Hope walks back down the path. Sarah is quiet as the sound of steps becomes more distant. Nathan holds out his hand and she takes it. He is safe.

'How are you doing?' says Sarah. 'I hope you're not going overboard again.'

Nathan laughs. 'What does that mean? We're doing God's work, here.'

Sarah stares at him. Her eyes are blue and beautiful and full of faith. They burn bright against all the nasty rain. 'You know what I mean,' she says. 'You know what I'm scared of.'

He takes her into his arms. She comes into them like a cold sheep. He kisses her forehead. He wonders about those in the library who may have caught a glimpse out of the window, and what they might be thinking.

'You don't need to worry about anything,' he says. 'Other than getting those tight students in with that free lunch.'

Sarah laughs and kisses his neck. 'I'll have them begging for more quiche,' she says.

'I know you will,' he says. 'I love you. That's what makes me believe. I hope you know that.'

'You say it enough,' says Sarah, but she kisses him anyway, rain and saliva mixing on their lips.

As she walks away, Nathan again feels the old pangs of guilt that so undermine his beautiful, certain faith. He tells himself, as he so often does, that Martin Luther King had mistresses, that it was the one vice he allowed himself. Augustine had to confess. Adam raised a Caine. Everyone has something for which they need to seek forgiveness. Nathan touches the promise ring. He still means that promise. That much is certain. The rain continues to fall. Nathan pulls his leaflets to his chest and paces, waiting.

CHAPTER SIX

The light of late morning cracks through cloud and leans gently in through Glynn's window. It splits and reforms as it passes through the shutter-blinds, but it is not that which wakes Josephine. It is the howl of wind, and the slap of rain hitting glass. There is the soft yellow of the ceiling, arms under her neck and over her chest, and the sense of someone else. The memory emerges. She did not go home afterwards, and this surprises her. They are both naked, their skin sticking together from the sweat of being too close. Everything is too close, here, too hemmed in. Glynn's bed is small. She can just about glimpse some space on the mattress. His body is firm and large. For a moment she considers letting herself fall back into it. There was a certain way he held her. Nausea waves through her body, dragging away new feelings and leaving behind old ones. No, it was just the drink and the music, the drama of the storm and kissing under the clock tower. She simply got caught up. She shifts slightly, trying to shimmy out from under his arms. He stirs, opens his eyes, looks at her, his pupils widening.

'Morning,' he says. 'Did you sleep ok?'

He runs a finger softly along her neck. She could tell him to let her go. He could do anything at this moment. She tenses a little at the thought.

'I guess so. What time is it?'

Glynn pulls away and she breathes. He leaves one arm beneath her neck as he reaches over to the bedside table. He picks up the phone and tells her what it tells him.

'It's late,' she says. 'I don't usually sleep in this long.'

'I've got a habit for it,' says Glynn, grinning, putting his other arm around her again. 'It must be infectious.'

Deciding not to nod, she smiles instead. 'I should go soon,' she says. 'If it's already so late.'

He tightens his grip round her. 'You don't need to, you know. You could stay here.' He places a kiss on her shoulder. It is soft and good and reminds her of last night. She considers the proposition. Then he kisses her again, just above the spot before, and again.

'Ok, Glynn, enough, please,' she says.

Glynn moves his arm from under her and pulls himself up. He looks at her. 'Sorry, I didn't mean to… is everything ok?'

Josephine turns to take him in. His earnest eyes. The way his bottom lip has dropped slightly, leaving an o shape all vulnerable and delicate.

'It's just, this isn't really my thing. All this laying together and cuddling.'

'Right,' says Glynn, trying to hide the sting of her words.

But already he is seeing the mistakes he has made again. It was the same with Anna, all over again: wanting love too quickly, wishing it to be massive immediately. He could have sworn, under the rain, the clock tower and the lamplight, that this was the same feeling but truer, something he could really believe might just come good. He looks up at the yellow ceiling, focusing on its pale brightness.

'I'm sorry,' he says. 'I'm not trying to push you any which way. You can go if you want to.'

He pulls away from her and moves over to the edge of the bed, so all the space of his mattress and its grey sheet stretch out between them. The rain begins again, and a little stream pours from holes in the gutter down onto the window. The waves come in on south beach high and darting, kicking up over the promenade and the jetty. In the distance, other waves crash over the harbour light, and beyond are flashing lights and signs of something happening. Glynn looks at his phone again and sees a text from Jake.

'Jesus,' he says. 'No way.'

'What is it?' says Josephine.

'A *whale's* washed up on the fucking beach. Jake says he saw it this morning, before anybody else. Apparently, they've cordoned everything off now, but you can still see it.'

Josephine remembers whales drifting in water over smooth voices on television, the sound of their song echoing out over the vast space of the oceans. 'Do we even get whales here?' she says.

'I don't think so.' He drinks in the blue light of his phone. 'It's on Tan-y-Bwlch.'

'Where is that?'

Glynn turns to her and rises an eyebrow. He smirks. 'You don't know Tan-y-Bwlch?'

'I won't unless you tell me,' Josephine says, unwilling to play.

'It's that beach past the harbour light. Haven't you been there?'

'Vic just calls it the secret beach,' she says. Glynn is grinning at her. She finds it annoying. 'I just didn't know its actual name, I guess. It's not a big deal.'

Glynn shrugs. 'Do you want to come see it?'

There is a brief pause where they remember the previous conversation as the waves hound the land.

'I don't mean anything by that,' he says. 'It's just, it's a fucking whale. I feel like you can put your awkwardness on pause for this, right?'

Josephine laughs. She leans over toward Glynn, surprised at herself. 'I guess we can,' she says.

*

The three of them stand on causeway, next to the harbour light. They look over the sweeping bay, its pale stone, its waves salting the beach, and beyond, hills, farm fields and the running river. And, upon the rocks, surrounded by orange tape, flashing lights and men wearing high visibility jackets and smoking roll-ups, is the whale, still and shored. They catch its stench from the gusts like too many tins of mackerel left out in the sun. Josephine gags, putting a hand round her mouth to keep attention away. The wind roars over her splutters. The whale looks as if it could simply roll back into the water which gently laps against it. Its bulking mouth is agape and glaring.

'And I swear, I was the first one to see it, I must've been. I just couldn't hack it. I mean – what's it doing here? You don't get whales in the Irish Sea. I thought that when I saw it, but then I wasn't sure, but now everyone's talking about how we don't get sperm whales in the Irish Sea. They reckon it beached itself, because the sea is so shallow here, you know?'

Jake is shaking, hopping from one leg to the other, his head moving back and forth.

Glynn steps forward. 'Do you think we can get closer?'

Josephine coughs and looks at him. 'Are you fucking mental?' she says. 'It's disgusting.'

Still, they walk back along the causeway and through the carpark. There are more cars than usual parked up where people shelter to point and stare. There's a small crowd of people wearing rain macs and under umbrellas, holding up flashing cameras and mobile phones. A man with a megaphone in hi-vis shouts 'stand back' every thirty seconds or so. The scent is stronger here, too. People are pinching their noses, screwing up their eyes, holding their breath. The mouth is visible, just about. As Josephine, Glynn and Jake walk further down, they see what they can of its jaw, the pointed teeth, the scream in which the whale seems forever silently entombed.

Josephine takes her hand away from her mouth. The smell is still there, but suddenly it doesn't hurt her so much. She just looks at this great, dead creature, and feels a soft sadness, like it should be mourned. She takes another step forwards and the man with the megaphone sees her.

'Do not go near the body,' he says. 'No one go near the body. Forget the body is here.'

'It's hard to know what to do,' says Jake. 'It sort of feels like we should spend all day staring.'

'You can't be doing that, can you?' says the man with the megaphone. 'If you need to get a look in, get it now, then go.'

The megaphone squeals with feedback under the amplification of his boorish voice. It makes Josephine's ears ring. The three of them turn away.

Taking a step back towards town, Josephine looks around. The crowd is large but beginning to thin. The demand of the everyday beckons; get out of storm and strangeness and return.

'I wonder what it would feel like,' says Josephine as they pass the harbour light. 'Running your hand along something like that, something so big and beautiful and dead. I wish I could.'

'I did,' says Jake, eagerly. 'It felt slick, shiny. And, and I know how this sounds, but it felt like it was alive.'

Josephine grins. 'Are you sure you're telling the truth about seeing this whale first?'

Jake launches into protests as they walk through the carpark. Eventually, Glynn puts out a hand to calm him.

'Ok, we believe you,' he says. 'You can tell me more once we find some place to get food.'

'I can't,' says Jake, calming suddenly, his face crunching considerably. 'Bill and I have a lecture soon.

'Lecture?' Glynn stops in surprise. 'You guys never go to lectures.'

'No sir,' says Jake. 'But they told both of us we'd have to go to a meeting if we didn't start. I'll see you soon.'

He takes a turn off the road and leaves them with the wind, and the distant sounds of the man shouting through his megaphone.

'Just us two then,' says Glynn, before looking at his shoes. 'That is, if you want to come. No pressure.'

Josephine smiles. 'No pressure,' she says, 'but I would like to eat.'

They walk away from the carcass, which continues to lie there, observed.

Glynn thinks about linking hands with Josephine, watches how closely their fingers dangle, when he sees a woman in glittery summer clothes, with long dark hair, wandering towards the harbour light.

'Shit,' he says. 'It's her.'

Josephine squints. 'Why isn't she wearing a coat?'

'I have no idea,' he says.

'And why is she dressed like that?' says Josephine. 'Do you know her?'

'She went by my house yesterday.'

The woman sees Glynn and waves. Her hair is long and brown, her features poised and sharp, but petite and fine, her skin pale like yoghurt. Josephine wonders what kinds of friends Glynn has. He could be one of the odd people on her course, perhaps one of the guys who dresses in old-time clothes and pretends to be some Victorian lord, she could see that. She hopes he isn't.

'Hello,' says the woman, showing bright white teeth that glimmer almost as much as her unsoaked dress. 'You're the boy that helped me remember things.'

Glynn stops and looks at her. 'Yeah,' he says. 'Did you find who you were looking for?'

She shrugs. 'Not yet. But I will. It is only a matter of time. I didn't ask your name.'

'I'm Glynn,' he says. 'This is Josephine.' He gestures to her, smiling a little, liking how it makes them seem together.

Josephine shakes the woman's hand. Her grip is light, the fingers delicate, as if she is made from something like air.

'It's lovely to meet you both,' says the woman. 'Quite delightful. I so rarely get to touch. People usually kneel or bow.'

Josephine and Glynn laugh unsurely.

'Anyway, I should keep looking,' she says. 'If you'll excuse me.'

And so she goes. Glynn and Josephine watch her move over the bridge and towards the harbour light.

'She is fucking odd,' says Josephine.

'Yeah,' Glynn agrees. 'But I almost did bow.'

*

Frederick can feel the metal pins in his wet earlobes and sweat soaking into his damp collar. His words are shaking and breathy. His hands gesticulate half formed shapes. 'And you see, that's why today, with all the various new networking opportunities available, the word of God is more accessible than ever. A tweet can be a prayer. A Facebook post a sermon. A picture on Instagram a stained-glass window. We need only shape the thing around our own desires, which in turn are shaped by the Lord's desires, to make social media the Christian media.'

There is a little pause where the man's eyes dart about nervously. Quickly, Nathan slaps his hands together and a smatter of applause follows. There are ten people in the room. Only one is new, but Nathan cannot see their face. They are in a corner, away from everyone else, their head down. They are dressed in black. On a table at the side of the room is a buffet of cheese sandwiches, cocktail sausages, pork pies, quiche, and vegan pizza slices. Nathan decides that, once everyone is picking at the food, he will approach the stranger. They look like a loner, and these are the sort of people Nathan enjoys offering company and help to. Outside there is a howling sound which makes Nathan feel this place is very much the warm light in a time of cold darkness. He stands and smiles, glad for a moment that people have come, not bothered that the numbers are below what he would have liked.

'Thank you, Frederick, for that wonderful talk. And another applause for coming all this way from Shrewsbury. The storm that rolled in last night has flooded the tracks. Frederick braved the rail replacement bus to get here, and we are all deeply grateful he did so. It was certainly worth it. So please, another round of applause.'

The room fills with more clapping and Frederick, sweat glistening from the top of his head, dripping down onto his shirt and into his eyes, smiles. He is pleased they have listened.

'I'm grateful to have spoken,' he says.

Nathan nods and carries on. 'Well guys, I'd love to carry on some of this conversation. I'm sure none of us really fancy going outside at the minute...'

There is a murmur of polite laughter as rain clatters against the large windows behind the speakers. Its suddenness scares the room into quiet, and even Nathan says nothing for a while, shaken a little, thinking about motifs and symbols and hidden meanings. Composing himself, he carries on.

'Let's talk some more. Let's debate. Let's be respectful and let's have a good time. We've a plan to go for some drinks this evening as well, so it'd be great to see all your faces there, yours included Frederick.'

Frederick smiles and nods. Nathan thinks he hears a snort somewhere distant beneath the storm's droning cries.

When he goes to the buffet table, Nathan finds the pork pies have been left for too long in the centrally heated room. The pastry is soft and the meat squelching. Putting a couple on a pink paper plate, he approaches Frederick and Hope. He chews slowly on a pie as he listens, grimacing at the lukewarm, salty taste.

'I guess what I'm wondering, Frederick,' says Hope. 'Is whether this sense of interconnectivity, of total knowledge and knowing, of total togetherness, is almost a – well I guess you wouldn't say the real thing – but a simulation of that which is to come. You know? As in, we are all, by the will of God, destined to be together again, to be one, to know each other instantaneously. And maybe we can see this thing, the internet, less as that which intercepts our authentic selves and more as something that allows us to be outside of ourselves.'

Frederick nods and continues chewing. He frowns, swallows, then opens his mouth to disagree.

'What you're saying is,' says Nathaniel, 'we can almost bring ourselves closer to God simply by treating the internet as something holy, as something gifted to us, just as we would the trees or the sky.'

Frederick takes another bite of his pie.

'Yes, yes,' says Hope. 'That's completely right.'

'I think that's wonderful,' says Nathaniel. 'What do you think, Frederick?'

Caught in the chewing, Frederick smashes his teeth down and bites his tongue. He lets out a little yelp and begins to choke on jelly, meat and pastry. His hands go to his throat. For a moment he wonders if this is how the Lord intends for him to die. Then, someone is slapping a hand onto his back, and he is coughing. Food jumps from his mouth in a spit-covered ball onto the paper plate in front of him. Frederick thinks of frogs. He takes a deep breath, feels his lungs ache, water in his eyes. He turns around. The man who struck him is tall, hair black with a gentle curl, his face wide and handsome, streaked with soft lines of sweat and rain. He wears a white dress shirt, black trousers and a black overcoat. Looking into those eyes, Frederick struggles to move. Something larger holds up his fragile body.

'Thank you,' says Frederick, feeling the pot of his belly around him.

The man nods. 'When you see a man in need, you do what must be done.'

Frederick nods. 'Quite.'

'Still, you do not need me to tell you that.'

Nathaniel pats the man on the shoulder and introduces himself. 'Thank you for acting so quickly,' he says. 'What's your name? Are you a student here?'

The man screws up his face. 'I am a preacher.'

Nathan raises his head. 'Really? Where?'

He smiles. 'Nowhere you would know. And to people long gone. I have not preached in a very long time. And the ways have changed greatly since my time spent speaking.'

Nathan falls quiet. Eccentrics come along to their talks regularly enough, but there is something that stops him smirking at Hope and rolling his eyes – something that makes him want to keep quiet and listen.

Frederick smiles and opens his palms. 'Well, this is less of a sermon, more of a talk. Less my thoughts on God, more my thoughts on spreading the word of God.'

'How complicated can it be?' says the Preacher. 'Simply open your mouth and speak what you have always known.'

'Yes, of course, but we have to get people to hear us, first.'

'You intend to sell them faith?'

'Not sell, but pitch.'

'God's word spreads like light. He does not need advertisement.'

By now the group are watching in a little semicircle behind Frederick. Nathan notices and takes a step forward, away from the crowd and closer to the action.

The Preacher takes them all in. 'What on earth are you? Barely a congregation in number or in spirit. You stand and listen to lectures on how to speak about the Lord as if He were not the first thing you knew upon birth, as if He is not the very breath and body that gives your life. You have divorced yourself from Him, and you wonder why this thin hall is empty. Who are you? Speak to me. Speak for yourselves.'

Frederick places a hand on his chest. 'Don't you think you might be going too far here? There is no need for anger – surely you and I can agree on that?'

'Anger is as necessary as breath,' says the Preacher. 'Look how far we have fallen. If that does not anger us, then what does? Do we just sit and smile at the streets' filth? If I must rage my way to the Lord's side, then I will.'

Frederick shakes his head and looks at those behind. 'What do you think of all this?'

Nathan steps forward again, so he is next to Frederick. He looks at this new man, into eyes which are black as darkness. Something deep lurks beneath, like a whale under the waves.

'Let's hear what he has to say,' he says.

*

Bill does not like learning. He thinks this as he hooks himself up the stairs, shifting right to take a seat in the back row. He likes to look down on all the other students and see how many of them are only pretending to take notes on their laptops. Jake slides down next to him, looking around the room like there is something for him to spot.

'What are you doing?' says Bill.

'Getting the vibe,' says Jake. 'Want to know where my exits are. In case something happens.'

Bill opens his phone and flicks the screen with his thumb. 'Like what?'

Jake turns towards Bill and nods. 'Shenanigans.'

'Ah, Jake, for fuck's sake, I'm sorry. You know how he gets me. I didn't mean to leave you.'

'You always say that, and it always happens.'

'Well, I'm not going to get in a fight in the middle of a fucking lecture, am I?'

'You said you wouldn't get in a fight at the club last night.'

'Well, no one's going to hit on my girlfriend here, are they?'

'I don't know. You can't make assumptions about the future.'

The door to the lecture hall opens and Dr Bernard Everett walks towards the lectern. In his right hand is one half of an egg mayonnaise sandwich.

'This wanker,' whispers Bill, shifting uncomfortably in his chair. 'I can't stand him, Jake, I actually can't.'

'Don't fight him.'

'Obviously I'm not going to fight him,' says Bill. 'He's just boring.'

'I like him. He tells stories.'

'We have an exam in three weeks. If he starts off with some pissing piece of piss chat then I'm going to scream.'

Dr. Everett turns on his microphone, setting off a slight squeal of feedback. Holding up his sandwich, he takes a bite and chews. The speakers softly echo the soft shifting of teeth across the hall. He pushes the mic stand down towards the lectern. He coughs, and then begins. 'A republic built on tulips and a town built on slate. Both pulling the ground up from beneath them, stuffing bits of it onto ships and seeing them sail off to new places. Trade in its essence. Here is us and there is you. Let's swap.'

Bill looks up at the ceiling and tuts. 'You have got to be fucking kidding me,' he says. A few faces look round.

'You're embarrassing me,' whispers Jake.

'Of course, things are more complicated now. But in its essence, you can see something almost progressive, almost metropolitan, in the exchange of goods between nations. I mean, take this town. Look around it. Ignore, if you can, the colourful houses along the seafront. Forget the shops and the streets and the various collages about local history. See the place as it is in its essence. There is the yellow of gorse, there is the green of the grass, and then there is only gloom. You can see it in the storm, this is a place of grey, grey like slate. But then comes a ship, stuffed with tulip bulbs. Have you ever seen a tulip? Oh, I know, they're everywhere, every M&S and every funeral. But have you ever really looked at one, in bloom and full of its own colour? Imagine planting a bulb deep in the earth, waiting as one waits and then, one morning: the sprouting, the flowering. Living in a familiar place with its own colour scheme, land such as this and seeing something so pink and pure and disruptive giggling back at you. You would see suddenly that the world is more than you could have ever thought it to be, that there are other places with other shades. Not just pink, but orange, red, and yellow, too. Cartoonish, I hear one of you mumble from the front row. Well observed, in one sense, but in a truer sense, you could not be more wrong. There were no cartoons then, forget them. Forget your childhood, spent rotting on pencil sketched characters and far too many digitally enhanced colours.' Dr. Everett takes a breath and a bite of his sandwich. He chews.

'I'm going to forget every fucking thing in this lecture,' says Bill. Jake laughs. Bill smiles.

'See only the gloom of this land, the rain coming down outside, the mist and the dank darkness, and then the pink of the tulip and what it offers: that is trade. The possibility of promise. There is more to this world than your lands, than the place you were born, than the things you have seen. If we are not striving for that which we have not seen, then everything is dead: art, literature, culture, history, and, of course, the most important of them all, the subject which brings us here for this philosophical discussion, business.'

'Finally,' says Bill. 'What I paid for.'

Jake nods. 'We all get what we pay for in the end.'

Bill looks at him suspiciously. 'What's up with you? Whose been in your ear?'

Jake shrugs.

'Those traders were the beginning of global corporatism. Skullcaps rather than briefcases, eyepatches instead of ties, but still. They were, and still are, the foundation of our economy. And like all good business ventures, it was not only an exchange of goods when the Dutch came to Aberystwyth, but an exchange of cultures. Did you ever hear of the villagers who killed a group of monkeys, mistaking them for Napoleon's men?' Dr. Everett tears a piece of his sandwich off and tucks it into his mouth. He chews it as he speaks, like it is gum. 'We talk often of the importance of the free market, but never do we speak of the flowing market, rarely do we warn against stagnant markets. They breed ignorance, they lead to cruelty. Take the recent, rather unpleasant vote. The truth is, we were all too used to Danish bacon. For a market to flow, its different members must constantly reintroduce themselves, must remind each other of their own individuality, of the potential transformation that comes from consummation. Are you following me? I notice many of you are typing notes and not paying enough attention to the details of my lecture, despite its convincing delivery.'

Bill looks ahead, hoping that Dr. Everett will look back at him, hoping that he'll ask, as so many have before, what Bill is looking at. The idea of hitting Dr. Everett hard in the face is very appealing. Bill wonders if he could get one of the teeth to fly out, or if a chunk of egg mayonnaise might fly across the hall. But Dr. Everett is focused on the people in the front and the middle. He gives only a cursory glance at those far off in the shadowy deeps of the back of the lecture hall.

'That's the problem. You're all brain dead, waiting for the next six-second jolt of electricity to re-animate you,' Dr Everett says. He smiles as a ripple of awkward laughter and whispers moves through the lecture hall. 'That got your attention, didn't it? It takes an attack with your generation, and then you wonder why we are always blazing our guns. What do you want? Facts without narrative? Content without story? Whatever it is you need to get out this room and waste your lives on the edge of your beds? Fine. The Dutch were fools. They put too much into tulips. Nobody likes flowers that much, even all those painters. Flowers die too quickly, they're fleeting. If you cared for narrative, you'd see what was coming before I said it. The economy collapsed when people lost interest.'

Dr. Everett looks around the hall. He picks it back up. 'What's the moral of this content? What's the inference from this fact? The small-minded say it's to keep the product fresh. Make it new, as somebody whose name escapes me said. But, no matter how many flavours and adverts, we always remember the glass bottle and the promise to buy one for the world, do we not? I see some nodding, you are not all quite as deadened as I feared.' Dr. Everett pops the last of the sandwich into his mouth.

'Nothing's as deadened as you fear, man,' Jake whispers to Bill. 'Been thinking about that a lot recently.'

'The lesson is this: everything ends. People lose interest. That caused the end of tulips. The brief promise of colour they gave Aberystwyth long trodden into the dirt by the foot of history, which is of course business, making this class the study of figurative feet. And as we all know, tulips were seen no more.

'And where now are your shaking heads? Pull yourselves away from your phones. Wake up and see the flowers. Tulips returned. They come back again and again, not just with the Spring but with the various trends of the market, which for all their unpredictability are as steadily moving as the seasons: fixed in a certain spot only for a second, ever evidence of time's movements which are of course not linear but in fact slipping and shooting back and forth, up and around, all over the place. And if we were to look down and see that strange line it would look less like a line than a series of different things all happening at once, contradictions sat next to each other – no, inside one another. And that brings us to what you all need to think about. Here, I see eyes turn to the front, perhaps realising that there is indeed some message you can all take to your start-ups and your banks when you leave here and go out to that much fabled real world. Business is not about making a new thing out of thin air. Make *it* new, is the quote from the poet whose name I cannot remember, not make new. You are not magicians. Magic is not real. Your job, your duty, is to take that which is dead and make it not so. Vinyl records. Cornettoes. A child's grandmother. And you can bring them back with ease, if you only believe. Yes, as bizarre a word as that is to use in a degree that is, at least by our classifications, a scientific one, belief is at the centre of business. Belief, imagination, the dare to dream that nothing is gone, nothing is permanent and that everything is sellable. Remember, again, the way the world would have been only Aberystwyth to those who lived there. Grey and mountains, sturdy and still. Till someone brought them a flower, soft and colourful.'

Dr. Everett nods. He looks at them all. 'And none of you can see it, anymore. None of you can see the change.' He walks away from the lectern. He switches off the screen, looks around the room. Then, he takes his microphone from his lapel and drops it onto the ground. Looking at his students, he says, 'I can't be here anymore.' Then, he leaves the room.

'Huh,' says Jake.

Bill looks at his phone. 'That was like ten fucking minutes,' he says. 'He can't just fucking do that.'

Dr. Everett is walking towards the doors when Bill gets up and shouts it.

'Hey wanker! Give me my money back!'

The lecturer turns round with a little smile. 'They already sold it, you idiot.' Then he leaves the room.

'What,' says Bill, his voice suddenly dry.

'Cold,' says Jake. 'Game respects game. Etcetera etcetera.'

Bill thumps back into his chair. The rest of the lecture don't seem to have noticed a thing, packing away in their same half-comatose apathy. He sits and stares at his phone as the others pack up and leave. He likes to look as if he has all the time in the world, as if whatever he must do next will wait for him. He flicks through his phone for a couple of minutes.

'Another fucking waste of time. I'm going to the café. Are you coming?'

There is no response. Bill looks to his left, but Jake's already gone, run off with the rest of them.

CHAPTER SEVEN

They go to a place on Pier Street which only serves jacket potatoes. Glynn likes all of it, from the warm potatoes to the synthetic leather stools. It reminds him of those places sitcom characters frequent. Josephine is less impressed.

'It's just the same sort of stuff you can make at home,' she says, pointing to the menu.

Glynn shakes his head. 'Just wait till you try it. The flavours are so good. You'll fall for it.' He can't quite get it across, the sublimity of the tangy cheese, saucy beans, crispy skins and fluffy mash all together.

'For cheese and beans on a potato?'

'Yes,' says Glynn. He taps his finger on the counter nervously.

'I don't get it.' Josephine looks out the window. The weather is doing its icy, gloomy thing, the streets quiet and empty.

'Wait and see,' says Glynn. 'This place will surprise you.'

When the potatoes turn up, they are ok. Not quite as Glynn promised, but better than Josephine's expectations of cardboard-dry skin and lumpy, not-quite-melted cheese. When the waitress, straight-haired and light skinned, placed their food on the table, Josephine asks for salt and pepper.

'Excuse me?' said the waitress, as if the words could not be penetrated.

'Do you have any salt and pepper?'

'What?' said the waitress. 'I don't understand.'

'Salt and pepper,' said Glynn. 'If that's alright.'

The waitress apologised, blaming her misunderstanding on a busy day and a long shift. Now, chewing on potato, Josephine decides to mention what she felt.

'It was just strange,' she says. 'Like I was suspicious. Like I didn't belong.'

'What?' says Glynn, feeling himself tense. 'Just because you're English?' He has had these conversations before, tiresome debates where Wales is pressed to apologise for just being. He readies for it.

'I'm not just English,' says Josephine. Then, not quite sure what else to do, she holds her palms up flat, and circles them round herself. 'I don't always feel like people here are used to seeing not white people.'

'Oh,' Glynn looks down at the table, not sure what to say. 'Do you feel like that a lot?'?' he says, his voice hushed, concerned.

Josephine wonders whether she trusts, likes or feels there is the potential to like and trust Glynn enough to ever tell him about the extent to which she feels always watched, here. She stares into her potato and says, 'sometimes.'

Forks press into yellow mash as steam drifts. The wind gurgles outside like a long ball of spawning phlegm.

'It's bad out there,' says Glynn, nodding to the grey cold. 'Must be tough for you city lot.'

Josephine rolls her eyes. 'We do get rain in London,' she says. She does not remember the cut of the wind or the splash of rain ever being quite this hard, but she does not want to give any ground to this boy pretending to be from a darker place than what he is.

Glynn goes quiet, trying to separate what he should say from what he thinks.

'But yes, it's bad,' says Josephine. 'You start to forget where you are when it's this bad for so long.'

'There's more to come yet,' says Glynn. 'Another day, they reckon.'

Glynn feels comfortable talking about the weather. It's like keeping to the script of some daytime television show.

'This place can be fucking miserable,' says Josephine. 'You can't escape when it's like this. Even when you're inside you can feel all of that waiting for you.'

Glynn's mouth dries. He wants to defend his home.

'It's lovely in the summer,' he says. 'All ice creams and sun and beer gardens. You can stay outside forever. As a kid, this place was like Spain to me.'

'You should get out more,' says Josephine. 'Wales isn't Earth in miniature.'

Glynn scrunches his shoulders defensively. 'You should stick around more. Have you ever stayed here past term-time?'

'No. When was the last time you went somewhere further than Shrewsbury?'

'I know the place I live in. What's wrong with that? I'd rather that to moving around as if I own the whole place without knowing the name of the next village over.'

Josephine bites her lip.

Glynn gives a blink of shock. 'You do know the name of the next village over, don't you?'

Josephine pokes at her potato. She shakes her head.

'Jesus. It's Borth. They go through it on the train,' says Glynn. 'Have you been walking around here with a hand over half of each eye?'

'Don't you think that's a bit of a rude fucking thing to say to a person?' says Josephine.

A quiet comes over them. Each sits furiously as the minutes tick away. When they finish their food, they agree to split the bill. They keep a distance from each other as they leave the shop.

'I better go to the library,' says Glynn.

'I need to see my boss,' says Josephine.

They leave each other there, things seeming less wondrous than they did before.

*

To get away from Glynn, Josephine walks the long way round. It is strange to be walking to Yoko's from a different way, to not walk up the long spine of the high street, to not spot it looming behind the clock tower which seems always to have its gaze settled on her. When she left Glynn's earlier, she looked at the boats in the harbour and how they shook with the wind, heard the strange ringing of their bells, seeing beauty she hadn't before. Before, the pleasure crafts, the large yachts and the sailboats all caught her attention, but now she looks down towards the big fishing ships. They are, in fact, quite small, but tower over the rest of the marina like old, weathered giants. They tower over her, too, and suddenly it seems the whole town does, like this tiny fragment of a place on the edge of things is its own hole she has fallen into.

*

What has she fallen into? Smoky rooms of clinking glasses and booming laughter. Something to do with stories like this one.

'You remember the story of the big man, of course?'

'He was big.'

'So big.'

'Bigger than big old Brian who's out doing scaffolding. Bigger than that whale washed up on the shore, wasting away. Bigger than big old Consti and those other, larger hills out in the long old distance.'

'Rwy'n cytuno, he was big. Used to walk along North Road and you'd reckon he could see the sea. That's what my Tad-cu used to say.'

'Where's all this reminiscing about the big man going? Are you wanting to tell the famous big story?'

'Yes, with the horses and the falling and the rest. But let me tell it in my own time – it was I who asked if you remembered.'

'But we do remember. We were all told the same tales by our Tad-cus too, at least in this case.'

'Memory isn't a bank in which your assets sit, boys. It's a wild woodland with plenty of spots to camp, some regularly used, some rougher, some rewarding, some not.'

'He's going far off again. Ydych chi eisiau dŵr, bardd?'

'Stop, paid â bod yn wirion. All I mean is we must re-remember these things, repeatedly, telling all those that might eavesdrop or sit in, or they go away, disappear. Become like that tree in the empty woods.'

'I didn't know you needed a philosophy for being a droning old man.'

'What do you think our Tad-cus were doing in the first place? This is the final phase of our learning, boys. Then we complete the course and head up to whatever's next.'

'Enough of that. Less said about it the better. Don't like to think about it.'

'Get enough practice for that bit when I go to sleep. Don't need it now.'

'Iawn, iawn, I'm not trying to push you towards all that. I just mean to tell you why I'm telling you what I'm telling you.'

'Go on then. Say that old story again, making it your own way, of course.'

'I ain't heard no story about no big man.'

'There you go. There's your audience, boy.'

'Listen in and I'll tell you about big man. Big man was big, and he'd walk the town in all his bigness, reaching sometimes it seemed right up to the skies. When the elephants came around, he could run a hand high up on their wrinkly skin, could rest his palm on their heads. They knew he was the closest a land like ours had to giants.'

'Closest my Tad-cu said he'd come to seeing Bendigeidfrân. Reckoned you could see him charging across the shallow sea, getting to the shore on the other side and smashing up towers. Sitting on Cadair Idris and using it as a throne. He had a love of exaggeration, mind, and that is a high hill.'

'And a deep sea. Just not the deepest.'

'But this fella, big man, he wasn't a king like Brân. He was a man like us, walking and working and all the rest. And he did lots of little odd jobs, bits of building and lifting and things. He was strong, too, big man, as big men often are. Big arms that could lift lots. And he would help at carnivals and fairs sometimes. Play along with the locals, arm-wrestling and things like that.'

'There's that fella in *Captain Corelli's Mandolin* who's a bit like that.'

'It's possible Louie lifted him to lovely Cephalonia. Didn't fancy making someone touched in the heavens all flattened by the rain. Of course, it doesn't rain here that much, not that you'd guess that now.'

'It rains enough.'

'Yeah, enough, it rains enough. That's all you can hope that it rains enough. But he had his days bathing in the sun. It was a day like that when what happened, happened.'

'What happened?'

'Big man had been boxing back then to pay the bills. Couldn't get much normal work. Didn't like it much, either. But after a while big man had beat all the boys there were to beat in Aberystwyth and Ceredigion, so he could either head off to Birmingham or London or somewhere larger to try out his fists or stay in this quiet place and keep his nose in check. He stayed and started work again. Normal work. Work without punching. As it happened, the council had just got some money to do some. Forty years before, a big flood had come along, and the town's pipes were all smashed and shaken and done. But finally, the town were spending money and making new pipes and sewers, so big man joined, hammering away at pipes, lifting things.'

'Stink worse than after twelve rounds, doing work like that.'

'And I suspect big man probably thought the same thing many times. But he was in love by then, had a boy, loved to watch him run around. He worked well. Along the road...'

'Where was it? I can't picture the scene till you say where it happened.'

'Bridge Street, weren't it?'

'Yeah, Bridge Street. That long stretch down to the old bridge and the River Rheidol. And there was a man, Sam Bach, walking down it, little fella with a big horse that dragged along a milk float.'

'A what?'

'Used them to sell milk. Sam Bach sold milk. He was a milkman.'

'Horse milk?'

'Don't be daft.'

'Sam Bach was leading his horse down the incline when somebody dropped a single glass bottle containing a pint of milk onto the concrete. The smash was enough to send the horse scared. Big man had left his trench, so down fell the poor mare, cart and all, into this grave of filth and mud and water. Sam Bach was weeping and begging for help, the horse was kicking at the trench walls, couldn't right itself. Milk spilled in with shit. And big man approached, just finishing his fag, peeked over and looked at the fallen animal. It just started to rain, but the sun was behind his head, so he cut a glorious shadowy silhouette, staring down upon the beast like some angel briefly descending to save its soul.'

'Surely you're not going to tell me he lifted the bugger, cart and all, from the sewer. No big man can be that big and strong.'

'And yet he did. He got on his hands and knees, he wrapped his arms around the horse's belly. He whispered *easy now* and *come on now*; he lifted hard, felt the pulse of the beast's blood, the strange shapes of its organs, the wetness of the coat from all the different liquids about. He held so tight the beast wouldn't slip. And then it rose from the ground. He shifted it up, so its front hooves clopped ground above the trenches, and at that metallic clang there was a round of applause from all those watching on in hope and horror. And so big man jumped down in the trench, and he pushed the horse up from the back, and the horse pulled itself from the ground, and the cart begun to rise, all broken milk bottles and things, and suddenly the creature was up, standing, snorting and shaking its mane like those beauties tend to. And Sam Bach was kissing its nose over and over, saying *thank you thank you thank you*, crying tears, and he bought plenty of drinks for big man afterwards and always gave him his milk for free. And everybody was clapping and cheering. And big man, who up until then had been a tough lad but nothing more, became a real hero to the whole town. Somebody worth nodding to in the street. Somebody worth shaking hands with. He never told his boy, who himself became as fast as his dad did strong, as sprightly as his dad was tall, but his boy heard from stories in the playground and from men who drank with Sam Bach and big man. And he always looked at his dad after and wondered what other wonders he might yet do. And he never did do any more. But that one was enough. I think there's no doubt there.'

'Jesus, that's quite the one. Rubbish again?'

'Not that one. Everybody knows the story of big man.

'Biggest thing anybody's ever done.'

'Yeah. Don't go disgracing that story by calling it lies. Just keep quiet and keep a thought for big man.'

'Biggest of men.'

'Least that I ever saw.'

*

This is not what Glynn is thinking about. On campus, the wind moves through the brutalist loggias, brushes the concrete pillars and builds from this contact into a wailing song. Glynn is sat in one of the comfortable new green armchairs the library has put next to the windows, occasionally looking at the grey skies and the falling rain, marvelling at how the storm seems to have wrapped itself around things, wondering if it is like this anywhere else, meaning to check the news on his phone but for some reason never quite getting to it. He has an open book on Owain Glyndŵr and a notebook on his lap. It is a struggle to focus, and this is a source of guilt for Glynn, who loves to study. At least he thinks he does, and yet can never do it for more than an hour without getting bored. He just drifts sometimes. He is drifting now, and what he is drifting to is not so bad; the thought of Josephine, the feel of her skin against him and the way she kissed him, how he could run a hand along the curve of one of her thighs and let it go on. He felt real, then. At the café, he felt his usual sense of fragmentedness. Glynn has always believed himself to be nothing more than a few scraps of a self. He thinks of that day in his first First Year, when he properly collapsed, where things had stopped, where the terror of what he was dealing with really occurred to him.

He was in bed, staring at a spot in the wall where the wallpaper had been chipped off; staring for forty-five minutes. The wall against which the single bed was pressed. The chipped wallpaper was beneath the nail of the index finger of his right hand. There was a gentle throb from where it had cut at his skin and lodged into him. He was breathing heavily. Absently, he thought about getting something to dig the plaster out. Outside, the sky was a circus-light orange with candy-floss clouds drifting across, but Glynn could not see outside because his blind was covering the window, and he was staring at the wall. From beyond the door, he could hear hallway voices in talking about nights out and girls. His books were strewn across the floor next to his bed. Something in the studying had made him stop, made him petrified. If he stayed still, he could cease to be. Glynn blinks and remembers where he is. Those things have happened, now.

*

The Preacher is preaching in the rain, standing in the middle of the road. He is at a crossroads, between the coffee shop and the potato bar; behind him the street, lined with shops and takeaways, strewn with litter left by careless revellers, and seagulls that have torn through various rubbish bags. But ahead of him is the triangle of the Old College's low roof, and beside it the watching tower of a church, Anglican but a house of God all the same. The Preacher has changed slightly from what he once was. Above his top lip is the slightest etching of a moustache, and his hair, now black and luscious, points as if towards someone. He is wet, droplets of sweat and rain staining him like kisses. His shirt is all billowing black in the wind. His arms are open wide. The four members of the Aberystwyth University Christian Society stand evenly on either side of him, listening, nodding, occasionally clapping and even cheering.

'Lord, can you hear me speak?' he cries. 'My people, come listen as I shout up to him. As I offer my penance for our crimes, for how far we have fallen, for how many of the souls that were once mine to guide have become lost. Sin saves us by testing us. But my people seem to see it now as a virtue. And I, Lord, am sorry to see this scene play upon your stage.'

Across the road, in front of the carpet shop, a builder smokes his cigarette and watches, his eyebrow raised. Two students walking to their flat from class stop by a lamppost.

'These streets are violent and carnal now. They are crime-strewn, full of drugged up minds and sex. Liberation has become confused with sensation. Judge them but let them hear me and let them have the chance to change, if you still see them as worthy, as I perhaps might yet.'

Jake is walking down the street to the pier, his headphones on. He is coming back from the waves. He likes to watch the sea on hungover days and think of fish swimming in the water. Now, he can't stop thinking about all that bigness in the deep unknown. It scares him, scared him so much that he had to walk away from the water, that he felt himself shivering against the cold wind and against his own fear. When he sees the man standing like a cross at the junction, something about his poise and darkness makes him stop and take the headphones off. Something in him says the man is worth hearing. It is the first time Jake realises that he has longed for guidance.

'Lord, you told me you were not yet finished with me, and sent me walking again. I believe it was for this purpose. I ask again, Lord, can you hear me speak? People, will you hear me speak? Will you heed as I call for you to commit to something greater than yourself and your sad impulses? Or will you fall away, falter, taking the easy way until your sad deaths come and you find that the low path led lower than you ever knew, and that lowness leads only to lonely damnation?'

A Ford Focus slowly comes to a stop behind the Preacher. The driver slaps his hand against the steering wheel. The car emits a pitched exclamation. Then another. Then a long, droning, howl. The Preacher turns.

'I will not be moved,' he says. 'My own howl is far louder than yours, friend, and it shall last longer. Stop and hear me or go elsewhere.'

There is silence, then the sound of a window rolling down. The Preacher makes shapes in the air, strict circles and strong points, his hips twist and turn, spittle flies from his mouth. It looks, to Jake, like some beautiful, ancient dance. There is a final honk from the driver. Then, the car rolls back, moves right, turns again and drives away.

'And there is the proof, Lord,' says the Preacher. 'Any one soul might stop and listen. And if enough do, then there might be an army. And if there is an army, there might be a conquering.'

*

Past the pubs on the south side of town, Josephine hears day drinkers chatting affably. The awning over Yoko's club is dripping with overflowing rainwater. Outside, Bryan, one of the bouncers, is smoking a cigarette and glaring up at the sky from beneath his hood.

'You ok?' says Josephine, smiling. 'On tonight?'

He nods. 'Bit early for you, ain't it?'

'Not working, just here to pick up my pay. Then back to hiding out from all this.'

'Ay, fucking pissing it down. I'd get out of here quick as you can, if I were you. Always messy on the stormy nights.'

Josephine remembers four of the football guys in fisticuffs in the rain, slipping over each other, swinging and missing and falling. 'Yeah,' she says, softly.

'They'll try and get you in tonight, you know. They need people.

Becky's already called in sick. No one wants to work when it's like this.'

'I'm not going to.' The hauntings are always worse after she's been working.

*

There was so much to know and so much he couldn't. So much expected of him: the first in the family, the usual pressures facing a son from a house with few books and little money. But that was then. Now he is in the library, and while it is warm from the heating, there are no beautiful candy-floss clouds moving past him. The world is grey and dark and full of sharp water. He is desperate not to be a failure. The people might be gone but the pressure is not. His heart is thumping against his chest at a speed it should not be. Glynn takes a breath and looks around the library. No one is looking at him; all are focused on their own work and its attached anxieties. He curls his hand in his fist and smacks against his chest a few times. This has become a ritual, a way of reminding himself to go on, a small piece of physical pain for him to overcome. And it works. Glynn looks down at the book and the words seem less terrifying than they did before. He reads on and things seem to make sense. The scratching of pen and paper starts up again. Something in Glynn's mind rests.

*

'And then two fives makes it a hundred,' says Mari, slapping the plastic on top of the paper. 'That's the last week sorted, love. We need overtime if you want a boost.'

Josephine looks at the wad on the sticky counter and prepares for the Velcro-like peel that will come with lifting it.

'I think I'm ok for this week,' she says.

'Still struggling from last night, are we?' Mari shakes her head and smirks.

Josephine's conversations with Mari are the closest thing she has to a friendship with a local, and she isn't even certain Mari is from Aberystwyth – just that she has run the Yoko's club for longer than Josephine has been working there. Josephine peels the money off the counter and feels a renewed disgust for her place of work.

'What do you like about this place?' says Josephine.

'The customers,' says Mari. 'They keep coming.'

Mari cackles and Josephine laughs politly. She puts her money in her pocket and walks away. She wonders if there is anything more to life than the accruing of assets over periods of time. Love makes it more than that, her dad would say. But Josephine doesn't believe in love – she's not sure she has ever really felt it. Except from her dad, of course. But it didn't seem to do anything.

As she walks back out into the howl of the storm, she thinks of Glynn. Why is she thinking of Glynn? He's nothing to her. Well, not nothing. But people do this all the time. She just wonders what he would say to Mari, with his wide-eyed idealism about this place and its people. What does it matter what he'd say? From here on, she will do all she can to avoid him.

That's when she sees someone new. Nathan, standing by the clock tower, calling for the awakening of grace and love, his bright eyes peeking through his dark fringe. He is stood in the spot where she kissed Glynn last night. A wince. How many people have kissed right there? She really must not let it happen again.

Nathan is wearing a rain mac, but the sharpness and proportions of his features are clear. His small nose; his large eyes; his beautiful lips. But his voice teeters, unable to keep still, lacking stable pitch and command.

'Join our great beginning,' he is saying. 'You do not have to go the way you are going. Jesus loves you and he wants you to be better. Change like me.'

He looks at her. He wonders if this is the girl the Preacher told him to look for.

'Join us,' he says, looking at her still. 'We will accept you as you are, and we will make you better.'

'What are you doing?' says Josephine, a little amused by his fervour. She has never thought of Aberystwyth as a very religious place. 'And does it have to be so loud?'

Nathan starts for a moment. He lowers his hands. 'Sorry,' he says. 'We're trying to be a bit more persistent, these days.'

'Well, good luck,' says Josephine. She remembers people like this back home; Jehovah's Witnesses knocked on her door most weeks, hoping they would get Dad. He would talk with them for hours, sometimes, just out of sheer politeness. Josephine turns towards the street's downward slope and begins to walk away.

'Wait,' says Nathan, holding out his hand. Josephine looks round. The skin is all pink and dripping, soaked and chafed by the cold. She stands still and waits.

'Hear me out,' he says. 'I don't mean that you aren't living righteously. Well, I do, but only, it's not your fault. Well, it is, and it isn't. We are all responsible for how we are all born. But we can fix it. Not everyone but ourselves. As in, yourself and myself. Does that make sense?'

'Not at all,' says Josephine. 'You're a Christian?'

Nathan sighs at the sight of familiar ground. 'Yes, exactly. Are you?'

'No,' says Josephine.

'When was the last time you entered a Church?'

'Eighteen months ago.' Josephine scratches the back of her head. 'My mum's funeral,' she says, surprising herself.

'I'm sorry,' says Nathan. Don't ask if they don't want to say. He presses on. 'Have you ever considered God in any way? Ever thought about how all the things, even the dark, awful things, seem to be bound by some sort of sense? Some poetry?'

Josephine laughs. 'Do you really believe that?' she says, thinking of her mum.

Nathan nods solemnly, thinking of things, too. 'I do, yes, I do.'

'Well, I'm jealous.'

Nathan straightens himself, clears his throat, and tries to remember what The Preacher said. 'Something is coming. The whale washing up on the shore is just one of many signs of what is to come. And I want people to be on the right side when it does.'

There is a rumble of thunder in the distance. Nathan arches his eyebrows as if to say, you see. Josephine smirks.

'I'm not sure I'm your audience for this,' she says, turning back towards the sloping street and its streams of rainwater.

'But you are!' shouts Nathan desperately as she becomes distant from him. 'You are! You are! Oh, you so are!'

*

People are coming out of the shops to watch now. Those in the coffee shop and the potato bar are watching, listening to snatched phrases pierce through the bland drone of music.

'If we rise together, if we take our souls, forged independently as they were, and gather them, we might yet see the end of this long night, this painful storm, this great punishment we have assumed by now is never-ending. And He might yet forgive us.'

The wind sings like a choir.

'It is a hard life,' says the Preacher. 'And it should be no other way. We should feel every piece of pain given to us, and know it is necessary. It is that, or it is nothing but the alleviation of pain, which is a sedative to life itself, a way of numbing out the Lord.'

Jake steps a little closer and asks a question, but his voice is cracked and croaking, and nothing but a bare whimper. But the Preacher turns. He hears something, and points to Jake.

'A question?' he says. 'I welcome them.'

Jake clears his throat and speaks again. 'But what do we do? How do we commit ourselves?'

Sarah, from across the road, steps forward earnestly. 'You need only believe,' she says, repeating those lines she has rehearsed so many times. 'It is enough to know in you…'

'No,' says the Preacher. 'No, no, that is not enough. You must sacrifice, while knowing your sacrifice is a mere fragment of what the Lord's own Son gave. You need only sacrifice those vices which you lean upon and love so corruptly. You need only throw away the bottle, you need only love the person you marry, you need only work and help the land in the way your soul demands. You need only help your fellow man and try to guide those that sin even as they refuse you, and understand that they will, that this is part of his test, that Jesus kissed the cheek of a sin filled world and so must you.'

The rain falls and the wind blows.

'Will you?' asks the Preacher.

'Based,' says Jake.

CHAPTER EIGHT

Perhaps it is time to take a longer look at Robbie. He hasn't seen the whale. He says he wants to, but Ellen has been next to him in bed all day. She has walked around in his Mark E Smith t-shirt, no bottoms on, like she owns the place, like he gave it to her sometime during the sweating mess of their fucking. For the whole morning and now a fair part of the afternoon, he has pondered her being here, while they cuddled and kissed and touched each other. Now, he wants her to leave but is scared of what she'll do. Were they anywhere else – were they out there – he would not care what he caused, would enjoy seeing her eyes well up with tears, hearing her ask how he could be so cruel. But in here, his little safe paradise, it is different. There are things she could break. He has been trying to gently dislodge her, like some wobbling tooth not quite ready to fall. And what better thing to lure someone away than a washed-up whale?

'I mean I'm comfortable here,' he says. 'And I've got lots of work to do. Otherwise, I'd be there, looking at it. I mean, it's a once-in-a-lifetime thing, you know?'

He is laying on the bed and she is sitting in front of his dresser, combing her hair for the sixth time today. She looks at his reflection in the mirror. 'Why don't we go for a little walk to see it before, then? And then we can come back here, and you can work?'

Robbie nods slowly. 'And what would you do?'

'I can stay here,' she says. 'It's just such a long walk back up the hill in this weather, 'specially if we're already going to get soaked looking at the whale. I could cook you dinner while you study.'

Robbie nods slowly, his heart beating like a trapped rabbit's. 'Don't you have stuff to do?' he says. 'Vic seems pretty snowed under at the moment.'

Ellen shakes her head and keeps combing her hair. 'She just works too hard. I've got plenty of time. I want to enjoy you.'

Robbie nods again. His phone buzzes. It is a text from a girl he slept with last week, inviting him to a house party at Afallon, the hangout of some locals and postgraduates he has befriended. Escape beckons. He shakes his head.

'You know, Ellen, it's just I've got a lot on. I mean, I'd really like to see you, but maybe later in the week might be better.'

She stops combing. She turns to face him. Mark E Smith stares open mouthed like some trapped warning. 'Are you saying you don't want me here?' her voice warbles, its own omen.

'No, no, no, no, no, no, no,' Robbie trills. 'How could I think that, baby? I just mean I want to be able to give you my full attention. You get that, don't you?'

'But I don't need your full attention,' she says, her eyes beginning to fill with tears. 'I just need to be around you.'

Robbie closes his eyes. A man's home is his castle, that's what Uncle Rory always said. But what do you do when the castle has been infiltrated? Perhaps sometimes the peace must be broken to be restored. He gets out of bed and walks over to Ellen, wearing only his underpants. He takes her chin in his hands and pulls her face, so she looks up towards him as if in prayer.

'Listen,' he says. 'I know that this obviously means a lot to you. But it doesn't to me. And you've got to accept that now. I can see in your eyes that you already know. You know you're trying to cling to something far too slippery. No, not slippery. Something too large for your tiny hands. I'm bigger than anything you can know. I stretch over this whole fucking town like a tidal wave. If I happen to pick you up in my fucking current or whatever, then get pulled and be grateful and know you'll have to fall away soon enough. There's a fucking whale laid out on the beach right now, so go look at it, tell yourself and your friends that you couldn't stay around with someone as lazy as me when there was something so glorious and large like a whale to see, and get the fuck out of my room, my flat, my life. I'm not anything you can own. Do you understand that? Do you feel what I'm saying?

The tears in her eyes have begun to slowly fall as he has spoken. He thought she might scream and shout, curse him, perhaps hit him. But she does nothing like that. She nods slowly. Her tears are hot and leave thick, fat, watery streaks.

'Good,' he says. 'Now give me my shirt back.'

And she does. She takes off his Mark E Smith t-shirt, lays it out on the bed. He watches her half naked form coldly as she picks her clothes off the floor. Her mini skirt is stained with ketchup from the chips Robbie had last night. Her jumper has a tear in the right shoulder from where he pulled at it. She looks at him one last time.

'I knew you might be a bit of a bastard,' she said. 'But I didn't know you could be this horrible.'

Robbie laughs. 'Yes you did. You've seen me. You just didn't think I could do it to you.'

And she is gone. He watches her from the window as she climbs the hill. Her purple raincoat is far too thin for these winds. Her skirt is already soaked and slicked back by the elements. She is shivering. Robbie touches his right cheek, where Bill aimed to hit him. That is all he wants, really. But he can't make it easy for anyone. He looks at his phone, replies to the text from the girl asking if he can bring some friends. She writes back that he can. Robbie smiles.

*

'You blond, smarmy, little, tight-lipped, lucked out, lurking, leachy prick. What the fuck are you calling me for? You got me barred for three weeks, did you know that? You and your chatter and your fucking tricking.'

'Trickery, Bill.'

'I don't give a shit about words!'

'I do. And so do you. Look, I really am sorry you got barred. I feel bad about it. It was all a genuine misunderstanding. I wasn't going to do anything with Anna, and she certainly wasn't going to do anything with me. It was a classic mix-up. Do you forgive me?'

'Why would I believe you?'

'Bill, I can't advise you on your own thoughts and feelings. That's your domain, I wouldn't dare take it from you. But what I would say is that I can offer you something far better than Yoko's if you'll just let me in one more time.'

'Is it a fucking house party?'

'Yes. But not one of these awful ones up in some university accommodation flat. We're talking a real party at a real house with real people. Plenty of drink and plenty of other things, too. You need a new experience, Bill, and this will be it. They'll love you. Bring along the whole gang, why don't you? And then we can have a laugh and put all this away.'

'I ain't seen anyone today. Anna's in a strop with me, still. Glynn was shacked up in his room all morning, then he went to go see the whale with that bird, your flatmate. Jake's gone.'

'Josephine? So that's got going, has it?'

'Apparently.'

'Interesting. Well, let them all know. I'm sure they'll be keen. Have you seen the whale yet?'

'No. You?'

'I've had a problem with my room I've been trying to fix all day. I might go now. You're welcome to come.'

'Seriously?'

'Bill, there's a whale in Aberystwyth. What's a couple of arguments next to a miracle like that?'

*

'He seems nice to me, Josie,' says Vic. 'I don't see what your problem is. You could at least go out with him again.'

Josephine sips her tea and shakes her head. 'It's fucking patronising. Just because he's Welsh, it doesn't make him some kind of fucking seer does it? Like he knows this place so much better than me. He's still in the same shitty clubs and flats as the rest of us, isn't he?'

'I just think it wouldn't be a bad idea for you to maybe give him a go. It seemed like something different when you were with him last night.' Vic places her hands on the counter behind her. 'And he's a nice guy. I've got a seminar with him, you know.'

'Yeah, and you said he talks too much and wears polo shirts.' Josephine takes the last cigarette from the packet she bought last night. 'Do you reckon I could get away with having one here? It's fucking miserable out there.'

'We have that inspection on Friday. Maybe best not to.'

Josephine puts the cigarette on the table and takes another sip of her tea. 'Look, he's nice enough. But I just don't want anything right now.'

'Polo shirts aside, he made you laugh,' says Vic, smiling a little too knowingly at Josephine. 'It just seemed like you got on, that's all.'

'People are allowed to get along.'

Vic looks out the window at the rain, shaking her head. 'I just…'

She stops. 'You don't have to be so afraid of people knowing you, you know.'

Josephine goes to say something but finds she can't. She just looks at the packet of cigarettes, thinking of that unknowing growing thing, killing itself with every breath.

Robbie comes through, wearing his Mark E Smith t-shirt and a pair of blue shorts. He knocks on the kitchen door and then leans against the doorway.

'Hello,' he says, looking at Vic. 'Up to much?'

Vic shrugs. Robbie glances around the kitchen and sees the back of Josephine's head. 'Returned at last. We were worried. How is old Glyndŵr doing? You manage to make him fall to the English?'

'Not now, Robbie,' says Josephine.

'Ellen went by earlier,' says Vic, turning her gaze back to the window. 'She looked really upset.'

Robbie shrugs. 'I've been invited to this house party tonight,' he says. 'This is my real crowd. The hippies and the postgrads and the locals and that. Should be good. Should be mad. You guys should come. Might get your minds off whales and Glynns and Bills. I could certainly do with it. Broke my heart seeing that beautiful beast lunge at me.'

'What?' says Josephine.

'Just after you left,' says Vic. 'Robbie was holding hands with Bill's girlfriend, so Bill went for him. Missed and got barred.'

'Bill's girlfriend,' says Josephine. 'Was she there last night?'

'Not for long,' says Robbie. 'Bill saw me talking to her and saw a bit of the red mist. Probably reminded him of what happened to Glynn.'

'What happened with Glynn?' Josephine says the words before she can catch herself. A little shudder. She doesn't want to know. She wants all of this far away from her.

Josephine looks at Robbie, and from the smirk she manages to guess it. And then she thinks about hurting him.

'Alright, Robbie,' she says. 'Let's go.'

Vic looks at her. 'Seriously?' she says. 'Do we have to?'

Josephine ignores her. 'Just, none of the guys from last night, please.'

Robbie nods and smiles. 'Very good. A night for strangers only.'

CHAPTER NINE

Up a little street, near the empty tennis courts, a house of mismatched colour waits like an unsolved Rubik's cube. Music and light pulses from within out into the empty streets, vibrating and colouring the rain which, as ever, falls – this time steady and straight. Josephine and Vic arrive as the song changes from Kanye, with its screeches of destinies, to Mick Jenkins, weathered and knowing. The bassline crips around the street, a tired voice stretching over and above, as if headed up to the same place from which the rain comes down.

'I didn't even know there were people that just lived here,' says Vic. 'You know, our age.'

'Yeah' says Josephine. 'I thought it was just students, lecturers, and old people.'

'How does Robbie even know these guys?'

'Drugs,' says Josephine. 'Obviously.'

Vic walks up to the door and knocks. Nothing. She knocks again.

'The music's too loud,' says Josephine. 'They won't hear us.'

Through the blurred glass they see people in the hallway, drinking from plastic cups. The rain is pelting, hurting them, and they crowd close to the door to try and get a little cover. Vic knocks on the door, harder this time, as the wind rises along the street. The door slowly swings open, no hand pulling it on the other side.

Robbie is leaning on the banister, halfway up the stairs, talking down to a blond girl by the kitchen doorway. Turning and seeing them, he opens his arms wide.

'Ladies!' he says. 'The women we've been waiting for.'

The blonde girl raises an eyebrow and Robbie smiles. 'Nothing to worry about there,' he says. 'Just my flatmates. No risk. Not how I roll, darling.'

Robbie slides down the banister, leaping off just before he reaches the knob, which he grabs with his hand to twist round, so that he is standing in front of Josephine and Vic.

'Glad you came,' he says. 'This is authentic Aberystwyth, here. All the fuckers that have been here for more than three years. This is where the real stuff happens.'

'Robbie, do you ever even really say anything that isn't bullshit?' says Vic, but her eyes are wide and taking the place in.

The house has green wallpaper and fairy lights, with a grey, stained carpet and posters declaring allegiances to Catalonia, Anarchism, Communism and the Kurdish fight for independence, among other factions. From upstairs a yellow light stretches, but down here the faces are shadowed, features difficult to distinguish. It is too dark to see the mould and damp, but you can feel it.

The blond girl wanders up behind Robbie and puts an arm over his shoulder. 'Are you going to introduce me to your friends?' she says.

'Yeah, of course,' he looks awkwardly over. 'Vic, Jose, this is Tara.'

'Ellen not here tonight then?' says Vic.

Tara laughs. 'Is that the girl I saw you off with last night? The big one you ran away from to come talk to us?'

Robbie shrugs. Josephine thinks she would usually see him smirk, but the darkness covers any hint of such playfulness.

'Yeah, her,' he says. 'It's not serious. She went to go see the whale.'

He doesn't want to tell them about how he took Bill to the whale, watching that ape gawp.

'I saw it,' says Josephine. 'There were men with orange jackets trying to keep people away. Like we aren't meant to see it.'

'Too much on in this town at the moment,' says Tara. 'What with that raving old man walking around.'

'Who?' says Robbie.

'He's been preaching at people all day, drawing crowds and everything. I caught him by the Mountain Warehouse.'

Josephine remembers earlier. 'I saw a young guy earlier, he was saying stuff like that,' she says. 'He wasn't old, though.'

Tara laughs. 'Oh yeah, he's got all these recruits now. Little zealots. Uni students, apparently.'

'I saw him,' says Vic. 'By the marina. He was telling everyone to stay out of the pubs.'

'Worked, then?' says Robbie, nodding to the can of gin and tonic in Vic's hand.

She ignores him. 'It nearly had me for a second. And I think he had some people properly.'

'What's his name?' says Josephine.

'I didn't catch it,' says Tara.

'I can't remember what it was now,' says Vic. She turns to Josephine. 'I thought you'd have heard about him.'

'Jose's been busy,' says Robbie, his shadowy face staring into hers. 'How's little Glynny boy doing?'

'Robbie, if you're just going to go on about this all night, I'll leave.'

He puts his hands up. 'No, no, don't worry. I'll keep quiet. I'm being misinterpreted again. I'm cheering for you two.'

'There's nothing to cheer for,' says Josephine. 'We're not seeing each other.'

*

Glynn is walking with Bill and Anna, the rain now soft and the air rich and cool. Freshly showered, there is something in the rain that seems to cleanse him further. The memory of the night before has softened, now is gentle and warm, waiting for him to occasionally turn to it in brief moments of quiet. As of this moment, however, Glynn is listening as Bill recounts strange news.

'And that's when he said to me – I'm not doing it anymore, none of the drinking, none of the dancing, he said he was out, out completely, no longer sinning, then he went off on one about God and all that, so I just walked out the room. Bizarre fucking puff. It's so typical of his sort of guy, man.'

'Bill,' says Anna. 'Careful what you say. He's your friend.'

'What sort of friend snakes you to go to a fucking prayer session and drink orange squash?'

Glynn is trying to pretend this issue is as pressing to him as to the others. He puts his hand onto his chin, scratches thoughtfully. 'And this is all because of that bloke in the streets?'

'Yes,' says Bill. 'I can't believe you haven't heard about him. Suppose you been busy wrapped up in sheets and other things.'

Anna looks at her shoes and lets out a gasp of laughter. 'Between this and the whale, you're missing everything. Stuff's finally been happening over the last day and you're nowhere.'

Glynn goes quiet and looks up at the sky. 'I've seen the whale,' he says. 'Have you?'

*

'From what we know, this house,' says the lad with the shaved eyebrows, looking pointedly at Vic, as if she might glean some extra knowledge from this special secret, 'Was once a house of love, a brothel. And that is the kind of ethos we have tried to maintain, even if not through the same practices.'

Robbie lets out a squeak of laughter and repeats the sound four times. Josephine rubs her ear. The music has blurred the falling rain, even here in the white-lit kitchen with its door open to the garden, but it is still low and thudding like something comfortable, some kind fabric that Robbie's sounds rip at.

'You have a lot of piss-ups, then,' says Josephine. 'Is that what you're getting at?'

The lad with the shaved eyebrows grimaces as if he has just been hurt. 'Not *piss-ups*. The greatest parties you can imagine. Parties so glorious they're all people can think about.'

'I've never heard anyone talk about them,' says Josephine.

'You've been hanging out with the wrong kinds of people, then,' he says, again looking at Vic, who smirks.

'These two girls have been sheltered away, Shivy,' says Robbie. 'Students living like students do. This is their first taste of real shit.'

Vic laughs sarcastically. 'You've got to stop saying that, Robbie. We're not sheltered just because we don't live like you.'

'I'm sure,' says Shivy. 'There are all sorts of roads to experience.'

'Alright,' says Josephine, bored. 'I'm going for a fag.' She gives a little glance at Vic which she thinks is knowing.

As she steps out into the night air, Vic grabs her hand.

'I'm not interested in him, Jo,' she says. 'He's just weird, that's all. I happen to like eyebrows, thick ones at that.'

Josephine laughs. 'Sorry,' she says. 'I just didn't want to get in the way, in case you were.'

'Ok,' says Vic. 'It's just, I'm fine. I don't even think I... well, you remember.'

A conversation had one drunken night. One of the first she had told. *I don't think I'm really attracted to anybody like that.* The fact Josephine forgot makes her feel cruel.

'Of course. Vic, I'm sorry.'

She laughs. 'It's ok. Let's just have a cig.'

They walk under two bare trees, other darkened figures around them, rain coming down. Drips from branches slowly form into something larger.

*

Josephine's nostrils tingle from what she has taken off the bathroom sink. Soon the drip in the back of her throat will start. Next to her is a man with a long mane of curly brown hair, a thick moustache and a green floral shirt, like some Californian gangster.

'I can't believe you just go about like that, man,' she says. 'Like something out of *Big Lebowski*.'

He laughs, and his voice is soft and strangely naïve. 'What do you mean?'

She laughs too, then, and they kiss as part of the exchange. She walks out the loo holding his hand. Across is a podgy man with greasy long hair, looking at them with a pained expression. He has a little beard stretching across his face.

'I've been waiting ages,' he says. 'Please.'

'Alright,' says the man. 'No need to worry, we're out now.'

Josephine decides to move away from the man, quickly. They go back down the stairs, and the man puts his arm around her. She asks his name again and he says that it's Brendan. She says she'll remember it, this time. They go to the kitchen, which is long and stretches out into the garden. Revellers stand on either side, chatting with each other, music bleeding out from speakers and seeming to shake the walls. Vic is by her side, putting a hand on her shoulder, her eyes wide.

'How are you doing?' she says. Then, with an excited, faux-dramatic, gasp, 'did you know Glynn is here?'

Josephine looks around the kitchen. 'Where?' she shouts back.

'In the garden. What do you reckon, hello or no go?'

'Who's Glynn?' says the man who gave her the ketamine and whose name has slipped from her mind.

Deferring, Vic looks at Josephine, who says that he's a friend she knows through Robbie. His name is Brendan, but Josephine doesn't remember that. One of Brendan's friends comes over and starts a conversation. Brendan introduces them but does not say his own name, so Josephine points to Vic, who introduces herself, and Brendan once again says his name is Brendan. Brendan starts chatting to his friend, so Vic and Josephine talk to each other, turning away from the two men.

'Do you want to see him?'

'Why would I want to see him?'

'You spent all day with him, Jo. It seems like you're a bit more interested than just a shag.'

'Not all day,' says Josephine. 'We left each other after lunch.'

'It just seemed like there was something, last night. I mean, you can't be so into this other guy that suddenly Glynn means nothing.'

'Can we just move on?'

'Ok,' says Vic, and without anything more, the two walk back to the living room, where green and blue lights and new music offer themselves up through the doorway.

*

The concrete in the garden is slippery from long hard rain. On two bare apple trees, candles burn in small, secure boxes. Beneath the tree is a table made from old pallets, where three smokers sit and talk, their clothes damp, their bodies shivering. Next to the kitchen, a makeshift cover has been put up to shield yet more smokers, who sit on mouldy green furniture. There are fairy lights burning along the walls of the building. The rain glistens as it falls, light passing through liquid. Glynn stands at the doorway, very cold and quite sober, listening to a man called Erik.

'The thing you got to understand, right,' he says. 'Is it's not just minesweeping. It's like an art, right? It's an art I've mastered.'

Glynn's eyes are half closed against the rain and the cold gust of wind that makes the cover next to them billow and shake off its collection of fallen rain. 'Right,' he says.

'I stand there, and I'll just stand there, with my own drink, and I'll look around the club. The clubs are the best places to do it, Yoko's, Pier, these are the places where people are distracted because of all the music and all that. I'll look around, and I'll just see who looks a little bit like they're not looking. Maybe they're talking to a friend. Maybe they're about to dance. And once they move, I calmly get myself round to their table, almost like I'm meant to be there, and I gulp.'

Glynn can make out the gleam in Erik's eye, see the wide smile and yellowed teeth.

'Is that it?' says Glynn.

'Oh no, mate, here we're just getting started. That's just the warm-up. I mean, that's the easiest stuff. Then you get your more ambitious projects. I see some people approaching a table with loads of left-over drinks on it, I ask if I can take those glasses. Guaranteed they'll let me have it. That's where persuasion comes in. A little bit of the gift of the gab.'

'Are you sure it's not just because people think you work at the bar?'

'Yeah,' says Erik. 'Because of the gab. But that, again, is just to sort of get the brain working. Then you start to give yourself challenges. When you start looking at people that have full drinks, or half full ones, and you start thinking how you might be able to get them. That's when the night starts to become proper cheap, suddenly you're just paying your entrance fee and the money for your chips home.'

'Isn't it just stealing at this point?'

'No, you wanker, shut the fuck up,' shouts Erik, spittle flying hot into Glynn's face, mixing with the cold rain. 'It's not stealing at that point, it's stealing from the beginning. That's all minesweeping is. Legalized thievery.'

'Is it legal?'

'Well, its thievery no one gives a fuck about then. Now do you want to hear the rest of this or not?'

Glynn takes a drag of his cigarette and looks up at the sky, then over to Anna who is talking to someone under the cover. Strangely, he finds he does want to hear the rest, even if it means getting soaked to the skin. He takes a sip of his lager and nods.

'Sorry,' he says. 'Continue.'

'Thank you,' says Erik. 'Let's get to the core of things, the whale of minesweeping. Getting a full drink. Or a nearly full one. Or one that has more than just the ends in it. Some think it can't be done. Some... Sorry, what's your name?'

'Glynn.'

'Some, Glynn, lack the will and courage to do it. But it can be done. I've seen it and I've done it. Grab a half empty drink, swap it round with the full one, knock the emptier one over. Guy thinks they've spilt it, you've got a pint, he might even buy you another one in apology if he thinks its yours he's knocked. Or, you start swapping your drinks. You start with a near empty, swap that for one slightly fuller, go up all the way till you've got a whole pint and left a trail of people with slightly less of their drink than they should have. And no one's any the wiser.'

Glynn stands there, looking at Erik as the rain falls, the small silhouette cutting through the light of the candles on the trees. 'Thanks, mate,' he says. 'I'll bear all that in mind.'

'Yeah. No worries,' says Erik, taking a pause, looking suddenly vulnerable. 'Do you want some 2C-B?'

STORM

*

Earlier that day, one of the boys who lives in the house snuck back into the community hall he had just been employed to clean, and stole their stage lights. Now, the blue of the stage lights, dragged sneakily from the town hall to the house's the living room, pulsing and cut through with lines of white, reminds Josephine of being underwater. She moves like some slowly falling, gracefully drowning thing. There are only a few of them – maybe six or seven – dancing in the living room. There's one couple on the sofa kissing, and the man who was waiting to use the bathroom earlier is sat on the armchair watching everyone. A woman behind the mixing desk nods her head and places her headphones to her ear, treating her role as house party DJ with an unearned level of focus. Josephine does not want to observe any of this. It pulls her up to the surface and places her on somewhere far too solid. She keeps looking up, enjoying being beneath, moving and unthinking.

Someone puts a hand on her shoulder. She looks around and it is the man from the toilet who gave her the ket. He is smiling, nodding his head in time to the music, moving his arms back and forth.

'How are you doing?' he says.

'Good,' she replies. 'Pretending I'm under an ocean.'

He nods and she remembers that his name is Bryn, Ben – Bryan!

'I see what you mean,' says Brendan. 'Because of the blue.'

'Yeah,' she says, grounded again. The fantasy feels suddenly very small and very dead.

She looks down and sees they are holding hands. Just as quickly, he moves one hand round to the small of her back and brings her close to him.

'I've been thinking about you,' he says. 'I've not been able to stop since you kissed me.'

She laughs. 'You're a bit of a charmer, Bryan.'

He stops. 'Brendan.'

There is a lull, and she kisses him before it can become anything more. He kisses back, and she likes the way his mouth tastes, the way his hands are firm against her phantomed body.

'Do you know this house well?' she says.

'Yeah, there's a spare room upstairs, if that's what you're…'

'Yes,' says Josephine.

They move out into the hallway. Looking straight down through several doorways, Josephine sees the back of Glynn's head shining wet from the kitchen light. Something in her kicks, and she thinks about going to him. Then she feels a slight tug on her arm, and she follows what's-his-name. She thinks Brian, but it's Brendan.

*

Yellow squares squish upon each other. Beneath, a background of green limes become blue waves. Twelve degrees left and four degrees up from the centre, a simple eye stares back; Glynn certain that it shifts ever so slightly every now and then. It is an ugly painting, but one made, it seems, for Glynn and this very moment – just as the hallucinogen is reaching its climax. The thing is revolving, and he is certain that he need only reach his hand out or step forward and the whole world of those odd colours would be his.

'It's my mum's,' says a girl with wide eyes next to him. 'She's a local artist. People really know her name round here. Angela Coe. Have you heard of her?'

The girl's voice is delicate and pitched like the chime of antique clock. Glynn shakes his head.

'I don't know much about the art scene here,' he manages to say, the words slow and blurred, strange sounding.

'Oh, it's wonderful,' she says, and her voice seems faster, as if while he loses pace she gains it. 'You see, everything art-wise is just much more authentic when in Aberystwyth. It's like, you know, things are so real. They're not real in London. It's too far from nature, unless you count those fake little parks.'

Nature bursts up through the wrinkly bits in Glynn's brain. Leaves and trees and things. Vaguely, animals that roam predatorily, perhaps killing rabbits or something small like that. Nothing like this town and its banks and trains and the farms and hills that loom in the darkness, like something alive and dangerous and living. Like a sleeping giant. Maybe nature does seep in, too.

Glynn points at the painting. 'Is this nature?' he says.

'She based it on this walk where she saw a pigeon's egg cracked between a bed of leaves and a river. Apparently, she was obsessed with the yolk.'

'Yes,' says Glynn. 'The yolk. You can see it now. You can see why. Life spilling out just as it ends. On a bed of more abstract life, but also rotting life, all shifting in the wind but briefly in this moment still.' Glynn feels as though he has never been more intelligent or coherent in his life.

'You should meet my mum,' says the girl.

'Oh no,' says Glynn, now feeling at one with the painting. 'She is too heroic for me to meet.'

The room they are in is somebody's bedroom. It's on the ground floor between the kitchen and the living room.

'Come join me?' she says, sitting on the edge of the bed whose foot faces the painting. 'We can look from here together.'

Glynn stays standing, looks over at her. 'But I'm standing,' he says. 'Can't you see I'm standing?'

'But why not move?'

He takes a pondering pause. Looking up at the ceiling, wondering if he might glimpse the sky, he awaits a message from the universe. That is something Jake taught him. Whenever you feel doubt, you look to that strange cosmos and wait for it to speak the answer to you. Glynn does, and it comes.

'I am not meant to move over there,' he says. 'It's not the right place for me.'

The girl gets up. Beneath the painting is a plush, blue, colonial-looking sofa.

'What about here, then?' she says. 'This sofa is an antique, you know. Come lay on history with me and see what we make with it.'

Glynn blinks. 'Is this your room?' he says.

'No. But the person who lives here is somewhere else. It might as well be ours in the meantime.'

Glynn takes a step towards the sofa and feels for the cosmos again. 'Sorry,' he says. 'I need to go somewhere else, too.'

He walks out the door and into the hallway. Light flashing. Cigarette smoke from those who have given up trying to reach the outside. Something in his spirit tells him to go upstairs.

*

Brendan opens the door to the spare room. It is just a little bigger than Josephine's room. There is a sink against the wall, and a full-length mirror next to the wardrobe. A single-glazed window shivers against the wind by the single bed, which Brendan gently lays her down on and begins to kiss her neck. She lets out the moans she knows he wants to hear as he runs his hands up and down her body. She pulls him up to kiss his lips, keeping her eyes closed. This makes her think of Glynn last night, of how he held her that morning, how he said he saw something in her that she claimed was not there. She opens her eyes, suddenly keen to get away from him, and looks at Brendan. But Brendan is not there anymore. There is only Mother, staring down at her, white gleaming bone and flesh that stinks, drooping and dripping down on her face. Flies buzz around her skull. Her teeth are yellowed and wonky, the gums scabbed and pink.

'Darling,' says Mother. And then that scream again. Pitched like a whale song, vibrating across her whole body, shivering up and down, beginning to distort as it reaches its last shrill notes. And again. And the hands are still on Josephine but now they are skeletal and strong and they are pressing Josephine down so hard she cannot move, and that mouth opens wide as if to swallow her screaming still, so Josephine screams back, the same painful sound and they both shiver and shake and Josephine closes her eyes but Mother is still there, reaching for the blackness, coming ever close, and she is sure she is going to be swallowed whole.

And then her eyes are open, and Glynn is sat there on the bed next to her, his hand on her shoulder, shaking her softly, and she is coming to. There is no sign of Brendan other than his jacket draped over the wardrobe.

'Are you ok?' he says. 'You were screaming.'

'I wasn't...' she stops. 'I'm fine.' She breathes deeply.

'What happened?'

And, surprising herself, she tells him that she saw a vision of her mum, a dead woman who, when alive, had been abusive and cruel. She says that her mum haunts her. She tells him how she never cried for her mum and begins to feel strength in the saying of things. And he listens, nodding, eventually sitting on the bed with her and wrapping an arm round her, offering his shoulder as a place to hide her face from the world.

*

'These baron bans of ours. This lordless land. It is a wonder that it stays, somehow stable, somehow not stumbling into the sea. Barely recognised, barely alive, but still here.'

'It would hardly be easy to kill, would it? This place is permanent.'

'But you take my point?'

'Not at all, man. You've pasted something onto this town, not thinking about it at all. I mean, this place had a Lord, as it goes.'

'It did?'

'The Lord Ystwyth. He was as steady in this town as the flow of the river for a good while. Father of the House. Father of the town. A man of all the pomp and pageantry you'd expect from such titles. Loved a top hat and coattails. Liked to cut ribbons and wax his moustache. You know the type. Not around so much anymore – considered eccentric if they ever appear in the wild, outside palaces or televisions. But then, that was what you wanted in a leader. Somebody who looked like they might remember the last century.'

'Now we like our leaders to look like men pretending to be less than they are. Lords calling themselves things like Georgie and Dom just so they fit in even with their blue air accents. But Lord Ystwyth wasn't like that. He was a Cardigan boy, who grew up to be a Cardigan Lord.'

'Sounds a bit grand to me.'

'And like all grand things there's bound to be a fall. He was a police officer. Probably used to enjoy breaking the noses of boozers like us. Then he was a Tory for a while, but he went Liberal before he won election. But none of that matters. He doesn't matter till he becomes Lord Ystwyth.'

'The only one.'

'That's right. No children. No wife. No family. A title bequeathed upon and led to extinction with him. Lord like water, flowing and gone and eternal.'

'Strange thing is there's not much to remember him by. Sort of thing you'd expect to see a statue for, a big old cast iron thing. But not here. There's nothing other than some portraits.'

'Except the film of the war memorial.'

'Oh yeah that's something.'

'Ghosts upon ghosts, there. All black and white and ethereal. Dead upon the dead.'

'What's so special about it?'

'It proves your theory about lordless lands wrong, for one. There he is, our Lord, moustache nice and waxed, hat all good and proper on the top of his head. And around him are all these Union Jack flags. Crowds of people standing and looking sad. You see it these days and it all looks a bit too much like lots of people trying to prove how much they care. But then you're looking at people who had their sons and nephews and the rest blown to bits or killed by disease or what have you. The whole thing is sombre. And the Lord Ystwyth stands in front of his people, and he speaks. And then the camera cuts. God knows what he said.'

'You have no idea?'

'Not a clue.'

'What would you guess at?'

'If I had to guess he said anything, I imagine it was the usual stuff about final homecomings, about the bravery of men who went and fought for their country and all that was good and right. But at this point the War had been finished for five years. He must've been sick of talking about it. Must have known, as everyone who lives on the edges does, that those who make their decisions in the centre don't do it for goodness, but glory. They do it for sinful things all wrapped up in their own ego. So, maybe there, standing amongst his own people, he put down his placards, told them to switch the cameras off. Had the journalists put down their pens. Looking up at the strange monument, he might've said that; might've said how in this place we are all looking West, waiting for the homecoming of something. The dead are coming again, and we are waiting for them. Those of us who live here truly, anyway.'

'Even the students?'

'I'm talking as the Lord Ystwyth here, not as myself.'

'But you must have something to say on that.'

'They tread on the dead, the students. Think because they're dead it means they don't matter. But one day, when things move again, they'll find their ankles have been grabbed, they'll find all that skipping and dancing will be a lot harder to do.'

'I fear thee, Lord Ystwyth.'

'Come off it, now. We've had enough of all this silliness. It's just chatter anyway. Getting a little too ghostly for my liking. They're ringing the time bell with sudden fervour. Let's stop while we're ahead. And I'll see everyone and everything tomorrow.'

'Bella will be cleaning the bar, washing all the remnants away. Unless some droplets of beer form a hand to grab her ankle, I suppose.'

'Don't make fun, man, it's not on. Not after this many beers. I can't be responsible for what I say after this many beers.'

CHAPTER TEN

Out on the edge of land, water comes in cloudy waves spitting at the shore. Josephine and Glynn walk, shaking themselves from the evening, their hands gently linked. Josephine feels something dripping at the back of her throat. Glynn sees all the colours of the egg painting pulsing in the black water, and watches the white foams of a wave gallop to shore like horses.

'I'm glad to see you,' says Glynn. 'I feel like things were awkward, earlier.'

Josephine laughs. 'I guess it all got a bit much. You know, you saying all that stuff about hands and eyes.'

Now, though, she realises he might have been touching on something real. Since he said it, she has keeping her eyes open, looking at the people and places around her.

'Maybe I got a little carried away,' says Glynn. 'It's just, I thought you'd get what I meant. That's my problem. I expect everyone to see things my way. I'm sorry, anyway.'

The wind is soft, nagging at their bodies, icy and tender, letting out a low moan. It makes Josephine shiver. Then, feeling Glynn's grip around her hand loosen, she interlocks her fingers with his and squeezes tight. He looks at her like she is the sun come unexpectedly. He pulls at her arm, and she stops, looking into his eyes. Their bodies are lit by the firm brightness town and, beyond that, the twinkling lights of other towns further away. They both hear the familiar patter of rain before each feels it on their skin. They feel their clothes grow heavy on them.

Come into me, thinks Glynn, and she does. They kiss as the water comes down, long and slow.

A man is turning from the north beach to south. He sees the couple kissing and recognises them. There is no bitterness or anger in him anymore. He knows what he is following. The Preacher has built his congregation, knows what there is to do and how to do it. The plan revealed itself like that very same sun Glynn saw just now in Josephine. As he approaches the couple, he enjoys the feel of being washed again, how it reminds him of the final wash, the one that once almost wetted him. They are kissing, and soon he must kiss too, but not now, not till things have reached their fever pitch. They do not notice as he moves towards them. Something about just drifting by seems wrong. He speaks.

'It's good to see passions rise so high.'

Josephine and Glynn break apart, step back and turn to face the Preacher. Each feels embarrassed, alarmed, and a little curious as to why anyone else would go wandering on a night like this.

'Can we help you?' says Glynn. He takes the figure in. The Preacher wears a brown leather jacket and a white dress shirt. Black denim jeans. Dark curling hair and the slightest shades of a small moustache above his lips.

But the Preacher is looking at Josephine, who is looking back into his eyes, which seem icy blue like the rain, or those rifts in the clouds she watched the other morning. They recognise each other, though Josephine does not know the who, where or how of it all. She gets the feeling that this is someone whose gaze has been on her for a very long time. Now, she wants to gaze back at him.

'I'm sorry to interrupt,' says the Preacher. 'I shouldn't have said anything, should have let young love burn amongst all this dampening wet. But I couldn't help myself.'

He walks on and, and they watch him leave. Once he is in the distance, falling into the darkness hulking beneath the Old College, turning the corner towards the pier, they link hands again and move south, towards Glynn's flat.

'He was a weirdo,' says Glynn. 'Did you see how he was dressed?'

'Yeah,' says Josephine. 'And I think he knew me.'

As they turn the corner, south beach stretches out in front of them, and the rain darts in over the colourful houses, the harbour light flashing in the distance. Josephine looks right and then left and sees the war memorial, the angel pointing and the naked woman beneath her.

'Now I'm looking properly, it is a weird statue.'

Glynn laughs. 'I can't believe you're just noticing.'

Josephine laughs and they link arms. 'Shut up, I'm trying!'

And they hold each other like lovers always have, like lost souls finally found, like – like men holding each other while dying in the mud and rain, hiding from bombs and guns, or men in beds in hospitals dreaming of lost lovers – or men missing home, here, not here and here at the same time.

This story is being briefly taken over by other voices. Josephine and Glynn walk on, but we must stay here. Listen to them, the voices in the names guarded by the angel and her friend.

Dear Father, Grandfather, Mother, Grandmother, Brother, Sister, Lover, Friend occasionally Cousin, perhaps even Neighbour, in rare cases, son or daughter, and, in even rarer, grandson or granddaughter,

It is wet and sunny here at this part of the front or middle or back or hospital we have been sent to fight on or wait by or rest in. There are many other men, and we are sick of the sound of gunshots and screams or laughter and screams or doctors and screams. In the evenings, or whenever it is that calm descends, we play cards. We will be back home soon, or in a while, or we don't know when, or never. It was good to be sent out with those that we know, though many of us are separated now and we are sure you know of the ones that are separated for good. We miss you, and the sea, of course, and wish that we, too, could come in on a wave, though we would not retract, taunt you with our presence just to go off to some unknown place again. Despite our constant wanting to escape we have never missed home more than now, when we are the furthest from it we have ever been. Or, alternatively, we always knew we were in the right place from birth, and all these damned deaths and bombs only confirm the fact. We miss everything, even the students – we miss how they meander and talk of their own things and live little lives of innocent beauty. What we wouldn't give to see one walking the prom, worrying about whatever essay they have due, or working through their most recent ontological crisis. There are no ontological crises here: we are too worried about keeping alive to think about being it. It is hard to remember where Aberystwyth is when we are here. It is not like fishing out at sea, where one simply looks east and knows over there is home. We tend to just look around and hope that our glance at least briefly crosses over the Ystwyth and the Rheidol, dancing over Trefechan and back to you. And sometimes we feel you, looking out towards us, out from the coast like some still angel, albeit looking not to France, but to Ireland, where they have their own troubles, from what we've heard. And we might be there too. Do you like that idea? That you could look across the coast and divine something like that? We like you as an angel, but we like you more as something beneath, with all the beauty and none of the pretence. We have been stuck here for longer than we expected we would be. Far longer. But we are wanting to come out now, come home, emerge all shelled and blinking at all the strangeness that has taken place since our time. And we will be, soon, believe me there, whomever you are. We will be coming home soon, all of us. And we walk our streets again after so many years.

With love, best wishes and kindest regards,
With sincerity,

The Dead.

*

Did you forget why we're really here? Take a breath. Move along. We can catch up with them.

Josephine and Glynn are walking along the seafront, their hands linked, their blood warm and their hearts beating quickly against cold and rain. Josephine wonders, holding Glynn's hand for the second night in a row, what might come of this. She wonders with a numb sense of dread. She is sure it will bring only trouble. That is what anything other than the narrow act of existence seems to bring. They turn a corner and they are standing on the marina, looking over the boats.

'It's funny,' says Josephine. 'I'd barely even noticed this part of town before yesterday.'

Glynn shakes his head. 'I just can't believe how much of this town you've managed to miss.'

'I get it,' she says. 'Like you're so wise.'

She turns around to kiss his cheek and stops. Standing just behind Glynn is the boy from outside the flat yesterday, still in the same blazer and cotton trousers, his sleeves rolled up, a cigarette in his mouth. His foot is up against the metal railing between the marina and the water, miraculously dry. Josephine feels an intense sense of intrigue. She lets go of Glynn's hand and moves towards him.

'Hello,' she says. 'I saw you yesterday. You borrowed a light.'

He looks up and bites his lip uncertainly. He nods. 'Yes, I remember you.'

She gestures at his outfit. 'Are you not cold? You must be freezing.'

The man briefly wonders where all this concern was yesterday, when he first went walking. He keeps such thoughts to himself. 'I'm alright, thanks,' he says. 'I don't seem to feel the cold so much these days.'

Glynn looks at him from behind Josephine's shoulder, his body a little tense, his hands slightly clenched. 'You'll get ill, you know,' he says. 'Even if you don't feel like you will.'

The man nods his head and laughs. 'I'm not sure I need to be worrying about that. But thanks.'

Glynn catches him in the glow of the lamplight then. Sees the green eyes and the ginger hair. Thinks of the woman from before.

'You're not looking for someone, are you?' he says. 'Or maybe being looked for?'

With sudden seriousness the man nods and looks directly at him. 'As it happens, I am,' he says. 'Why? What do you know?'

Josephine looks at Glynn. 'Oh yeh – that woman. You've got the same vibe, kind of.' She looks from Glynn to the man, nods.

'You've seen Alice?' he says. 'Where?'

'By the harbour light,' says Glynn. 'Over on Tan-y-Bwlch. But that was this morning.'

The man nods. 'It's enough.' And then he is gone, moving towards Trefechan bridge, leaving only smoke from over his shoulder.

'They should just text each other,' says Josephine, linking her hand with Glynn's again.

*

'One more story.'

'Yeah, one more. It doesn't even need to be true.'

'I've lost my need for a true one. Just let it be good.'

'I'll do you one better. I'll do you one good and true.'

'Can it be?'

'It is known that in Aberystwyth, a summer three years before the First World War would briefly wipe away wonder, there was a wondrous sight to behold upon the town's north beach. Pictures populate the walls of pubs, restaurants, shops and museums of the place still. Two Indian elephants bathed in the calm waters of the Irish Sea, stood towering above the prom and its people, seemingly unbothered by the clamour of children and adults alike. Except not quite unbothered, for suddenly and simultaneously, the two plunged their trembling trunks once more beneath the waves before bringing them to the surface, pointing them high up towards the sky, spraying salt water for the adulation of the crowds, droplets of water falling like rain. Those watching had only ever known descriptions and black and white images of such a creature: had never felt the wrinkled grey of its skin, never marvelled at its grandeur, at the way it called out to the sky like some preacher.

'A little further back, his corduroy trousers rolled up to his knees, his top hat perched at an angle on his head, the Master watched his beasts earn their keep. At times, he felt a jealousy toward those who touched their trunks, how the giggles and shouts made some claim of intimacy. They were his creatures. He raised them as calves, taught them how to pull his cart along the country's highways, built cages with which to cover them from rain and protect them from those who meant harm. In a moment of conviction, the Master knew with full surety how he might prove his mastery to his customers, how he might make them reverential of himself as well as his creatures. To his right he could see the great Constitution Hill, looming like some dragon – or, indeed, an elephant. And he saw himself and his creatures at its peak, and he thought what a wonder it might make. He let the man with his big camera take a picture of the elephants in the water. Then he approached and said, "surely you want something better than that?". This was how it began, the side of the story that not everybody knows.

'The crowds followed and cheered as the Master led his creatures up the hill. As he went up the path, he was pleased to see how much space the paths left for turning. He began to think that something like destiny could be at play in his great ascent. Someone shouted from behind, "how will you get them across the bridge?" and the Master replied, "by walking them."

'When he came to the bridge, its narrowness surprised him. He saw the second bridge above. He saw nothing else except the peak and its glory. He urged the elephants on, keeping one ahead of him and another behind. He moved in the middle, his two iron-chain leashes steadily pulling on their necks. Smiling, he took a breath. Things seemed secure. It was then that the railway beneath burst into action, ticking to a timetable unrestricted by fate. One tram moved down from the top and another moved up from below. The master did not see, but the elephant behind him did, just as she stood in the middle of the bridge, her companion having safely crossed, and the sight of something so loud and slow and large, almost as large as her, made her descend briefly into a madness.

'But before any more of that, I must tell you of two of the passengers upon the rising tram. A couple in love, unsurprising on a summer's day like the one in question. A couple so in love they were the only two people in the town to not notice the elephants at all. One was Dewi Gruffydd, an apprentice baker from a baker's family. The Gruffydds worked the shop on Terrace Road that shut down not so long ago. He was a good baker, in the end, but back then he really had the soul of a poet. He had a thin frame, beautiful red hair, and grey eyes that could really see. He used to love listening to things: the tweeting of birds, the hushes of the sea, the chatter of customers in his father's shop. And he listened to her, too, the woman in love with him. That was how it happened. She was older than him; eleven years in fact. Married with two children, too. But she escaped all that to be with him for a little while. People of her position could do that. For this woman was Princess Alice, a grandchild of Queen Victoria. Later she would rule colonies and meet a President. In our story, though, she felt like another piece that, in her marriage, had been played.

'She'd been sent there a week ago, on behalf of her uncle, the King, who himself was due to visit, to open the National Library. She went into the bakery and they did not know her. She took a shine to the boy behind the counter. She saw him again on the beach when she went walking on her own one midnight, having escaped her chaperone. Dewi offered her some wine from the bottle he'd taken with him. They drank it on the sands, watching the moonlight glimmer. And they'd made love there, and held each other in the darkness, and the Princess was struck with the sudden and specific heartache of knowing this would be the last time she would feel real and true love like this, and that it was the first time for her partner. And for Dewi, this love made everything fresh and new, but he felt guilt, too. The guilt of knowing this woman was married. When he told his brother, Alun, of the affair, the man's fury confirmed this. Dewi taught Alice fragments of Cymraeg. They saw each other every evening and made love in what places of privacy they could find.

'One night he took her to the Ystwyth river, and as they watched it pull hard and fast along the banks, he spoke of his love for her and his hatred for himself, and he tried to mimic the preacher he listened to every Sunday. Without his Cymraeg it was strange, but he tried. In English, his sentences spilled over into each other. He said their love was like a hatred pushed from God to Satan and back again, that it was Judas kissing the cheek of Jesus. And the Princess heard all this and was breathless, and more in love and fearful than ever, and once again the two made love with the tragic beauty that comes from knowing they were destined for some impending doom.

'And the two of them stood on that carriage, rising above the town, and each in their own mind began to think that perhaps they would rise above the difficulties of their births and their places and what they were bound to and rise to something new and different, something that would let them live with their love for each other. And then a great shadow descended over them, and Dewi looked up, expecting to bemoan a cloud, but instead saw something else.

'The Master lost his grip on the leading elephant's leash as the one behind roared and stamped. He tried to calm her, but she refused. He gave the leash one final tug, and the elephant veered left and crashed through the wood of the old narrow bridge. The other elephant watched as his companion and his master fell.

'In a matter of seconds, wood crashed against the station at the foot of the hill. When the ambulance arrived, a woman was dead. She'd been crushed by the weight of one of the creatures, her bone split and her body flattened. Two others were injured. The Princess and her baker's boy were shaken but safe. Not long after, she kissed him goodbye and returned home. They covered this part of the story up, the powers-that-be, who still very much existed then, and had us all believe nothing more happened than a friendly paddle in the sea, so the King's visit could go on unimpeded. The story was re-told, kept alive overs the years by witnesses, then the descendants of witnesses, all changing slight details, but all of them, when drawing to the tale's end, shaking their heads, taking a breath, and mumbling, "you should've seen the way that fucker fell."'

'Come on, now. You can't expect us to believe that.'

'What's not to believe?'

'The whole thing, fella. You've pulled this out of somewhere other than what's around us.'

'It was Alun, Dewi's brother, that told my grandfather. Alun died in the Somme. My father told me. I've not pulled anything out of anywhere. All I'm doing is keeping the story alive.'

'Well, either Alun or your Tad-cu or your Dad was underestimating how much shit you'd swallow.'

'Maybe you're right. Maybe we've finally gone out too far. Maybe it's time to head back to the shore.'

*

Nathan and Hope are elsewhere. Jake has walked Sarah home. Sarah puts her phone in her pockets and looks up at the sky. The rain drips. The moon's glow dimly lights sheets of cloud. Jake is looking at her, wondering how he can help her feel less sad. He longs to see those sharp cheek bones move higher, those soft lips move up into the shape of a smile. Music thumps slowly, playing from the building behind them.

'I can never sleep anyway, when he's not there,' says Sarah. 'With the music it'll be worse.'

'What does he even do?' says Jake, knowing that Sarah and Nathan are not the kind to share a bed, much less sleep together.

'He talks to me till I fall asleep.'

Jake wants to say that he will talk to her till she falls asleep, if she would listen and like it. He wants to say, you know what I mean when I'm asking what I'm asking. But he doesn't. He just looks at her while she looks back, the rain between them.

'I'm sorry.' Sarah puts her head in her hands. 'I'm being dramatic. This has all been a lot to take in.'

Jake nods. 'Do you believe this guy? Do you believe him about who he says he is?'

'I don't know.' Sarah laughs. 'Of course, I know. He's crazy.

Absolutely crackers. And we're doing everything he says. Nathan's obsessed. It's like…'

Jake instinctively holds his hand out and, to his surprise, she takes it. 'It's like something is going all kinds of wrong,' he says. 'I know what you mean. I didn't expect to get into all this. Marches and banners and the rest. I just thought – well, to be honest, I'm not even much of a believer. I just wanted some friends.'

Sarah shakes her head and laughs. 'That's very sad, Jake.'

'I never thought it would lead to this,' he says. 'But a lot has happened.'

They are looking at each other again, now. Sarah is aware, more than ever, of her hands. The way they are held in Jake's, and do not feel uncomfortable there. But the weather is worsening. She says a hurried goodnight and goes in, leaving Jake out in the rain. He wanders for a while, looking at things. He looks at the lamplight reflected in puddles, drenched trees and shabby apartment blocks. Then he goes home, worried he'll catch a cold.

*

They are standing outside the Academy, watching the drinkers go into the Angel. The Preacher has his hand on the old brick. Nathan watches. He still does not understand what he sees.

'Tomorrow, we shall have the gathering,' says the Preacher. 'Then the march. Soon after, the storm will break, and I shall leave you. Do not think I am ungrateful for what you've done.'

'Where will you go?' says Nathan.

There is a shout of glee from across the street. A man has stubbed a cigarette out on his friend's arm. The friend grabs him and presses him against the pub wall. The Preacher looks at the scuffle, then back at the stone.

'Nowhere you can understand,' he says. 'But you must try: just as you must try and understand your fear of God. There is great fear in you.'

A friend is breaking the two men apart. They are shouting at one another, threats of smashed faces, insults directed at girlfriends and mothers.

'There is no fear in me,' says Nathan. 'I promise.'

'There is, and you would be a fool not to fear God – not to fear the Father. But you must seek to understand the fear rather than hide it, hide from it. Your life is too chaotic.'

'What do you mean?' says Nathan.

The men are being separated by security, now. They are being pushed up the road, toward the kebab shop and the clock tower. Their friends let them go, start apologising to the security, negotiating their entry to the pub.

The Preacher looks at him, his hand still on the stone. 'Cease these silly liaisons with Hope. You are betraying your duty. But more than that, you are attempting mastery over God, who cannot be mastered, and whom is he you are meant to worship.'

Nathan looks down. He is scared. The Preacher seems to know everything. His head is full of noises, hissing sounds that remind him of boiling water and steam. The Preacher looks at the two men who are sat by the clock tower, hugging and crying.

'She is the key,' the Preacher says. 'She and I. A point of meeting. Forgiveness. Then departure. And a new feeling of faith. Faith, which is of course in truth the oldest feeling we have.'

'Sarah?' says Nathan. 'What does she have to do with anything.'

'No,' says the Preacher. 'I've told you what you need to do.'

The Preacher walks away, towards the castle and the seafront. Nathan walks up the hill toward his home. He finds Sarah waiting for him. They hold each other, and she asks where he has been. But he tells her not to worry, and he kisses the lips that made him a believer. Then he goes back to his own bed, across the hall.

STORM

*

You feel tricked, of course. Don't worry, you might as well get used to it. Once death comes, of course, you realise the sham of everything. All those days you thought you were late for work, you were really nothing for nothing. There is only space, and it is infinite. Laid out in this space, among other things, is the totality of your own life, and very often you find yourself recognising, finally, those failures you never wanted to look at directly. You wander.

Wandering, you come across another. They are weeping for people they could not save. You are weeping, you realise, and the other asks why. You tell them it is because you did not love the person you were most supposed to love. Other things got in your head, things that now, in darkened death, reveal themselves to be nothing. They nod. 'There are many like you,' they say.

You wander together for a while. You do not know why they choose to be with you, when there is so much space and so many spirits. You are not a person, now, you would ever choose to spend time with. You say this to them, once.

'We are not people anymore,' they say.

That is something you are having a hard time coming to terms with.

The other directs you, and you see something for the first time since you have died. Endless stars. Brightness. If you had a heart, it would be beating.

'That was all we were,' they say, 'not even that, but the smallest fraction.'

You say, solemnly, 'so why does it matter, what we left?'

'Because there were other fractions, too.'

And like that, it happens. You are both together, and then you are fracturing. Now you are two tiny pieces of what you once were, spinning out, past planets and rocks and suns, until a small little blue dot grows larger and larger, until you recognise its particular patches of green, yellow and white, until you realise you are coming home, and then you are building, in the atmosphere, amongst the clouds, with all those others restless souls.

And all you want is forgiveness.

THE THIRD DAY

CHAPTER ELEVEN

Now, the storm has wrapped itself around the town, sapping its stability, making it other to what it should be. Tan-y-Bwlch is changed: tree trunks and carcasses along the shore, water over the footpath and into the nearby field, grass boggy and squelching. The fog is thick and surrounding. There seems the town, the hills, and then nothing. No one has managed to leave the town since the storm first came in. The railway tracks are flooded and the rail-replacement buses have all broken down. Bus drivers and cabbies have disappeared, got sick, and even walkers who attempt to stray further than Tan-y-Bwlch find themselves strangely pulled back as though the town is some great black hole on the edge of the west. The sea still comes crashing in at the shores and, if one were to climb the peaks of the hills, the bones of building and places could be seen.

By now, the promenade is covered in sand and pebbles kicked up by the wind. There is a digger kept somewhere that is dragged out for events like this that will gather up the grains and throw them back toward the beach, but that is not for now – not when things are still so rough. Not when the dog-walkers are still suffering gallantly as they walk their dogs, smiling and wishing each other good morning under hoods zipped up to chins; when there are still people getting up, stretching their joints and making coffee, looking out the windows and grimacing, eventually making that dreaded journey to work, perhaps allowing themselves to be a little less punctual than they normally would.

The whale lies on the beach. By now word has got around. The men in the orange high-visibility jackets will arrive with something to take it away, though they do not yet know what. But in spite of the winds, crowds gather regularly around that fallen beast, pointing and whispering, marvelling, committing its shape and its position to memory.

Not so much as a picture has been taken, though many have tried. People have slipped phones from their pockets, pointed their lenses towards the body, but never quite found the courage to set the process in motion, to make this a thing that undoubtedly and unforgettably happened. And in huddled conversations in pubs and on walks, some of those who have sighted it have admitted that, as inconceivable as it sounds, as ludicrous as the suggestion may be, they have seen it take a breath. Just one, and so briefly that it could well have been a trick of the light. But the stories are beginning to gather, and suspicion is beginning to grow. Perhaps this thing is not quite dead even though it is washed up on the beach, out of its element, with nothing to nurture it other than the minute sustenance of far-reaching waves that still lap at its grey body, and the rain.

This morning, there is a small group watching, braving the painful weather, holding flasks of coffee and tea. The group are muttering amongst themselves. Their remarks are things that would occur to any of us if confronted with such a scene: exclamations of its hugeness, admissions of strange grief that it has come here, dead as it is. Some of the more observant have pointed to the marks on its skull, explained how these are certainly the battle scars from mighty fights with giant squids. This has happened before. Each time, it has ended with people looking out at the sea, thinking about the depths of water, knowing there is both a great voided depth beyond them and that there are things living in it, things they cannot know.

Once most of the group has gone, there are two people watching the whale who are slowly coming to know each other. Jake is thinking of how a beast so beautiful does not deserve to die, wondering if he might yet again see it breathe, but becoming slowly certain he will not. Now he mourns for what he sees. He finds himself wondering why it had to die, and why it had to show its death to him. He would like to see one breathing, swimming, promising him something like a continuation of things that went on before him, things that were bigger than him. And yet here is something bigger than him, dead, while he is alive.

Sarah has always found this town beautiful but boring: easily read. Yet here, lying on the sand, is something that imbues the whole place with a sudden and strange meaning. It seems to fit with the hills and the rain and the long, desolate beach upon which she is standing. She thinks about Melville and Murakami, and Griffiths too, and all the people she spends her days writing about. And then she catches herself, realising she is not really thinking about the whale enough, that she has let her mind drift back to the same old themes, and she curses what thinking has done to her. Then she stares again, really looking at the bleached grey of the wale, at its half open mouth and the bullet shape of its head.

They see each other then, a gust of wind pushing the Sarah's hair in front of her face so that Jake appears apparition-like through the strands. He smiles, his yellow jacket almost glowing, and she smiles back. He seems to just *appear* at all the right times. She touches the ring on her finger. She has convinced herself that nobody else is worth talking to. Yet the sight of the whale and how useless she feels next to it, makes her desperate to say something.

'How do you react to something like this?' she shouts over the wind. 'I mean, what kind of small talk do we make about this thing's dead body?'

Jake laughs. 'I don't suppose you can say anything. All I keep thinking about is how sad it all is.'

She puts a hand to her face and smiles. 'All I can think about is what other people would make of it. I can't even get a grip of the real thing,' she says.

'That's not true, you know,' he says. 'You've got to have something in you that feels something, don't you?'

She thinks and finds something. 'I think I just can't quite believe that of all the people in the world to have seen this, it's me. All those people who lived and died here, not even knowing something like this was out there.'

Jake nods. 'Since I arrived, I thought I knew this place. This makes me realise I didn't really know anything. But I'm glad it's happened.'

'Because it has happened,' says Sarah. 'We can't really argue with that.'

For a moment the wind beats against the carcass and the two share a quiet. Jake thinks about reaching his hand towards hers, again. There are the waves and the seagulls, hawking. There is the world in stillness. And then the whale takes a breath. Another. Great, deep gasps. A deep gurgle fills the air, roaring over the moans of the wind. Its fin begins to flap gently. Its mouth moves up and down like a seesaw. Its tail slaps against the shore. Jake and Sarah jump back. They look at each other, then look ahead. It is not only that the words won't come, but that they feel bound to some sort of strange silence, like speaking has been quite suddenly barred for the moments that this miracle takes place. The whale goes on, gurgling and thrashing against its own death until the gurgling ceases. From its open mouth it emits something sharp and piercing, something fragile and delicate that stretches across the land. Incredibly – impossibly – the whale begins to sing. The sound is as ancient and unknowable as the depths beyond them. Like the whistling of a kettle along a large cavern. Despite this, both Sarah and Jake feel they understand it somewhere. It seems to promise that something is preparing for an end, that some climax is coming, something it has been waiting for on this cold beach, something it has slumbered in preparation for, something it is itself a requirement of. And then just as suddenly it ceases, and the two of them are left standing in the rain, looking at the carcass, shaking against the cold and the impossibility of what they have witnessed.

*

The Aberystwyth University Christian Society are meeting in a new place at the insistence of the Preacher. There were fears about the proposed location: the shut-down pub on Great Darkgate Street, with its high ceilings and loud acoustics and a grand staircase. The legal objections were the first to be raised, obviously. The building was for sale: it was still owned, though no one was quite sure who by, and it could not just be used by anyone. But the Preacher insisted. It had to be there. The force of his speech made all counterarguments dry up, seem arbitrary and useless. Then came the second wave of objections – the anxiety of who would attend and whether the walk down the hill would be enough on its own to put most of the first year members off, claims that the loss of familiarity would make people lose patience with a group that was already struggling to stay relevant. But the Preacher smiled, shook his head and said that anyone not willing to make such a comparably gentle journey was not really equipped for the struggle to come: the struggle to save oneself and one's world from sin. It seemed to resist would mean to be one of the damned, and with that, any opposition was silenced.

An emergency meeting was called. Emails were sent out and

group chats were alerted. And, on this morning, Nathan, Sarah, Hope and Jake walk into the disused church of the Academy Bar and see the Preacher standing atop the staircase, dressed in black, his arms spread out, a smile on his face, his eyes closed. To their shock, they find many people have arrived before them. The hall is full of whispers, some they recognise and some they do not; young and old, some students and some locals. Nathan, reflecting on the usual thin attendance of his own meetings, feels as if he is watching his own deposition.

'We need to get to the front,' he says. 'It's important we're close.'

They try to cut their way through the crowd, but everyone seems so set in place. Nathan looks around the room and remembers the drinks downed, the girls kissed, the sins he has indulged in this old place of worship. Something about his own soul seems to be mocked here.

'Many years ago,' says the Preacher, his eyes still closed, his face tilted slightly towards the ceiling. 'I led hundreds through this town. We marched for Eden. For divinity, for a better humanity, one closer to that which God created – one closer to that which He desires us to be. Some of you marched and sang with me that day.

'It felt, then, as if we were on the precipice of some great change, as if we might yet overthrow the vice-driven oppression that was gathering around us. And yet, now, we must look honestly upon what we did and what it did. It failed, friends. We died and sin went on. And we stand now in the centre of our failure. A church turned into a pub, a place of worship become a place of sin. My own memorial, the singular thing commemorating the hard battle many of us fought, is surrounded every night by drunks and perverts. We failed, and our world fell further, fell closer to Hell than it ever has been before. Many of you are part of its failure. Many of you have consumed and indulged, have held some private, harmless, weak faith that has not expected anything of you, that has been bent and twisted by your own self-centred desires.'

And yes, it's true, they all have. Their guilt comes home, brought by this strange figure, this man they do not know, who says he has waited in a clock tower. The people are confused and captivated, all at once.

'But take heart: we are all corruptible in such a corrupted world. By coming here, by braving the storm, by standing in this room, you have declared yourself worthy not of forgiveness but of redemption, of re-earning your place at God's side in Heaven. For on this day, we will recommence our striving. We will begin again our attempt to cleanse. We will once again march along these streets. We will once again *canu'r caneuon o rinwedd*. Join me now, see me as the saviour I have been sent here to be, and let us lead this place *yn ôl i'r golau*.'

There is a great cheer from the crowd. Nathan turns to Hope. He has heard enough. He will put his foot down. Who is this man, really? Just some stranger wandering in from the streets one rainy day, who found that he suddenly had the gift of the gab. They had believed every word he said, but not anymore. Nathan is ready to stop it. But when he looks at Hope, she is cheering and clapping; she is moving through the crowd towards the Preacher. Then Sarah, who is crying into her hands. Spinning, he tries to find Jake, but he has disappeared, swallowed by the crowd. Nathan realises he is no one. He is alone. He cannot turn the crowd, just as he can't stop the storm. There is only the Preacher, his words, and his masses. Nathan cannot be alone, again. He claps with the rest of them.

*

And, of course, there is Josephine and Glynn. You need only know that as they hide away from the storm, wrapped in quilts, Josephine finding herself once again softening into his arms, feeling in his warmth a reason to believe in something.

Meanwhile, those wailing winds rouse those spirits which we have been hearing so much about. Those spirits stir as the whale breathes and the Preacher moves. They stretch and yawn and screech up, asking, 'won't you come and remember us?'. The rain is falling and people are listening. As night falls, and it is winter, and the nights fall oh so early, and it is the time of warmth and sipping hot chocolates and looking out windows and saying oh I shall not go out in that, the people do begin to go out, almost as if under hypnosis, almost as if called by some higher cause. Perhaps, God has come to Aberystwyth. No, it is a simpler thing. History. History is screeching through this town, on some tract from some distant place. History is shifting and shaking, and it is made from water. It is speaking from the walls. It is coming from the walls. It is persuading people that things should not be as they are. In short, while Josephine and Glynn fall into each other, the present falls into the past. The town begins to go mad.

Again, she wakes to him, his chest warm against the chill of the storm which has seeped through the single-glazed windows and the cheap walls of Glynn's house. Josephine knows, now, that she has never been safer than at this moment. The sound of his soft sleeping breath, and the feeling it leaves on the back of her neck. It almost makes her eyes water.

Glynn pulls her over. She closes her eyes, puts a hand on his face and kisses him slowly. His breath smells of tobacco and pizza. They rest their noses next to each other and she smiles.

'This is quite scary, you know,' she says.

'How scary?' asks Glynn. Josephine's eyes are still closed but she can hear his grin.

'Only a little,' she whispers, opening her eyes, expecting his warm breath and his soft face, wanting again to kiss him slowly.

But Glynn is gone. The first thing she notices is the cold hardness in place of the soft skin on her fingertips. The smell of rot and dirt, the feeling she needs to gag, as if the scent itself had filled her with some kind of poison. And there is the face of Mother, half skull and half rotting skin, tufts of hairlike wisps of cloud taunting her.

'No,' says Josephine. 'Please, no, please, not here, not him, please, just leave him, take everything else, just not him.'

Mother shakes her head. She smiles. She opens her mouth. Josephine puts her hands over her ears, preparing for the scream that will split her. But instead, something happens that has not happened before. Mother speaks.

'Sorry, Josie, dear,' she says. 'It's all or nothing.'

Josephine jumps from the bed. Ludicrously, despite the racing of her heart and shivering of her body and the sweat on her forehead and the fear everywhere around her, she puts on her clothes, quickly, as Mother rises and reaches out a hand for her.

'Don't run from me, Josie. I'm everywhere.'

'Fuck off and leave me alone,' says Josephine, opening the door and running out into the hallway.

'I can't, Josie!' cries Mother, her voice wailing, banshee like. 'And you can't leave me!'

Storming down the hallway, Josephine sees Anna coming from the kitchen, an eyebrow raised, a plate of buttered toast in her hand, the slightest sense of satisfaction coming off her.

'You guys ok?' she says. 'I heard shouting.'

'I need to get out,' says Josephine. 'I need to get out now.'

'Christ, what did he do?' Anna lets out a laugh, before catching the shock on Josephine's face. 'He really likes you, you know,' she says.

But Josephine is already pulling open the stiff door, looking up the stairs, seeing Mother walking down slowly and waving, head perched to one side. They catch each other's eyes, and Mother's are black as the sea at night. Josephine's breaths are too quick for her lungs. She feels light-headed and scared. As she steps over the threshold and into the storm, the rain wraps round her. She does not look back at the house, does not even shut the door. But she hears the scream. It is like the burning out of a star.

Josephine runs down to the Marina, along the Rheidol River, over Trefechan Bridge, till she reaches Tan-y-Bwlch. The wind rises high and hard over the great flat expanse between the two great hills. The waves are hard and running up the rocks. The footpath in front of her leads towards the hills. And she sees it, up against the rocks, white and shimmering in the grey, still and solid and sleeping, the washed-up sperm whale. Standing on the rocks are two men in high-viz jackets. Behind them is a small crane and a pick-up truck. She didn't know she was going here. She didn't really know where was going at all. But now she is here, it feels right. Something beyond directs her here, there and everywhere, and always has. Josephine walks towards them, regaining her breath. When she reaches them, she finds she has nothing to say. She smells the pungent stink of something deceased follow the salt into her nostrils. It reminds her of Mother, but she keeps her gagging and her breathing under control and carries on. Looking up at the hill ahead of her, she thinks about escaping Aberystwyth. She continues walking, towards the hill.

The rain and wind beg her to stay.

And I'll make her.

*

At the bottom of the high street, the Preacher stands next to the café, nursing a coffee with one hand and holding a megaphone with the other.

'Do you really think we'll need that?' says Nathan.

The Preacher nods slowly, says nothing. Faces from the earlier meeting begin to appear, lining up along the pavement without care for pedestrians who step out onto the road to avoid them and then, hypnotised, join them. As the minutes tick by, the whole stretch of pavement from the café to the turning fills with people standing and waiting. Some are holding signs, others eating sandwiches or sausage rolls. They are zipped up in coats and woolly hats cover heads and ears. There are other others in justacorps, frocks, ulster coats. They wear leather boots, loose clothing and wear strange hats. There are children among them, but even the very youngest has a look in her bright eyes, a way of taking in the place that suggests she has seen something very like this before. Briefly the sun is glimpsed through a crack in the sky, and a ray of warm light covers the crowd. But the winds are cold, biting and unceasing, and the rain will only be away for a little while.

The Preacher looks over the group and smiles. 'The word that struck me shall strike us all!' he shouts into the megaphone, his ancient voice crackling and amplifying over his followers. There is a smattering of applause.

'Should we start?' says Nathan to the Preacher, trying to grasp some sense of control. 'There are quite a few people here. More than we've ever got before, I think.'

Despite his fears, Nathan can't help being moved. Looking at this vast swell of people, all here for God. He simply didn't know faith could still do things like this. He looks again at the Preacher, in his dark clothes, his fringe slicked with rain, the slight stubble on his face; almost as much a rockstar as a minister. And Nathan can't be sure, but he thinks he sees the man glimmer, almost like a drop of rain in lamplight. Perhaps it is true. Perhaps this man is a spectre emerged from this place.

'Not yet,' says the Preacher. 'More will come.'

And they do. Rather incredibly, even inconceivably, the group swells until it blocks the way of cars, until people start getting out their cars and joining. Signs in the air proclaim: 'water is the drink,' 'love over sex' and other strange slogans. On either side of the crowds, cars line the pavement. The high street is clogged with appeared believers demanding deliverance. It takes fifteen minutes for there to be enough that Nathan, with some hesitancy, says the thing on his mind.

'It's like we have an army. I mean, there must be thousands here.'

'Seven thousand,' says the Preacher, looking toward the uphill climb of the high street, staring up at his own monument on the clock tower. 'There are seven thousand.'

Nathan squints at the crowd. It stretches on and on, almost seeming to blur into one big mass. He can see people stretch round the pavement, emerging from roads and alleys. He watches water form into shapes, shapes form into bodies, bodies join the great swell. He knows, then, that everything happening is both real and unreal. For a moment, it is as though Nathan's soul has left his body and he can see from above, up in the cloud-covered sky, the heaps of heads below, the sheer force of what is to come. Then he is back in himself, and hearing the Preacher shout down the megaphone that the march will begin, and everyone is moving, and Nathan moves too, in a daze, unsure of whether what he is doing is right, wrong, Godly, ungodly or something more surreal and other.

The Preacher looks up at the sky, closing his eyes against the rain. He looks forward, towards the clock tower and the castle. Centuries of stony sleep, for this. He points. As the Preacher leads the marchers up past the high street, figures not seen before emerge from alleys and doorways. At the first they are quiet, watching on without a word, their faces fuzzy, their features blurred. Faced with such awe, there is nothing to do but follow; Nathan looks to his new commander.

'Who are they?' he says, knowing the Preacher will know.

'Doubters,' he replies. 'Pay them no mind.'

But already they seem to be coming more into focus. They are glaring men with long hair and large beards and pints of beer in their hands. They jeer and point. They laugh with each other. It takes a moment for Nathan to realise that they are laughing at the march.

'Caewch eich cegau!' shouts one man. 'Gadewch eich geiriau yn yr eglwys.'

'What are they saying?' says Nathan. 'I don't understand.'

'You should,' says the Preacher. 'How can you spread the faith here if you cannot speak to those whose words you are meant to give to God?'

Nathan falls silent and walks on. The men line the whole top of the high street. They are all wearing white, and circular hats, like the men in that Gene Kelly film his mother always watches.

'They are the doubters. They are sailors,' says the Preacher. 'They worship alcohol and the sea. They see us as fools and bores. They are emptier inside than the bottles they drain.'

And Nathan tries not to. But others do start to pay mind, so that by the time the march reaches the top of the street, nearing the clock tower and the Preacher's own plaque, some of the sailors and some of the marchers are shouting at each other, declaring all kinds of curses. The Preacher says nothing, just walks on, his cassock billowing in the wind, a slight smile on his face.

'You should get back to your fucking chapel,' says a young sailor with just a little stubble over his cheeks. 'Stop telling us how to live.'

'Wynn,' says the Preacher, saying the name slowly, indulging on its whistling sibilance. 'I baptised you with holy water under God's eyes. What has happened to you?'

'Deuthum ataf fy hun,' he says. 'Rather than the man you told me to be.'

'Ydy wirod yn eich gwneud chi'n dyn?' says the Preacher. 'I believe there is more to one's independence than trips on boats and empty glasses.'

Everything has come to a stop now. Participants on either side are glaring at each other, baring teeth, preparing for something that is coming. Those like Nathan who remember again the strange absurdity of this world they have found themselves in. They wonder if they should take this chance to run. They hold their ground. Something is making them. I cannot tell you what. I'm beginning to tire. It's harder to see what I'm supposed to see.

The rain renews, coming down harder, thicker, whipped around by the wind. It is pouring now, and the clouds block out the light and fill the place with gloom. Wind howls down the street. The air filling everyone's lungs is sharp and painful.

*

Hope and Sarah are behind the Preacher and Nathan. Sarah feels like she is on a train, her stomach full of butterflies and her face hot from all the motion. She is shivering from the cold winds, and sweating from the heat of all the surrounding bodies.

'This is too many people, isn't it?' says Sarah, her eyes flicking over to Hope, sure that here, at least, they can find some sort of common ground. 'Something about this just doesn't feel right, right?'

Hope flicks her hair, keeps her eyes fixed ahead, not looking at Sarah as she speaks. 'You need to get on board with what we're doing,' she says.

'But I don't understand what we're doing,' says Sarah.

Her phone buzzes. She pulls it from her pocket, but her hand is so slick with rain it falls and hits the pavement. She kneels to pick it up, Hope walking on beyond.

Before she knows it, the whole crowd is moving through her, as she stares at the ground, the lines in the pavement, the puddles, looking for her phone. She sees it just a few inches to her right and reaches just as a hard boot comes down and crushes that metal, glass and plastic.

Another boot hits her face. The world goes white then dark. She remembers when, as a child, she went too far out in the sea when visiting Brighton Beach. She was pulled under a wave, pinned beneath the surface. Helpless, aware she would either die or resurface, she had no control over either. It is the same now as the crowd marches over her, boots, trainers and shoes moving over like rain, the sky tauntingly above it all, water mixing with blood, before the crowd clears and she hears a kindly voice asking if she is alright. She turns and it is Jake, his face red. The great crowd moves ahead. They are singing something.

She cannot make out the words because they are in a language she does not speak. They are dŵr yw'r ddiod. Water is the drink.

'Are you alright?' Jake pulls her up and puts her arm over his shoulder.

She leans on him. Everything hurts.

'Where did you go?' she says. 'You disappeared.'

'I had to get out of there,' he says. 'This is all too much, too mad.'

'Yes,' she says. 'Is this actually happening?'

'I don't know,' he says. 'It feels like it is.'

'Where are we going?' she asks.

'We're going to mine,' says Jake. He pauses, remembering the hungover takeaway from two days ago. 'It might be kind of messy.'

*

For a while, there is just the watching, the marching, and the sounds of the storm. The Preacher reaches the clock tower. He touches his own name, smiles at the feel of cold slate against his palms. Behind, the people are moving in a homogenous, many-headed mass, swarming the town. It feels unbreakable.

What breaks it is the cracking of a glass, thrown from the Angel pub, just ahead of the clock tower. As its sign swings forward, the glass flies through the air, tipping amber liquid which mixes with water. As the sign swings back, it smashes at the Preacher's feet. He feels a shard of glass go through his ankle, a strange emptiness, an absence of pain, an absence of anything, where the wound should be, before he fills again. He looks up and sees a boy who became a man: Wynn, his lost sheep.

Wynn stares back, glaring.

Nathan feels a hand on his shoulder. It belongs to a large man in a double-denim getup covered in stitched badges. The man pulls Nathan back and steps ahead of him, just behind the preacher.

'Who the fuck,' he shouts, and it echoes across the town, 'do you think you fucking are?'

This is how it all starts. The people unleash themselves on each other. Bits of the crowd break off and form little scuffling groups. Alarms blaze as bodies are thrown into cars, and more glasses smash.

Something pulls at Nathan. He turns to face a woman in long breaches and a puffy dress shirt, who smacks him in the forehead with the handle of an umbrella. Blood drips and he falls down, crawling into an alley. He lays next to a pile of litter already picked at by the gulls. From there, he can still hear the cries. He pants and looks up at the sky, wondering where God is in all of this.

Then he thinks he might be in hell. Collecting his thoughts, he thinks it again: Aberystwyth is hell.

And of course it is. Everything connects, now. Nowhere to go, nothing to do, nobody who believes, nothing to believe in, not a single pleasure unspoiled by seagulls or bad weather or bad people or bad hygiene or bad building-work or bad upkeep or bad landlords or bad local politicians or bad local journalism or bad students or bad locals. Everybody just bad bad bad. And now, all those bad people beating the shit out of each other. Yes, he sees it now. Aberystwyth is hell.

But what is he doing in hell? Nathan, who knows that he is a good soul, if one occasionally led astray.

He stands up, looks around. The sky is darkening, the great ceiling of clouds blackening. Beyond all the rows of cellblock houses are the hills, and beyond the hills is elsewhere. He is Dante. He is Jonah. He is chosen to crawl back towards the light. So, he starts walking down the alley, further and further from the fighting.

Let him go. We need to look for someone. We need to look for how this will end.

For we have reached, now, reader, the pitch of madness. But there is more to come, yet. These scrapping spectres are not really our story. Still, drink this image in. Aberystwyth at war with itself, times coming into clash with each other, cultures tearing themselves apart. No putting the book down, looking to your partner across the pool while the children splash about, and saying, 'well, it's all got a bit far-fetched for me.' You've made it this far. It's almost over, now.

*

'I'm just saying, all I heard and saw was her telling you to fuck off and leave her alone, then running out the house, claiming she needed to get out like the place was some sort of torture chamber.' Anna puts a hand on Glynn's shoulder. 'What did you do?'

He is sitting on the middle step of the stairs, and she is just above him, a plate of toast at her feet.

'It doesn't make sense,' he says. His hands are pressed together, his forehead resting on his thumbs. 'She seemed happy.'

'Glynn,' she says it again and he looks up. 'What did you do?'

He realises, then, what she is asking. He puts his hands out and up. 'Nothing, Anna,' he says. 'Nothing like that, I promise.'

Anna is quiet for a moment, unsure whether to ask what she is thinking.

'Maybe you just got a bit intense?' she says. 'Only, and not to speak from personal experience, you do have a tendency to do that.'

Glynn looks up from his hands. 'No, it wasn't like that.'

'It's always like that,' Anna sighs. 'You need to stop getting so carried away. It sounds to me like the girl slept with you twice and got weirded out.'

Glynn stands up. 'I'm going to find her.'

'You'll get swallowed up by the sea before that,' Anna laughs. 'There's nothing dramatic going on here. She's probably gone home, and she'll be telling her friend about how she's not a relationship person. You'll see each other in bars and supermarkets. You'll catch eyes, look at your shoes, and you'll barely believe you had sex in the first place. That's it.'

Getting up and heading downstairs, Glynn says, 'I don't think so.'

He opens the door. The storm once again whips and bites and promises pain. The marina bells ring out over the boats. The town is all swirling grey and clouds and wind and crashing waves and Glynn realises suddenly he has no idea what time it is, what day it is. He has lost all semblance of everything but the storm and the way it rakes his body and his need for Josephine.

He sees Jake walking towards the house, a girl leaning on his arm. She looks hurt.

'Is she ok?' says Glynn.

'Just needs some rest,' says Jake.

'Who is she?'

Jake moves past Glynn into the doorway. 'You've not met?'

'I'm Sarah,' she says, panting. Glynn sees blood on her.

'What is going on out there?'

'Glynn, I don't even know where to start.' Jake guides Sarah down the hallway, towards the living room, calling over his shoulder, 'but I wouldn't go back out there, no way.'

From the staircase, Anna nods. 'It's too dangerous, Glynn. You met get hit by some roof tilling, or…'

'We are way past roof tilling,' says Jake from the living room, laying Sarah on the sofa.

'What do you mean?' says Anna. She turns back to call Glynn over.

But he is gone, pushing against the winds to slam the door shut.

CHAPTER TWELVE

The angel and the woman stare out to sea, reaching out for the horizon, as if trying to pull back the names, bodies and lives of those lost soldiers whose names are written below them. Around them is chaos, but while everyone is battered in by the winds and sent shivering by the rain, these two are still as the mountains surrounding them.

Glynn is looking for Josephine. He looks up at the two statues, briefly caught by the details. A naked beauty, curved and ample, looking almost as if she has come from the earth itself, like she has laughed late-night laughter and tasted the early morning air. A towering spirit, almost too tall to be seen, watching over everything, graceful and wise. Both here, irrefutably.

He should be looking for Josephine. Shaking his head, he carries on, his shoes squelch against the gravel path, his jeans caked in mud, water dripping from his fringe and his lips. He is exhausted and desperate to find her. Moving past the memorial, he looks up at the castle ruins, up at the turret across the wooden bridge, up at the rocky tower which once served as a look-out post. A head appears over the bridge. Glynn blinks. A flash of lightning bursts up over the hills in the east and Glynn sees the shadowy silhouette of a figure moving quickly. Then there is no one in view and yet Glynn feels eyes and perhaps something else on him, too.

'Pwy sydd yna?' says a voice that feels like the turret itself.

Glynn shakes his head. He should just keep walking and yet he feels somehow bound to answer to this sudden authority. 'Glynn.'

'Ffrind neu elyn?'

Glynn squints and can see what looks like a stick pointing at him from over the look-out. He walks closer, squints, sure he knows what it is but not wanting to believe it. Some sort of weapon, its sights trained upon him.

'Stopiwch! Atebwch fi! Ffrind neu elyn?'

Glynn realises he has never had a weapon pointed towards him before. He is grateful to be shivering from the cold already. It makes him look less frightened than he is.

'I bwy?'

'I Dywysog Cymru, Owain Glyndŵr!' The head of the speaker appears now, a man with a long beard and a green jacket. Glynn drops his hands down and relaxes.

'For fuck's sake, I don't have time to be fucking *larping*, alright? You can't just go around pointing plastic pistols at people. You're asking for trouble.'

Glynn walks on and has almost reached the doorway through the turret when he hears the bang, different to the clap of thunder, deeper and harder and like a punch in the gut and catches the scent of fire and smoke.

'Arhoswch!' shouts the voice.

'Iawn! Iawn!' shouts Glynn, putting his hands up. And looking through the doorway, he sees something that no amount of blinking can prove to be a hallucination.

A man stands with brown hair to his shoulders, a harsh forehead and a protruding nose. He is wrinkled and wears a beret. There is a red cape over his shoulders but he wears a camouflage uniform beneath. Glynn recognises him instantly – God, he's a good likeness. Standing in front of him is the man he has spent summers obsessing over; the figure whose shadow, has loomed over his nation, his home, since his disappearance that great many years ago. Looking longer, Glynn knows, in some inexplicable way, that the watchman had not lied, and these people are no re-enactors. In front of Glynn is Owain Glyndŵr. And, in front of him, a group of thirty men, all with long hair, beards, rifles and berets are kneeling.

'Cymru am byth!' cries the Prince, and his men repeat the cry back. There is a flash of lightning. The rain is hard, and the wind seems to howl with the chorus of the chant.

The Prince turns and sees Glynn standing in the rain, looks up and nods at the watchman on the turret. He draws a pistol from his trouser loop and points it at Glynn's chest.

'Shw mai, ysbïwr Saesnig.'

Glynn loses his words and feels the hurt of the accusation. He is suddenly a subject at the mercy of his monarch. He kneels. 'Dwi ddim yn ysbïwr! Dwi ddim yn sbïo!'

The Prince shakes his head and smiles. 'Amhosibl. Dwedwch y gwir.'

There is no silence, not really: there is the wind and the rain and the sea bursting over onto the roads. Glynn, wide-eyed, has forgotten all about Josephine and stands fearing execution at the hands of his hero. But a sudden chorus of shouting rises from the hill leading into town. The Prince turns from Glynn to see a group led by a man in black. The Prince lowers his pistol and holds it at his side. Glynn runs to a nearby bench and takes cover behind it.

'They... They have weapons,' says a voice Glynn recognises from somewhere..

'I don't know if this is the sort of thing we should be getting into,' says a girl with a Texan accent.

'Mae'r castell yn perthyn i ni,' says the Preacher.

The Prince smiles and twirls his pistol. 'O dan ba awdurdod?'

'Duw.'

The Prince shakes his head, and the Preacher nods his. A flash of lightning streaks the sky, just over the castle's tower. The wind pulls at the world. Then it begins. The Prince fires a bullet, the Preacher ducks and charges in a strange zig zag motion. More bullets fly, and the followers zig zag. Remarkably, the bullets all seem to miss their fleshy targets.

The Preacher leaps at the Prince and lands a punch square on his jaw. The Prince falls, gets back up, spits water from his mouth.

There are screams and bones breaking, and rain. Glynn takes it as his chance to flee. Down the hill he goes, onto the South Beach, and face-first into Robbie.

'Fucking hell, man, mind where you're going.'

Glynn has never been so happy to see someone he detests. 'You won't believe what I've just seen,' he says, gasping for breaths. 'Fighting, up at the castle, and it's…'

Robbie laughs. 'There's fighting everywhere. This town has lost the fucking plot.'

'No you don't understand. I've seen something that I'm not sure I've seen.' Glynn is blinking back up at the castle, the shooting stone of the tower standing tall and steady against the buffeting elements.

'It's that kind of night, mate,' says Robbie, pulling a packet of cigarettes from the back pocket of his jeans.

'No, this is different. Really nuts. Really impossible.' Glynn looks at Robbie as if his eyes might communicate that which his words cannot seem to grasp.

Robbie takes a cigarette from the packet. He recognises that Glynn's face is paler, his eyes scared. He's intrigued. 'How so?' he says.

'I've seen someone no one has seen in a long time,' says Glynn while Robbie attempts to spark up a light and is foiled by the whip of the stinging wind around them.

'This fucking wind,' says Robbie, kneeling and covering the

cigarette with his mouth. The two of them are still for a while, listening to the clicking sound of the zip lighter flint. Both men are so soaked that all the rain coming down and sea spray spitting up seems to slide right off them. The wind cuts, but that too has become familiar, like the sound of the sea coming in or the hourly ringing of a clock. The cigarette catches the light and smoke blows east from Robbie's hand.

'That's why I bought straights,' he says, the light having distracted him from any concern he had for Glynn. 'All the rocket fuel and stuff in them, they never go out. Anyway, I know what you mean about long-disappeared people showing up. I just saw George O'Keefe chuck a golf club through the SPAR window. Not been about since Black House two years ago. Haven't seen him raging like that ever, and he rages.'

They carry on walking. South beach opens in front of them: the rows of houses, the Rheidol pulling back into the town and providing a home for the rocking and shivering boats, the Ystwyth river running from it, approaching the hills, the hills shrouded in darkness and still like sleeping giants, the bright lights of another town across from the town sparkling like a beacon. Glynn knows then that his story is not for Robbie's ears. 'Yeah, right,' he says.

'You know what I *have* seen?' says Robbie, raising an eyebrow. 'You and lovely Jose cuddling up together and disappearing off into the night. What's going on there?'

Glynn feels a sudden pang of longing. He thinks of Josephine, the beauty of her naked back, the sweetness of her smile and the way he wants to know all of her and own none of her. These feelings drown Owain Glyndŵr, and everything else that could potentially come to mind like a flood.

'I can't find her,' he says.

The harbour light is spinning, shooting a white shafts across the ocean like a camera flashing. A patch of dark sea is briefly illuminated from a great distance, showing waves building and waiting to crash.

'You seemed stuck together like glue last I saw you,' Robbie says as smoke plumes from his mouth.

'Yeah.'

Glynn is watching the sea and its chopping waves. It seems to him as if everything around them is forcing them into stillness. If someone were to try and escape by boat, set sail for Ireland or America or anywhere, they would be wrecked before they were out of the harbour light's sight.

Robbie stops and takes a final drag of his dying cigarette. 'I shouldn't do this,' he says, before flicking the butt into the sea.

It spins over the banister, is pushed back by the wind, bounces off the sea wall and drops into the water just as a hard wave which has burst over the wooden jetty at the end of the promenade pulls itself back. The butt gets caught in the current, dips beneath, the paper falling away, the last of the tobacco floating and then drowning, the filter still somehow strong and buoyant and moving along like a single cheerio in a bowl of turbulent milk. It is washed outwards, and pops up again in the calmer depths just as the harbour light blasts its huge whiteness over the very patch of water the filter has found itself in. Briefly it is illuminated, this bizarre, small and irrelevant miracle spotted, albeit by another inanimate object, before a great wooden bow bursts into the spot of light and cuts through the filter and the water beneath it. The filter tears, splits apart, and sinks to the shallow grave at the bottom of the Irish Sea.

Over the marina to the west now, just coming by the harbour light, is a six-masted schooner cutting through the icy, riving saltwater. Glynn spots it, standing on the edge of the promenade where the sea splits into the Ystwyth and the Rheidol. Robbie is leaning on the barrier, pretending to look at the hills.

'The town is more interesting when it's like this,' he says. 'When the night is cloudy and you can't see anything. I love it. I love feeling lost in things. All this darkness is so fucking existential, man. It's so Sartre. You read Sartre? It's so fucking Sartre man.'

'What's that?' says Glynn, pointing at the moving fleet.

'Sartre? He's a philosopher. Aren't you meant to be the reader?'

'No, Robbie, that, over there. It looks like a ship.'

Robbie sniffs, shakes his head and takes another drag of his cigarette. 'Stop trying to work things out. You can't work things out, not in a storm like this. It'd be wrong. You have to embrace the unworkable-outness of it all. Do you know what I mean? Its dark and unmeaning and beautiful.'

They are coming in fast now, pushed in by the straight gush of the storm. White canvas sails billow. Men run around the decks. Glynn can hear singing in a language he doesn't know.

'Who are they?' he says.

'Who is fucking *who*?' says Robbie, looking round. And now he sees it, his eyes widen, his arms fall at his side.

'Fucking hell,' he says. 'Are we being invaded?'

Glynn looks at him and shakes his head. 'By a wooden boat?'

Robbie shrugs, not looking away. 'What else?'

*

The fishermen are loading caged fish onto a truck. The truck will freeze the gutted fish and drive them off to their various destinations. The fish will be sliced, offered up for various hungry customers in supermarkets, fishmongers and restaurants. Morgan lights a cigarette and leans on the wall. He has been up since the early hours and his body aches. The waves are hard today. For the first time in years, he was nearly sick over the bow.

It embarrasses him to know the water can still exert such control over him. As he puffs out a cloud of smoke, he thinks about going to the pub and getting drunk. The ship is all yellow light and ahead of it is gloom; a gloom where the two rivers pour into the sea, a gloom that seems to be a whole pouring absence just kept back by the electric light. And then something emerges from it. Something lightless. A bow, a huge one, on its own something that seems like it could quite easily swallow their little ship. As it sails on, Morgan sees the mast, sees men rushing around the deck.

'Fucking hell, man,' he shouts to the other. 'It's a bloody schooner.'

'What you on?' says Rhys, the young lad whose been working the waters with him for the past three years.

'There!' Morgan points. 'A schooner! What's it bloody doing here?'

And it keeps moving, a flag from the mast flapping, too high up into the dark to make out.

Rhys looks up and his mouth drops. 'Fucking hell. Must be Davy Jones. What is going on? Some gimmick or something?'

'Must be,' says Morgan. 'But what are they doing bringing out something like this at a time like now? I haven't heard nothing about it before.'

From the schooner deck they hear a voice call out to them. Morgan steps onto the edge of the dock and puts an ear out.

'Hello!' comes a voice from the dark that seems to dip up and down like the waves. 'We have come for ore!'

Wind mixes the words and spins them around. Morgan strains his ears as the voice repeats itself over and over. Eventually, Rhys steps forward.

'You want more?' he shouts, loudly as he can over the waves. 'What are you talking about?'

'Ore!'

'More?'

The ship is moving past them now, billowing and still in shadow, cutting through the water. Its crew begin to sing a song Morgan and Rhys have not heard before in a language they do not recognise.

'The kids will love that,' says Rhys. 'Whatever it is fucking is. I reckon they're dressing up as pirates or something, local history stuff.'

Morgan watches the ship and shakes his head. 'It's strange,' he says.

They agree and carry on packing up the van.

*

'I saw her,' says Bill, taking a drag of his cigarette. He rests his foot on the wall behind him. 'She was running down Trefechan Bridge. Didn't even say anything when I nodded and waved. Left me looking like a fool.'

Glynn nods. 'Is she alright?'

'Looked like she'd seen a ghost.'

'Bill, isn't that exactly what we've all been experiencing?'

Bill's lip pushes up towards his nose as he takes a disgusted drag. 'What are you fucking talking about? Not more of this philosophising mate.'

'Just look at what's going on!'

'Yeah. Exactly. All this fighting in the street and all you can do is talk, talk, talk. *Do* something.'

Glynn wonders if he could get away with hitting Bill, if he could catch him by surprise and manage to overpower him. He looks down Bridge Street and thinks about Josephine.

'I am,' he says. 'I've got to find Josephine.'

'Typical Glynn. Predictably away from the action.'

Bill throws his cigarette on the ground and heads towards the square, where a gaggle of wearied people chatter, holding sticks, traffic cones and other makeshift weapons. Glynn turns away and walks up Bridge Street, his pace quick now. As he breaks into a gallop, he notices that the tarmac on the left side of the road has been dug up to create a long trench stretching all the way down to the bridge. Moving close, he looks down and sees old, rusting pipes and muddy brown water, dotted from droplets falling from the sky. The smell is strong, centuries of waste that rise and mix, stinking of history.

He sees an old man in a top hat standing in front of the war monument, union jacks that were not there before now covering the plaques. Then he is in the air, descending, briefly convinced he is weightless, until his back hits the hard ground and his weight returns and aches. Water soaks his back. His body feels different to how it was before. Heavier first, with more muscles and strength, yet more rigid too. He finds his arms and legs will only kick straight, cannot reach up towards the trench's edge. His face is longer, and all the smells are stronger. Going to speak, he finds only the absence of words, and then a single sound, a long groaning 'neigh' that echoes up into the air. Language leaves him. He is a creature kicking in the dirt and the mud, alone and helpless. There are puddles joining beneath in the trench, making a river of sewage that will drown him. He sees his death, kicks and brays and tries to stand on all fours. Slipping, he hits the ground again, muddy water splashing up and covering his right eye. One final neigh into the night. Another kick against the wall of the trench. And then a sound from up above that makes him go quiet.

'Iesu Grist, beth wyt ti'n neud lawr fan na, ceffyl?'

With his left eye, Glynn sees a man standing on the edge of the trench. He seems to reach so far up that he could touch the moon. Muscles bulge from his white shirt. He rolls up his sleeves, revealing strong forearms, and adjusts his blue dungarees. Glynn neighs at him.

'I know, darling, I know. We'll get you out. Just stay still.'

The man leaps down from above, hooks his arms under Glynn

and lifts. Glynn feels his body's weight press back down, but sure enough he finds himself standing tall, his hooves squelching into the mud. He looks at this man incredulously. He is standing level with Glynn, stroking his face.

'Don't worry, now. You'll be safe, ceffyl. Just try to trust me.'

Glynn shakes his head and sneezes against the cold. The man pulls himself up out of the trench again. He gets on his stomach and wraps his arms around the horse's stomach. And then he pulls. Glynn feels the breath pushed from his lungs. He kicks and neighs and shakes, looking down the long line of the trench and wanting to gallop as far as he can from this and all its horrible strangeness. He rises through the air, feels the absence of hard ground, sees the moon in a gap between two clouds, noticing it is closer than it has been before. And then he is on the hard ground again, on four legs, but already shifting. He is shorter, standing on two legs, his upper limbs hanging with relative uselessness at his side. His muscles are gone, and he feels the thinness of his own body. He looks at his rescuer.

'What the hell is this?' the man says.

Glynn presses a hand to his throat and feels his voice. 'I don't know what just happened. But thank you. Who are you?'

The rescuer opens his mouth large and wide. 'They call me the Big Man, but I've got more of a name than that. I'm...'

But before the name can come booming from his lips, big man's form begins to dissolve. He looks down and sees his hands falling away into droplets of rain, then his arms. His feet and legs, too. Big man being made smaller by the second.

'What is this?' he says. 'What is going on? I feel like half a thing.'

Just before the last of him turns to water, Glynn can say, 'Thank you.' Big man nods, now just a chest and a head, and then disappears down the very trench Glynn was pulled from, following all that water and sewage towards the sea.

CHAPTER THIRTEEN

Who is moving now, and where? My eyes are struggling to see. Yes, it is Nathan again, on north beach. Seeing Constitution Hill loom, all dark cloud and bright lights on its peak, he is remembering the time when, late night at a beach bonfire, he'd become convinced it was a giant rising from the earth coming after him. He leans against the promenade railing, feels water seep through his three-quarter length coat. There is a roar, then a great burst of water coming over the wall, drenching him. Then there is another noise, almost an answer, higher and smaller, but ringing like a trumpet. A harder, narrow blast of water comes over from below and covers him. He falls backwards, swallowing gulps, eyes forced shut. Coughing water, lungs and ribs aching, Nathan pulls himself up. Going back to the railing seems foolish, but he does it, getting to his feet and steadying himself, ready to jump back when the next wave comes crashing in, feeling grit and pebbles skim his skin. He accepts it as all part of his redemption, his climb out of the underworld. Bracing himself for impact, he looks over the railing to the beach below. He sees them, just as the foam of another wave rises. Two elephants, black as the clouded night's sky, trunks pointed upwards, screeching like they are seeking vengeance from some ancient slight. The wave crashes around them, white fizzing flecks on grey skin. Nathan looks around for someone, a witness, proof that he is not just hallucinating.

Returning, he sees the elephants stomping up the old steps, towards him, towards the promenade, and he runs. Hell is strengthening itself against him.

He gets to the path which leads up Constitution Hill. He just needs to follow it till Clarach, then he's free. From there, he'll go somewhere, rest, and wait for a sign from God. For the first time in his life, he feels genuinely at His mercy. It is only now, running in the gloom, slipping every now and then on the wet path, tears in his eyes, his heart beating, that he realises he truly and deeply believes himself to be some kind of Messiah. On the other hand, fleeing, he knows, is not necessarily messianic behaviour. As he runs he builds reasoning for why he has fled. He has simply spent some time in the belly of sin, that when he gets past the peak of Constitution Hill and is past the borders of this strange place, he will become stronger, more holy, invulnerable to sin, ready to spread his message and really save the world. As he sees the bridge in the distance, he thinks it may even be possible that this town must burn for everything else to live, and this gives him a kind of comfort. He is the survivor of the lowest point, and he can rise to the peak, until eventually he is upon God's shoulder, perhaps even at one with God Himself.

There is a shape on the bridge, but Nathan cannot make out what it is. He notices its hulk, almost like a great rock that has landed on the bridge. Then he sees two. Remembering the story of Jesus and Satan in the desert, he closes his eyes and runs harder.

'Though I walk through the valley of the shadow of death,' he mumbles as his feet make a hard slaps against the wet wood, 'I will fear no…'

Nathan thumps into something that feels wrinkly and hard. It is skin, and Nathan realises this when he tastes the hair on his lips. He falls back and then he hears it, that great cry into the sky that seems to be giving some sort of response to the lightning's crack and the wind's taunts. In front of him, Nathan realises, are the two elephants, giant and black and bulking, as if from the depths of some place darker even than the hell he has nightmares about.

'Oh, God,' he says under his breath.

And of course, the elephants – well, you know. You've seen it before. They crash through the bridge, they go mad, they trample, they destroy. Carts go falling. Amidst the chaos, Nathan's body is flattened, his bones all split and cracked like wood under too much pressure, his muscles flattened down like pastry shaped for a pie top. Blood oozes from him. With his last breath, he thinks that this at least will be a death he is remembered for. And then he is gone.

*

That poor baker's boy and his lovely rich princess have been wandering this town for the last two days, always just missing each other, not quite catching the other's trail. The boy searched SPAR, seeing if she might be perusing the ready meals section, while she wandered the same street, about to turn a corner up the high street, so that when he emerged looking desperately she was beyond his eyeline. And earlier, she thought she might have glimpsed him by the clock tower, and she did, but just before a crowd of marchers burst up from Pier Street and covered her view. Each wants nothing more than to scream the other's name, and each has, in their own moments, attracted strange looks, rolled eyes, offers of help. None of it to any avail. Neither will be happy till they see the other, neither will be able to rest. And nor should they.

They have waited many years for their chance to be happy again, to hold each other for however brief a moment this strangely timed storm allows them to. They have borne witness to the events of the evening as well. The boy saw some soldiers gun down a few sailors. The princess watched someone turn into water before her eyes. They know that this is the fate that waits for them, too. A return to wateriness, to the lingering absence of thought, to the memories somewhere far off. But they think, each of them, in their different places, that this might not have been all there had been. They remember, at the moments of their death, something other than nothing. A last breath, a blankness, and then a meeting, a moulding. A moment of infinite, unfrenzied largeness. A vast comfort. But whatever part of them went there, it is not here. It has already gone. What is left, and each realises this, running their hands over their strange otherly bodies, feeling the lack of air in their lungs, the lack of blood and veins, the lack of a heart beating – what they are, is just a reminder of somebody who has gone long ago. But with the same certainty they know that they must act out the rest of their show. There is a script to follow. Finding each other becomes more than a desire. It becomes a duty. They go on looking.

The boy watches the elephant fall upon Nathan. He has climbed Constitution Hill to be in the final place where he saw his love. He runs over and tries to see if there is anything he can do to save a life. But it is too late. Remnants of the body have stretched out from beneath the elephant. The flesh is pressed, the bones cracked, the blood leaking out and leaving red puddles that slowly oxidise to brown. The creature snorts, putting its front leg to the side and pushing. It is standing. It looks up at the moon and calls up. As its call echoes over the hills, it turns, like everything, to water, nothing more than a little stream that runs down the path and wets the boy's ankles. And when he looks across, the princess is standing there, her hand on her mouth, her eyes wide.

'It's you,' she says. 'It's really you. I thought I'd never find you.'

He runs to her. She takes him in her arms. She kisses his forehead and his neck and then his mouth. It is the same as it was before, and briefly they forget everything about duty and absence and are just two lovers reunited, enjoying the feel of each against the other. And then the rain washes over them, and they feel themselves slipping away, two bodies becoming little streams that run into each other, and they drift after the elephant, down the hill. And the hillside is empty again.

*

Vic and Robbie are walking Tan-y-Bwlch. They, too, are looking for Josephine. Vic texted her when the storm got worse, called her when the fighting broke out, called Glynn after Josephine didn't answer. She assumed they were just together. When Robbie came in and told her Glynn was also looking for Josephine, she called the police, only to be told that the number had not been recognised.

The whale lies dead on the shore. Its smell has worsened. They cover their noses and mouths, but still when the gust catches the stench right they each have to gag and spit. It is like sucking back the left-overs of your own sick.

'This night, man,' said Robbie with a smirk, drinking orange juice from the carton while Vic looked out the window. 'I swear to God, I love this night.'

Vic told him to shut up. Then she said she had to look for Josephine. He said he'd come with her. Briefly, she was touched. She thanked him.

He smirked. 'I just got to get back out there.'

Now, they are searching for her. Vic is looking up and down the beach, as if Josephine might suddenly appear on a spot of stone. Robbie is looking at the sea.

'That is fucking nuts.'

'What?' says Vic, and then she looks.

They are seeing something impossible. The whale, its skin unpierced and unrotted, waves crashing against its bulk, is beginning to breath again, now so hard you can hear its huffing and wheezing, see its body bulking and shrinking.

Josephine is somewhere, but Vic can't help but stop. She can't even bring herself to speak. Her breathing seems to follow the whale's, shaky, shallow and uncertain.

Robbie takes a step closer. 'This must be some weird death thing,' he says. 'Maybe it's about to explode.'

'I don't think that's how it works,' says Vic, refuting Robbie being almost a habit. 'Actually, you might be right.'

Robbie walks closer towards the whale, holding out his hands. He stops for a moment to look at her. 'Have you ever seen that video of the whale blowing up in America back in the day? It covered everybody in its own innards. Fucking mint.'

Despite herself, Vic feels concern for him. 'If that's what's about to happen, we should both step back. We should call someone.'

'Who would we call?' Robbie shouts back. Vic doesn't know how he can handle the smell, when he's so close. 'The police don't even exist, anymore.'

'What are you doing?'

It is getting harder to be heard against the wind. Both are shouting. Robbie keeps walking. He wants to touch it. He want to feel what its like to feel something before it goes. He gets to its mouth. Long rows of sharp, tiny teeth. An open eye that looks right at him. Scars on its skin.

He kicks it and it stops breathing. The wind drops. The rain ceases. The storm seems suddenly to be over.

Robbie shakes his head. 'It always goes this way,' he says. 'This place has made my life so fucking boring.'

The waves soften, so that the last dribbles of foam slush softly against the whale's fins. They flap against its body. The whale takes another deep pull of air and exhales hard, so hard the gust pulls Robbie to the ground. Rain comes down. Winds pick up. Lightning streaks across the sky. Waves rush in. Robbie tries to get up, but is knocked over by the current.

Vic inhales the smell, salt and rot and the head of a newly born baby all in one. She calls, telling him to crawl back. Robbie turns to her, his mouth making a small o shape.

'Help,' he whispers, so softly that even despite the silence Vic barely hears him.

The whale takes another great breath, and as the air is pulled in Vic feels her hair rush towards the creature. Through the flying strands of hair she sees Robbie, dragged along the beach, his hands outstretched and clasping desperately. Then he has disappeared down the leviathan. His scream softly emanates from its stomach. Then it turns to a whimpering sob. Vic gags, and coughs. She calls Robbie's name and hears nothing in response. She walks around the whale, stares at its belly, how it seems to cover the horizon. She calls Robbie's name again. There is a pause, then the rain and the wind return. She thinks about how she can help. The whale breathes again. She steps back. The whale takes another breath, then ceases, its fins falling back to its side. Over the sounds, she is sure she can still hear him weeping. Like so many on this day, she turns from the trouble, and runs.

*

Scuffling clashes of steel and stick abound in the castle, but just beyond it the angel and her friend spot the homecoming they have been waiting for out in the storm-seared sea. They are coming on a wave, a wave rising and whitening, spitting salt and stone out at the prom. The wave crashes against the turn of the promenade, spraying the angel and her close companion. Every droplet contains the shard of a soul, and as each shard slides down the stone, it finds shape again. First there is the Lord Ystwyth, standing in front of the names of the far too many dead.

'And here they are,' he says, his voice grand and echoing over the turrets, along the chaos-ridden streets. 'The dead. Home again.'

And so, they come. Many men in green uniforms with deep pockets, rifles slung over their shoulders, some with cigarettes in the corners of their mouths, sending smoke up into the air.

'And here in Aberystwyth, the dead must be heard,' the Lord Ystwyth proclaims, raising his hands to the sky. 'They are always echoing from beneath. And this town has let itself tread upon their rotting flesh, their sorrowful bones, delicate and breakable as their bodies are. But no more. Their bodies are firm now. And now it is the dead who are making the present.'

The soldiers turn and nod their heads. They point their guns towards the Lord. He bows his head and removes his bowler hat. The gunfire echoes. The Lord Ystwyth lies briefly dead and bleeding, and then comes the rain and he is washed away, down gutters and back towards the sea, his body dissolving into water. Without a word, the soldiers march in single file over the bridge and towards the castle's one remaining ruined turret. A single shot and the sentry stationed upon the archway is dead; the arrow he was pulling back flies up into the night and lands sadly on the wet grass and sinks into the mud. They march through the turret doorway and encircle the great Glyndŵr, the Preacher and their many men, enshrouded as they are in shadow and rain. They take their aim and fire as one. The dead drop and join the sludging mud. Those left turn and charge, the Prince's company and the Preacher's followers briefly allied. The Preacher shouts as he sees the fire burst from the barrel of a gun. He ducks and drags a man down with him, crawls through a gap in the circle, takes shelter behind a piece of wall that hides the remains of a stairwell. He sees Owain Glyndŵr chop a soldier with a swing of his sword. He remembers: he is not where he should be.

'This is all some distraction,' he mumbles. 'And I've been distracted.'

Turning away from the circle, he moves slowly and with certainty down into the town, and moves towards Trefechan Bridge, Tan-y-Bwlch, the harbour light and Pen Dinas, which watches over everything with an oddly straight smirk.

CHAPTER FOURTEEN

We have found her. In a pub by the river, on the outskirts of town, where the madness has not yet reached, Josephine sips a pint of warm ale, staring at the sawdust sprinkled over the floor. There are others, sipping and chatting, who have somehow missed the madness of the day. Muscles ache and spasm. There seems to be no escaping this town. The hills are hemming her in, unclimbable in the rain, all wet mud. Trying to climb Allt Wen, she slipped and fell, was crying in the rain, the wind whipping at her hair, the peak seemingly further and further away with every step, the rocks looming beneath her. Reaching the peak, standing over the town made tiny, she felt something stopping her going any further, felt herself pulled back down the hill, almost before she could do anything to stop it. And then she was slipping again, and rolling, mud getting beneath her nails and in her mouth and all over her clothes. She can still taste it, beneath the bitter of her pint.

Somewhere, Mother is out there looking for her. Josephine wonders why she cannot stay dead, why she must rise, and why like this, all horror and no love. Then again, she thinks her mum never had much love to give.

The old door moans open. Out from the black comes through a group of men, all in black, all bearded. Josephine takes another look and realises they are all wearing various pirate paraphernalia, some with eye patches, tricorns, headscarves. They look like something from the films she used to watch, the ones everyone used to watch, with the well-choreographed sword fights and the wide shots of ships on the sea. But, she thinks to herself, they are quite obviously just a party of men in dress up, probably as part of a stag party or something silly like that. One orders a round of rums, and the rest let out a large cheer. Josephine watches them closely. Sees the scabbards and holsters at their hips.

'Those are good toys you've got there,' says the boy behind the bar, a preppy looking student with glasses and pimples. 'Where'd you get them? Charlie's?'

'These aren't toys, mate,' says the man at the centre, standing at the bar. His voice seems to twist, seems to become more gurgled and mixed, harsher as he speaks. 'These be weapons!'

A cheer rises and the boy laughs with them.

'Going as pirates, are you?'

'We are now!' says the man. 'I was a merchant captain, but I've been turned by the ways of things.'

The boy lets out an awkward gasp of a laugh. 'You're committed to the part.'

There is a murmur of agreement. Josephine watches on as the glasses are filled with rum. The boy tallies up the drinks, brings over the card machine, smiles again.

'That's £32.60,' he says.

The crew let out a cackle. Then the man at the front, the self-defined turncoat captain, pulls his gun from his holster and points it at the boy.

'We're not paying tonight, lad,' he says.

'Very funny,' laughs the boy.

'I told you we're not,' the captain says firmly, and now the boy stops laughing

Josephine feels in her gut a terror that lets her know that this group of strange pirates are connected in some way with Mother. People in the pub begin to look over. Josephine tries to shout but finds her mouth won't open. Dreaded seconds pass as the boy's eyes widen, the trigger is pulled, and a bullet is unleashed. The body drops beneath an explosion of blood that splatters over the bar and onto the pirates. They all let out a great cheer.

'Drinks on the house!' cries the captain.

There is a rush and Josephine finds herself in a bulge of people racing for the door, shoving and panicking. And she can hear, repeatedly, like some hastily and clumsily played refrain, the word 'pirates,' with panic, disbelief and horror. Shots ring out and she feels something limp and heavy fall against her. She keeps moving, squeezes through the doorway alongside a rotund woman, who falls away to the side and lands on one of the green benches. The rain is whipping into little whirlwinds and droplets slap onto Josephine's skin. From the pub she hears cackles and cheers. She runs.

*

Terrace Road is scattered with littered crisp packets, polystyrene takeaway boxes, tins of lager, crucifixes and daggers. The wind is like a spirit screeching, picking up what it can carry and spinning it into a tornado of rubbish. The rain spins with it too, and from this Josephine emerges, drenched, her leather jacket insufficient for the cruel weather, her heart beating fast. Josephine is scared and unsure if this is the sort of thing that happens in a storm, or whether it is something that could end up killing her. She hates the idea of her death being the front-page of a local paper, or one of the later stories on the ten o'clock news.

Amongst the spinning, Josephine squints and sees the ocean crashing against the promenade, salty spray bursting over the barriers, stones flying out like shrapnel from bombs. Faintly she hears car alarms squealing, not to deter burglars but as a cry for help, to save the cars from destruction. Seagulls screech too, except now the squeal seems like a song, mourning those lost to the ocean.

A crisp packet slaps Josephine's face. It seems to stick and makes a squelching sound as it comes loose. She looks for a bin, but they are all upturned, so it re-joins the wind and takes flight. It seems to cackle at her. Looking ahead again, Josephine sees another great splash of sea. When it settles, she sees a figure in shadow. She is about to turn and run towards home, lock the door and get somewhere safe and warm, but the figure keeps her still, the only still thing on the whole street. Even the lampposts are shaking, even the foundations of the strongest buildings move lightly, but Josephine and the earth are deadly still as this figure makes its way toward her. It walks straight through the whirl of litter, as if everything of this town has been demanded to let it pass unimpeded. It is wearing a dark robe with a hood covering the face in shadow, again unmoved by the harsh winds, but Josephine knows who it is from the hand with pale skin and the other of cold white bone. The hood falls and there, once again half formed, bald and rotting, is Mother.

'You're just a disgusting joke,' says Josephine.

'Not just me, and not just on you,' says Mother, and her voice is rasping and high like the wind's. 'This is far bigger than you, darling. You just happen to be at the centre of it.'

'You're not my mum.'

Mother looks up at the sky and laughs. It is like the sound a shell makes when pressed to an ear. 'What makes you think that, clever one?'

'You're appearing like how you did in my dream. That's not who you really were. Even in your last days, where you hurt us and hid from us and made sure you'd haunt me like you do, you were never that. We could dig you up and you'd look nothing like that.'

Mother nods, her teeth chattering from the force, her hair

shaking back, flecks of skin falling away with the wind, water dripping down white bone. 'Well done. I'm just an imitation dragged from your head. Still, you might as well make the most of me. Have you anything you'd like to say?'

'I wish you'd stop waking me up all the time. You're stopping me talking to Dad. He doesn't understand it.'

'You're talking to the imitation, not your mother.'

'I can't talk to my mum. She's dead. I should talk to my dad, but you keep fucking stopping me.'

Mother moves closer. 'All you have to do is stop remembering.' She places a hand, scabby and smelly, on Josephine's cheek.

   And Josephine like a flower finally opening
    And I   like a secret finally unveiling
    And we   like clicks in a lock unclicking

> You were right to hate me, Josie. You were right when you felt I did you wrong. I was not a good mother to you. I am sorry. So, so sorry. But I have moved as much of heaven and earth as I can, so that you might forgive me. Do you forgive me? Look at all I have unleashed for you. I have killed for you. I have made you feel the very things you thought I'd stopped you from ever feeling again. You know what I mean, don't you? That soft little thing in your heart that could move so much. It's love, Josephine. You are in love. And I made it with my love for you, my love for you, which I pushed down because I saw horror when I had created beauty. Can you forgive me, Josie? Can you forgive me, and in forgiving me, forgive the world? That is all I ask of you. Kiss my cheek, and in kissing, grant me forgiveness.

  And I   briefly whole, now unwhole again
    And you   Realising the monster you let in
     And her   No closer than before

STORM

Josephine looks at Mother. Mother is smiling, limply, a little anxiously.

'That's what you want?' says Josephine, slowly. 'For me to kiss your fucking cheek?'

'Bone or flesh,' says Mother, her voice now raspy and dry. Josephine realises she is trying to make a joke. 'And forgiveness, that's all.'

Josephine looks into her eyes, green, like in life. And she really sees her. Her mother, back from the dead. 'I can't do that, Mum,' she says. 'Not after everything.'

Her mother nods slowly. 'I understand,' she says.

The shaking of her bones echoes, quieter as she moves further away. She turns down a side road and walks over to the green Caribbean restaurant on the corner. She is let in and shown to a table for one by the window. She takes a menu from the waiter, reads it for a while. She turns back around to Josephine and waves.

Josephine walks away, from the sea, retreating to the high street. She looks at how the road slopes upwards. There is a broken-down car five hundred yards from her and on it, she can see two men, one wearing a hoodie with a crucifix on the back and the other a pirate hat, wrestling with each other. She looks behind her and knows that somewhere that way is the place she lives. She can picture her door by the barber shop, the feel of her green walls and the warmth of her single bed, but she cannot remember the walk to get there. Rain and fog are everywhere, and it is as if the streets themselves are being swallowed up. She stays very still and feels very desperate. She looks up and thinks of Tan-y-Bwlch. She keeps walking, just to do something, and she thinks of Glynn and wonders if he is thinking of her.

I cannot let it end like this. I take her to the whale.

*

There is the wailing wind, the flat beach, the great hills, the spitting stones, and the dead whale. The reek of it, now somehow softer than before. Josephine cranes her neck looking up at its fin, laying limply at its side. It breathes. She watches the body lift and fall. She hears the rasping, strange sounds of a body in the wrong place. It should be back home in the water. How can she get it back home?

Without thinking, she pushes at the beast's still body. Her hands slip, slick as they are with water, slick against the slippery surface of the whale's skin. Its body rises over her like a wave suspended in motion, unwhitened, a great yawning grey waiting to crash down. On the other side, waves come in, slap against the still flesh, shake its bones. The wind, too, blows against Josephine's efforts, pushing eastward as she pushes west. She starts mumbling to herself, then to something else, calling out for strength to whatever might be listening. A wave strikes the whale, and she feels the two of them move back a little. She takes a glance at the whale's body, fantasises for a moment about it tipping and crushing her, flattening herself, leaving the remnants to be gathered up by the sea. She realises that is something she does not want. She pushes again and imagines her hands sinking through the skin, her whole body entering the whale, what it would be like to be beneath the skin of something so great. Briefly, she feels something touch her hand which she is certain is a human finger. She jumps back and breathes out. The whale is still, the waves still come in, but something is different. The beast is ever so slightly closer to the water. It might be just her imagination, she knows that, but imagination has played little part in the night so far. She goes back and pushes at the whale again.

Again, she is pushing, and again she is pushing for a long time, but this time she feels the shift when it comes, the loosening of the whale from its patch of the beach. She notices the pebbles stuck to the newly released piece of flesh. She pushes again, and this time she feels again the finger, and realises there is a hand pressing hers from inside the whale. It is pushing at the whale's skin, almost as if to tear apart the blubber, rip itself out of the fate it is trapped in. Josephine wonders if she should help it. But something about the whale demands to be returned. She takes a breath and keeps pushing. Once more the whale rolls ever so slowly. And then it breathes. Its mouth now half submerged in the sea, it sucks up water, shoots it from the blowhole. Josephine watches the water shoot up towards the sky like a firework, or a gunshot against the rain. She goes back to pushing, getting the scent more now, still reeking yet saltier, fresher than before, and the hand is banging on the whale's stomach now, begging to stay on land. Josephine almost thinks she can hear the terrified scream of a voice vaguely familiar but not from anywhere she can place for now. She keeps pushing and suddenly she is knee deep in the water, foam and waves splashing up at her, shielded from the worst of the storm by the great carcass in front.

She continues to push, seawater above her knees, and the tail of the whale begins to flap gently, the fins begin to move, and then she is waist-deep in the sea. She gives one final push, slips, falls, is taken by the current. Under the water, all is green and filled with weeds. She is pulled forward then up, she sees the whale behind her, beginning to breathe, move and live again. She thinks this might be how she dies. A wave hits her as the whale shifts its face to the right. She goes under, shuts her eyes. In the blackness something hard hits. Strong and thick. The delicate, pleading hand again. She is stuck beneath the whale. Then another rush of current comes, and she feels her whole body shot forward.

When she comes to, she is blinking and gasping and shivering on the shore, waves lapping at her feet, the rain temperate on her skin. She coughs up water, lots of it. Then she is sick. She feels so sick she is certain there is almost nothing of her left. She has the wherewithal to wonder how this is something she could have ever wanted as she vomits until she can only retch. After some time, she manages to gasp at air. She feels the speed of her beating heart. The taste of salt on her lips, which feels almost sweet. Looking up, she sees the sky in all its darkened grey gloom. She looks east. The sun is still far away. Picking her coat up from the shore and wrapping it round her, Josephine shivers. She feels all the hurts inside of her raise up in a cacophony of pain. Then she looks out towards the sea to the whale carcass. It is no longer where it once was. She sees the water, and then the creature's bullet shaped head cutting through it, the tail splashing in the water. It cuts through, and as it does, it descends, till less and less is visible, and it has fled into the darkness and the waves, out of view. Josephine takes a breath. She looks around. Not even a dog walker to say any of it happened. She sees the harbour light flash up patches of dark water in the distance, hopes it may briefly illuminate the whale and its shining skin. But it does not. The creature is gone from them. Josephine walks along Tan-y-Bwlch slowly, limping. She walks past the harbour light and over the bridge. And then she remembers.

No. I'm going too far.

She should tell it.

*

'At her core she was a bitch who bore out all the bad pain and brought it, poured it, into me so that my own body was a shivering wake left in the wreck of her. She was a cruel, cold creature. I keep her far away as much as I can. But she could always make herself bigger than me; her will was stronger than mine. Her arms were stronger too. I was meant to be sad when we found out she was going to die and in a sense I was, but I was only sad for the certainty that she would die a monster, that my mum would always be someone that failed to love me. I didn't mourn her for herself. I never wept, and for that Dad has yet to forgive me, though he says he understands, his eyes drifting to the corners of rooms when he does. At the least, he chose to love her, was always head-over-heels, could never think of her as the all-bad thing she really was. He would say, even before the illness, that she was going through a lot, that we had to be delicate with her, that I had to think about the repercussions of my actions.

'The day after she died, I came downstairs and enjoyed the absolute quiet of the house. It was the first time I'd heard anything like it. There was not even the echo of one of her screeches. I ate cornflakes and watched dust motes drift down from a ray of sunlight that escaped through the closed curtain. On the mantelpiece over the electric fireplace was a picture of her and dad smiling. I was in the middle, with ice cream on my face. I turned it downwards and it felt like burying her. I put it back up again, worried about what Dad would say. I heard shifting from upstairs and not long after he was there, eyes dried out and baggy. During the night I'd heard him groan with grief and left him to it. His commitment to her was cowardly. She hurt him as much as she hurt me. And her hurting of me should've been enough. He could never bring himself to act. Could, at best, occasionally threaten divorce. Nothing ever happened. We stayed in a stasis, myself and my dad orbiting my mad mum, waiting for whatever would come next.

"How are you doing, Josie?" he said, and his voice was croaky and shallow, his face puffy. "Did you manage to get some sleep?"

"Yes," I said. "Did you?" I added, like a taunt.

My dad was too well-meaning for it to strike him. He simply nodded slowly. "All things considered."

'I felt guilty, then. I do not hate him. He is good. I once watched him dive into the River Wandle to save the toy of a stranger's child. He came up all thick with grime and weeds, spluttering and spitting, holding a Spider Man in his right hand. His phone had been in his right pocket, and that died there and then. It didn't even occur to him to compare the value of the two items. He was simply so ready to do the right thing. Mum couldn't help but be cruel to a man like that.

"Maybe you should take it easy today," I said.

'Dad nodded. "I'd like to. But there's things to do. The body…" His voice choked and I hated him briefly again. "Well, there's a lot of logistics to these things."

'I got up and held him for a while. It felt the thing to do. He pressed his face into my shoulder and then looked at me.

"We must do her proud now, I suppose," he said. "Stick together, the two of us. She'd love that."

'I looked at him and we felt the big and great chasm opening wider between us. His eyes flashed with something like recognition. He stepped back and shuffled away to some corner of the room.

'That was when I decided to get as far from this place as my grades could allow me. By then my exams were done, my middling results waiting to be received in a few weeks. I'd decided before that I wanted to reach somewhere far away but I thought Mum's death meant I didn't have anything to escape anymore. But when Dad gave me that strange look I realised she was still everywhere. Aberystwyth wasn't somewhere I'd even heard of, then, but when I saw it had a place for me, and I saw it put hundreds of miles between me and this place, that was enough. And I liked the emptiness, how it sat like a little outpost on the edge of the world, how it seemed like a place I could do what I wanted with.

'Before that, though, we had the funeral. It didn't surprise me that it was full. Mum knew a lot of people. She loved coffee mornings and dinner parties, liked to prove that she could do things in the way that things were expected to be done, could live life in that way one was expected to. It did surprise me how genuinely moved people seemed to be by her death. Mum was so performative but the idea people might fall for it had never occurred to me. Yet it worked. Everywhere I looked there were tears and I could not escape the sound of sniffles. Each one made me dig my fingernails into my skin.

'I get the train on my own when I go to Aberystwyth. Euston is a tin with too much squished in, all shops and people and pigeons standing around and waiting for something, whether that be customers, platform announcements, or scraps of bread. When I go there, I get a beef and bacon patty from the Burger King. I sit on the floor. I unwrap the pink paper and squish on the soft bread. I devour the thing. I like the way my teeth crush it. I like how the grease lingers on my lips and in my gums. The chips are crisp. Pigeons gather round me and peck at crumbs. I see their feathers shine rainbow coloured, made bright and dancing by the electric lights hanging from the low ceiling. That is usually when I move away.

'Moving north out of London, there are the long stretches of flat fields, the shires. I never see any farm animals. I see the castle ruin in Berkhamsted and it reminds me of the place I'm going. I stare out of the window and bore myself.

'When I remember the funeral, I like to enhance its absurdities. I imagine conga lines of mourners weeping and dancing, hear a hymnal version of Who Wants to Live Forever sung from the pews. But I can never see my Dad in these fixations. He was far too serious and still. He stood and talked of how they'd met and how it had sent his heart fluttering. I had to listen and not cry while others wept. I had to look up at the stained-glass windows and watch the Lord shine through and hear the Father's words and feel all its emptiness echo in my body.

'In Birmingham, I see teenagers walking around arm in arm, talking about things like school and friends. I am glad I am not one of them anymore, but I do feel a strange longing for something like that. The train to Aberystwyth is always early so I sit and wait for it to move. The land is dead with cityscape for a long time, all grey buildings that make me think of the inside of cars and hot, oiled air. With Shrewsbury begins the vast space, and then I still. The memories stop. I am distracted by encroaching mountains. There are many sheep that watch us pass. It is important to keep moving. Once a sheep got onto the tracks and the train struck and killed it. I did not know until afterwards that this was why we stopped. I keep my music loud in my ears. I wait. The marshes do something strange to me. I like the promise they offer of things sinking deep. There is the hill with the large tower pointing up in the distance. Once I step out from the station, see the Cambrian pub staring back at me with its ancient, decrepit second floor, with its smokers mumbling to each other as the painful pop music blares out, I feel far and free again.

'When they put her body in the ground, I knew she was still around somewhere. It's just on the train that she re-emerges. When I go home, too, but I don't want to think about that now.'

*

'Glynn might not believe this, but I did the walk to Borth once. It's just, when I get put on the spot like that, I freeze. My first seminar, someone asked me what my favourite book was, then my favourite film, my favourite song. I couldn't find an answer, but not because they weren't there. Because I was too scared.

'Everybody goes on about Borth, here. Nobody ever seems to leave the town except to go to fucking Borth. Everybody kept saying it was so lovely with the hills and the flowers and the rocks and the trees. It took me a while to do it – I don't like walking as a rule. I mean, everybody must walk: to the shops, to classes, to work. I guess if you have a car it's different, but I think even then you must be a real wanker to drive to the SPAR on Great Darkgate Street if you live on Bridge Street. I walk plenty. I just don't generally choose to walk.

'The hills on the way to Borth are very steep. I kept stopping to catch my breath, and I'd use these moments as chances to look at the views, which were admittedly quite pretty. The skies were cast over with a fluffy light grey but it was still warm. My jacket was tied around my waist. I followed the coastal path along from Constitution Hill, saw a lone sharp rock pointing up at me, watched the waves burst up over it, cover it briefly in green water and white foam. That was when the quiet first struck me. I'd never thought of Aberystwyth as noisy, but I realised then that there was always an engine humming, music blaring, people talking. Here there was only the waves and the wind. There wasn't even a bird to listen to. Not even the squawk of a seagull.

'Along that path there's a collection of trees, all leafless when I saw them. Many were cut down, the rest bent east by the winds, twigs sticking out from hard branches like so many hands reaching for something above the rising ground. Along the trunks were curving lines suggesting all the years that had passed. The branches themselves grew in twisting multitudes from the trunks, tangling with each other. I know it sounds strange, but I felt so certain that I was watching long, eternal torture. I could stand it for a few minutes but when I moved, I moved quickly. It felt like something that needed escaping.

'Not long after I reached a caravan site. The smells of barbeques, slush puppies and lagers reminded me of our own regular holiday spot. That was Eastbourne, though, the opposite side of the country. Except they're different countries, when you think about it. Opposite places, too. But no matter when the sun sets, the caravan sites are the same. The dodgems and the bar with its kids' club section. Another memory. A nice memory, as it goes. I won a free-style dance competition. Dad took a picture of Mum kissing me on the cheek. I was wearing a yellow hat with the word 'champion' emblazoned in red.

'After another hill there was a beach with a big brick building and nothing else on it. They say you can spot seals around there sometimes, but I didn't. It was all sand and waves. The silence was beginning to hurt me. Things kept resurfacing, kept coming up, horrid waves of memory, dragging in bits I thought I'd thrown far out. I thought my headphones might block out the sound but I'd left them at the house. I kept walking and tried to think of other things. As I climbed the hill, a rain began to fall, quite gently.

'By the time I got to the last hill, the mud beneath my feet began to move. I kept slipping, hitting the ground, caking my clothes in dirt. The rain was biblical now. It occurred to me that people sometimes died in this sort of weather, though I was sure I wouldn't. At the peak of the hill, I saw something. A little line pointing upwards. A figure. My mum, her skin so frail the bones pointed out of it, the contours of her skull pressing through the thin veil wrapped around it, waving to me. It was enough to make me think of turning back. But I knew I couldn't. It wasn't real, I knew that, but the rain was and Borth was, and Aberystwyth was far further away. I climbed the hill as she stood watching me.'

*

'The day she was given the diagnosis, I found her on the floor in the living room, her face pressed down into the carpet, as if waiting for something from below to come and consume her. She'd gone to the doctors with a complaint about severe headaches and dehydration. After the scans, they told her she had an aggressive brain tumour, that she only had a month to live. I couldn't help wondering, after everything kicked off, how long she'd laid in wait there. Because it wasn't until I called for her, until I said 'Mum, is everything ok?' that she started screaming. This high pitched, shrieking thing that rose up to a fever pitch from her throat and then fell to a low gurgle from the bottom of her mouth. I got on my knees and tried to pull her up. For a moment I cradled her head in my arms, and she stopped. I felt wet tears press from her skin onto mine, then a shift and then something very sharp piercing my skin. I yelped, a pathetic little patter of sound, and she took up her downpour of wailing again, falling back to the ground, stamping her hands and feet. There was blood running from my wrist. I kept asking her what was wrong. I tried to pull her up again and she scratched my face with sharp nails. She rose to her knees, reigned above as I cradled my face, pushed me to the ground. She resumed her position, carried on her performance. I crawled to the corner of the room and watched. Dad came home after about ten minutes, asked what was going on. That was when she finally said it.

"I'm going to die!" she shouted, looking up at the ceiling, perhaps mistaking it for the sky and all the holy things the sky contained. "I'm going to die and there's nothing to be done! Dead in a month! *Dead* in a month! Dead in a *month*!"

'Dad looked at me with a strange hurt. I really think in some way he was asking himself why I'd let this happen. "Go to your room, darling," he said.

'Later, he called me back down. Mum apologised and explained what happened. She said I had to expect and understand that sometimes she wouldn't have a filter because of the sickness. I didn't know that she had been supressing so much hatred. They both told me we had to get through this as a family.'

*

'I reached the top of the hill, my body fizzing like a shaken-up bottle of coke. Borth stretched out in front of me. The rain passed on and the clouds above were beginning to break, revealing the blue sky behind them. I felt a soft warmth from the sun. I took a breath and looked to my left, hoping Mother would not be there. And she wasn't. In her place was a stone cross with a list of names on it. A war memorial. A reminder of the dead.

'I had a drink at a pub before I caught the train back. I kept to myself, flicking through my phone while an old man chatted to the landlady. As I got up to leave, he asked me if I'd biked over, gesturing to all the mud that covered me.

"I got caught in the rain," I said.

'He nodded. "Well, be careful getting back, love. The weather will turn bad again soon enough. And there's nothing good to come from bad weather."'

*

'Hello, Josephine,' says the Preacher. 'What a miracle you've just performed.'

He is between her and the path back to town, his black hair glistening in the rain, a dark overcoat over his black shirt and white dog collar. His hands open in gesture of an embrace. Josephine recognises him as the man from the promenade. 'I don't know how I did that,' she says. 'Do you?'

He points up to the sky. 'He's always got something planned for us. Particularly those who need guidance,' he says. 'Why won't you kiss your mother, Josephine?'

She tenses. She felt it, before. Like he knew things about her she didn't want people to know. 'What the fuck do you know about my life?'

He laughs. 'I have been watching you for a very long time, Josephine. And I am your mother, in a sense. Our destinies are bound together. Neither is getting away from the other, not until what has been deemed necessary is done.'

Josephine takes a step back. There is a path to her right which leads up, up as far as you can go, towards Pen Dinas and its big copper tube.

'What's necessary?' she says.

The Preacher shrugs. 'Forgiveness.' He takes a step forward and puts out a hand. 'I can help you give it.'

Josephine darts to her right and runs. Her lungs burn and her body aches. Her run is slow and pathetic, her left leg lagging behind the rest of her so that it becomes a kind of hop. She looks behind her to see the Preacher watching her go, then walking very slowly behind her. He is playing with her. Letting her run on to catch her later. But she cannot think of anything else to do.

*

The soldiers have holed themselves up in the SPAR. They are firing on any that come near who do not wear their colours. Four at a time guard the sliding automatic doors, taking cover and aim behind upturned vegetable boxes. In the street in front of them are many dead who have tried to take their position, wanting, as people do, supplies such as orange juice, Spam and chocolate filled doughnuts. Behind the four, the rest of the soldiers stand around, smoking cigarettes, drinking cold bottles of beer from the fridge, watching stoically their prisoners, the SPAR's workers and customers, one of whom is dear Jake, having left the house to get some supplies. Shakily, he approaches the men.

'Can't you just let us go?' he says. 'It's not like any of us can do anything.'

But the men say nothing, made voiceless by gun wounds, by the distance of their deaths, by the writing of their names upon the memorial, that keep them dead as they can be.

The uniforms are woolly and green. The men have zippo lighters and hold old rifles. Jake has seen enough war documentaries to recognise their dress. He thinks of the Preacher, the odd people joining the march, the chaos of the town. It's all real, he realises with a shock. The dead have returned.

Jake looks to the corner where the three workers stand, wide eyed, shaking, their hands up always. He slowly lowers his.

'I'm sorry about everything that happened to you,' he says. 'I'm sorry you all had to die so young, and for a war that seems like it wasn't nearly as necessary as everybody seems to think these days and in those days. It's terrible. And you must be angry, and this must be a good chance to exorcise it, what with all your guns and fury. But we're all just scared, and none of us did to you what those other men did to you when they sent you away and then over the top and then didn't treat you properly and let you go to your deaths. We're none of us that powerful and we're none of us that bad.'

One of the soldiers watches Jake with a raised eyebrow, his face otherwise cold and still. Jake looks at him. He is holding a Red Stripe beer and a pistol, a Camel cigarette in his mouth, a Snickers bar tucked in the front pocket of his shirt.

The soldier with the raised eyebrows takes a deep breath of his cigarette and throws the stub onto the shop floor, stamping on it with his boot. The smoke drifts up to the ceiling and keeps going. The butt flattens and makes Jake think of slugs murdered by unseeing walkers. The soldier takes the Snickers bar from his pocket and pulls at the plastic wrapping. He scowls as the material refuses to tear, bites his bottom lip.

'Hang on,' says Jake. 'There's a trick to it.'

He takes the wrapper from the soldier, tucks his thumb between two pieces of wrapping so the white beneath shows, and pulls. No sooner has the nutty chocolate bar emerged from its covering than a bright flash of light bursts up from across the shop, then a bang, and then Jake feels something hard and strong hit his shoulder. He is on the floor, and he can feel blood trickling. The soldier runs to his side, presses the Snickers bar wrapping to his wound. The room is filled with smoke and stinks of tobacco and gunpowder. A high-pitched ring sounds out and Jake thinks this may be the audible quality of the experience of death. Water falls from the ceiling. Dully, just before he slips out of consciousness, he thinks of fire alarm protocols. The last thing he sees before total blackness, is that soldier kneeling over him, pressing the Snickers wrapping to his wound, looking up at the ceiling, frowning, before becoming a gush of falling water.

*

The dark sheet of cloud begins to crack open. Blue light swings in from up above. The scene below lightens. Those in scruffles see each other's faces, the eyes staring back frightened and enraged, the tremoring of lips, the softness shielded by beards and baseball caps. The rain softens and straightens, so that droplets run down necks and backs. People stop their striking for a moment, look around them, at the town in all its ruin.

That ancient hero, never beaten, never killed, Owain Glyndŵr, stands atop the smashed-in roof of a Fiat 500, shards of glass at his feet, the head of a man in his left hand, a gleaming blade in his right, a semi-automatic rifle on his back. He looks up and knows as certainly as he did those many years ago, when he fought his last battle, that the time to cease is coming and is certain. He drops the head, feels soft regret for taking another life, repulsion for so quickly taking up arms against his own people. To his right one of his men is taking aim with a bolt rifle. Wales' furious freedom fighter calls his soldier's name, points out to him, then lowers his hand. The man drops his weapon. The rain is still coming down. That great giant in all but size runs a hand through his flowing blond hair, strokes his beard. He sees his right-hand becoming water, feels skin melting as softly as well-cooked flesh from a bone. And that is all he is, something waiting to be scraped away. His weapons dissolve, and then he is dissolving, completely now, one with the water, rushing away. He feels himself become a droplet, feels his men near him, droplets themselves, lost in vast rainfall.

*

The pirates load themselves back onto their old rickety ship, looking up as their skull and cross bone flag turns to the red, white and blue of the Dutch flag. Their ship sways back and forth in the wind and rain as they unmoor; a few fall overboard into the shallow marina, manage to grab onto ropes or swim from the water back to safety. Others get caught in the tide and are washed away down the Rheidol. They go on regardless, working in silence, their shapes occasionally lit by the ever-spinning harbour light. As they get out into the open, onto the sea, the wind pushing them back and back, a great wave flies up and covers the ship in white foam. For a moment there is nothing but the wave. Then there is nothing. Just the darkness of the still night, the breaking clouds, three stars managing to shine from far out through the gloom, and many more drops than can be counted that have re-joined the ocean.

*

When Josephine reaches the summit, holding her knees and panting, she sees him standing by the monument, cutting black against the grey horizon and the brown metal. The rain still falls, it drips from her hair. It seems like nothing to her now. As natural as air.

'You knew, of course, I'd be here,' he says. 'All this has happened already or has at least been planned.'

Josephine says, 'I don't know what you're talking about.' But she thinks of that strange imitation of her mum, how the words seemed to come from something beyond, and she wonders, all the while keeping tight-lipped and staring straight ahead.

His voice is suddenly gentler. 'What is it you want?' he says. 'What are you tyring to escape from?'

Josephine drops to her knees. Mud and water squelch up from the ground, soaks through her jeans. The soles of her trainers are coming off. Her feet shiver.

'All I want is to be empty,' she says. 'To feel nothing like memory or pain. To have no one waiting for me. Is that bad?'

The Preacher moves towards her, his feet pushing against mud, the firm sticking sound softly audible beneath the wind's hard breaths. 'It is no sin, just a shame. You are ignoring your very bones, your very breath and blood,' he looks down and touches her cheek. His hand is wet. 'Your very soul.'

She looks up at him, towering like the monument, firm and strong. She feels weak and slippery, smaller than she ever had been before, emptier as well. But now it is an emptiness that sickens her.

'I'm sick of wanting to be nothing,' she says. 'But I don't know if I can forgive her. I mean, I'm still scared of her. What do I do? Tell me what I can do to fix things.'

The Preacher kneels. He takes her hands in his. Their watery lightness tickles her skin. She looks at him and he is smiling, shaking his head.

'I'm not sure any of us can do much fixing,' he says. 'But we can do living. Understanding. Trying. I think that's what forgiveness does.'

She takes his face in her hands. His skin is soft and wet, and as she holds it she feels wrinkles begin to form, roads of age carving their way across.

'What are you doing?' he says, his voice suddenly croaky and withering like some dying light.

She turns his face to the east. He sees the rising sun. She kisses his cheek gently. Blood pulses beneath old skin briefly. She sees a city of gamblers and adulterers burst into flames. Fat men in suits with cigars and grins and hands that seem to stretch far down. Her mother, hurting her, again and again. And between them, like gaps of light in a dark fence, she sees virtues. She sees a hand grabbing the falling. Then she is in darkness, and there are only the cool drops of the rain, which is softer now, and the mud slowly sinking beneath her weight.

THE FOURTH DAY

CHAPTER FIFTEEN

When she opens her eyes again, the rain has stopped, and the wind is whistling but weak. She pulls herself to her feet and looks at the sea. Other than the occasional white cap, the waves are soft, the tide receding. She looks east and sees the sun rising over the hills. Then she looks south and sees the town. The fires are gone. The screams silenced. Then she looks north and sees the stone and sand, and the absence of the whale. There is still the security tape, and two men in high-visibility jackets looking around, shaking their heads, likely mumbling something about impossibilities. The streets look empty again. A single car moves along the marina. A man in the marina inspects his boat. Josephine walks down the slope back to the main road, seeing cows grazing quietly. One moos her a greeting. Then she is on the main road, headed over Trefechan bridge. Rummers pub looks as it always has, devoid now of pirates, windows in place. A man in a tracksuit runs past her and nods.

'Been for a tumble have we?' he says.

She nods absently as he runs over the bridge. She wonders where everyone is, and then she wonders where Glynn is. She walks the streets. The first people of the morning emerge from their homes, blinking and unsure. As she approaches the seafront she sees sand and stones kicked up from the sea and is grateful. There was a storm, then, certainly. The pier stands short and modest. She looks towards Constitution Hill, sees the blue lights of an ambulance at the top of the hill, sees a helicopter and a stretcher. She shivers. She walks slowly along the promenade, going south now, not wanting to look at the destruction on the hill, hoping Glynn is alright, that she can make up for what she did, wondering what exactly she wants from him. And then he is there.

'I swear,' he says, laughing, his hands in his pockets, his hair shining from the gleaming remnants of the rain. 'I have seen absolutely everything tonight except you.'

She looks at him for a very long while, trying to take him in, all of him for the first time. She likes the way he smiles, how she can see the love swirl in his eyes. But she cannot see what he will be to her.

'I'm glad you finally have,' she says, and as she hears it she knows she means it. She places her hands on his shoulders, looks at the water dripping from his fringe, runs her fingers along his slick neck before locking them together. Then she embraces him, pulls him deep into her. He holds her, and they are very tight together like that for a while. She feels something, a kiss on her cheek. She looks at him.

'What made you do that?' she says.

Glynn shrugs. 'It felt right.'

They press their foreheads against one another. Josephine runs her hands down Glynn's back, rests them on his wrists.

'Do you want to walk?' she says. 'I feel like I could walk. Just a little more.'

He laughs. 'Haven't we done enough of that?'

'I just want to see what's left.'

Glynn nods. They turn away from the bridge. Walking along, the cars are parked and the windows unbroken. Outside the Castle Hotel a middle-aged lady sweeps up cigarette butts from the pavement, shaking her head and mumbling.

Glynn shouts over to her. 'Weird night last night, wasn't it?'

She looks up and squints, grimaces, shrugs. 'This storm gets in people's souls. Makes them do strange things,' she says. 'That's normal enough. But all that fighting. I've never seen anything like that.'

Glynn nods. 'Right.'

Josephine lets go of his hand and steps forward between two parked cars, so there is just the running of rainwater and the street between her and the woman.

'But what about the Preacher?' she says. 'What about all those pirates and soldiers and things? What do you think about those things?'

The woman shrugs. 'Strange folk about, for certain. Some sort of dress up thing got out of hand. Or gangs, perhaps.'

Josephine nods and steps back towards Glynn. She takes his hand, and they walk towards the horizon, a misted blue with lines of white crossing over it.

'Did nobody see anything?' she says. 'I mean, properly. Did nobody take anything in? Are we all just going to walk around like we weren't given some sort of searing vision?'

Glynn looks forward. The hut on the edge of the promenade stands steady, the shutters closed over it. In the summer it sells ice creams and drinks to the parched.

'You saw it, didn't you?' he says. 'I did, too. And we won't forget it, will we?'

They cross the road and the sea stares back at them, steel blue now, pushing forward with white-tipped waves, still strong, still looking to pull things back into the maelstrom, still dangerous, if dying, promising to return, even if going.

'What was it for?' says Josephine. 'What did it do?'

'I don't know,' says Glynn. 'What do you think?'

Josephine gulps. 'I don't think I've ever felt so small before.'

'Don't talk like that,' says Glynn, putting an arm around her.

'No,' says Josephine, wriggling free, taking his hand, looking at him. 'You don't understand. It's good. I'm so small. Everything I've ever known is bigger than me. It's all worth ogling at. Being astounded by. And I'm miniature. But I'm full. Full of things and thoughts and memories. And that's what I get to have.'

Glynn nods. For the first time, he feels behind Josephine, and it is with a little kick of shame that he realises part of his attraction towards her came from wanting to teach her things. But he finds he is no less pulled to her, as he thinks this he brings her into him so he can kiss her fully on the lips, savouring the way she kisses him back, how it affirms some feeling that neither of them quite knows the vocabulary of yet.

Upon the waves, four seagulls sit, squawking to each other, moving up and down, perhaps mourning their lost friends who could not quite get control of the wind. Glynn and Josephine watch them for a while. After a minute they take flight, flap their wings and skirt across the water towards the harbour light. On the other side, by the rocks, black as ink, a larger bird is still and watching.

'What is that?' says Josephine.

'A cormorant,' says Glynn. 'Scary things, you know. They could probably kill a person if they wanted to.'

Josephine elbows him in the ribs. 'You're making fun of me now.'

He chuckles. 'I'm not. They're huge. Big wing spans, sharp beaks, and they're clever too.'

The cormorant pauses its pecking, looks up at the sky. It turns its head towards Josephine and Glynn, looks at them a while, as if it is seeing something significant, something it recognises, something of note. Then it flaps its wings, shoots off back to the sea and its rough waters. The wings open, looking as if they could pick up the ice cream hut and carry it out to the unknown depths. It flies forwards, then left, then lands on the water. Making an arrow of itself, its beak the point, the wings closed now, it disappears beneath the water.

'Christ,' says Josephine.

'Yes,' says Glynn.

It emerges with a glimmer of silver in its beak.

'It's caught something,' says Josephine.

The bird turns and flaps again, disappearing into the morning mist. Josephine and Glynn carry on walking, now moving towards where the Ystwyth and the Rheidol pour into each other and the sea. As the rows of houses begin to fall away, they see dim pink in the east from where the sun rises behind clouds. A jogger goes by them as they reach the wooden jetty, nods to them as he charges along the pavement. They look at the rivers, all white with the force of currents.

'What happened yesterday morning?' says Glynn. 'I'm sorry. I know there's so much more that's happened since, all sorts of bizarreness, but you scared me.'

Josephine wraps her hand round his. 'I can't really explain it, not right now. Later, maybe. After some time.'

They pause where the rivers gush into the sea.

'It's to do with my mum,' she says. 'She died a year and a half ago. I don't know. She wasn't a good person, I guess. She used to hit me, and Dad. And when she got sick, I never ever felt bad about her going. But I did love her. And I miss her. But I also hate her, and I'm scared of her. And I guess I'm only starting to see it all as clearly as I should.'

Glynn nods slowly. Thinks about all the things he has not told her. 'Ok,' he says. 'That's ok. I mean, where are you at now, do you think, if you know?'

Josephine looks at the water. 'I'm a little better than yesterday. I think I need to go home. See my dad. I guess I've tried to not give him too much thought since I came here. I've not given anything too much thought to be honest. Not till I met you. I don't know quite what you did.'

Glynn laughs and looks up at the sky.

'I'm glad you did it though,' says Josephine, kissing his cheek.

*

Anna goes back to the house and packs a bag very quickly. She texts her mum and tells her that she is coming home, that she has broken up with Bill. Her mum, who met Bill once and found him not simply unsuitable but scary, will breathe a deep sigh of relief. She will tell Anna to come home, and when Anna arrives she will pull her into a deep embrace and say that as painful as these things may seem they are often the right decision. Anna will nod quietly. Later, the next day perhaps, over breakfast or on a walk, Anna's mum will ask Anna about Glynn, the odd, maybe a little overly eager, but undoubtedly good, nice boy. And this will really send Anna over the edge into tears, over scrambled eggs or while walking past a particularly impressive oak. She will fall again into her mum's arms and this time she will tell her mum everything, reveal she is heartbroken over a boy she had, over a boy she hurt, a boy who has moved on to better things. But Anna has a wise mum, one who will explain that these things are not fixed, that she is not doomed, that she can change and be better. She will refer to the incident as a learning experience.

But before that, and this detail is worth noting, Anna must get the train from Aberystwyth to Shrewsbury, which she does. She will sit in the front carriage, by the window, watching the landscape pass her by, thinking about all her pains, a rucksack at her feet. She thinks about where she is going to live, remembers that there is emergency accommodation available at the university. The possibility of new people makes her apprehensive, but her mum will put this right, too, will explain that new people is exactly what Anna needs, that she has fallen into what may be considered a bad crowd, and that these things have a habit of working themselves out. Anna will pull herself together, return in due course, complete her degree, move on to all the good things expected of marine biology graduates, spending plenty of time in the water alongside the wet and slippery things which she studies, hopefully far more time with them than she spends now, her academic interests having fallen by the wayside what with all the troubles of the last few months. We will have to wait and see. Well, not us. We do not have time.

*

The sun is a little higher in the sky by the time Jake walks by the tennis courts, but Bill is still there, sitting on the pavement, weeping into clenched fists.

'Hey,' he says. 'What's going on? What are you doing?'

Bill looks up, his eyes red and puffy like those spiky fish. 'Anna's left me.' As he says it a sob that feels like it is from his guts but sounds like his nose, emanates from his mouth up towards the sky.

Jake sits down and puts an arm on Bill's shirt. 'That's terrible, man,' he says. 'I thought she wouldn't go for another six months.'

Bill closes his eyes. His fists tighten so hard it feels as though they might collapse and crumble in upon themselves. Then he looks back up at Jake. 'What do you mean?' he says.

'You very obviously weren't right for each other. I'm sad for you, though'

Bill laughs. 'You weird fucking bastard.'

Jake laughs and pulls Bill in closer. Bill rests his head on Jake's shoulder and lets out a deep sigh of mourning.

'Where have you been,' says Bill. 'I've needed you these past few days. It's felt like a fever dream.'

Jake nods. 'I joined a religious uprising to turn Aberystwyth into a modern Eden. We were scuppered in our infancy. I was shot by a soldier from the First World War. Another bandaged my wound with a Snickers bar before dissolving into water.'

Bill laughs. 'You're full of shit.'

A little jingle squeaks through the fresh morning air. Jake pulls his phone out of his pocket. He holds it, intrigued, for a while, as it buzzes in his hand. Bill sees the name of a woman he does not know.

'Hello,' says Jake. 'Ok. I'll be back now. See you soon.' He puts down the phone.

'Who was that?' says Bill.

'Sarah. I helped her after she got hurt, she helped me after I got shot. Woke up in a hospital bed, she was right there, holding my hand.' Jake looks over his shoulders conspicuously. 'We even kissed.'

'That's big, buddy,' says Bill, and he means it. Jake does not, generally, kiss people.

'There's only one problem.' Jake does the look over each shoulder again. He waits.

'Sorry,' says Bill, realising Jake is waiting for him to ask. 'What's the problem?'

'She has a boyfriend.'

'Oh.'

'And they're mega Christian.'

'Wow.'

'Any advice?'

Bill holds out his hands as if to show the situation he has found himself in.

'Right, yes,' says Jake. 'Your heart is broken and you're re-evaluating the whole way you've chosen to live your life.'

'Yes, Jake,' says Bill. 'That's right.'

'I can stay here, if you want.'

'It's ok,' says Bill. Then, more awkwardly, 'Go get her, Tiger.'

Jake stands up. 'That does not suit you,' he says. Then, he walks away.

*

After saying goodbye to Glynn, Josephine heads back to her flat and packs a suitcase. Vic and Robbie are nowhere to be seen. Josephine leaves a note on the table for Vic, thanking her, promising to return soon, promising to be a better friend. She tells Vic she was right about everything, that she might even be some kind of angel, and that she means that in the most literal sense possible.

At quarter past ten she is smoking a cigarette outside the train station, watching old men slump into the just-opened Wetherspoons next to it. She is realising she has never really liked cigarettes, but that quitting them does not need to be part of whatever spiritual revelation she is having in this moment. There are two others waiting for the train, also students, also with big suitcases, but not for her to talk to, not today. Each steals a few glances at the others, knowing they all share some sort of strangeness that none of them have quite worked out the vocabulary for yet. A seagull sits on the tracks, screeching, the broken wings of one of its slain friends a few yards in front of it. As the train sounds its horn and comes in, the seagull takes flight.

Josephine steps onto the train and finds one of the four-seaters to sit in. The train moves as a soft rain begins to fall, the last spit of the storm. She watches the blurred colours, enjoys the green hills in the grey. The pale sun breaks between a hill and some cloud, shines yellow light down, lighting the water. As the train reaches Borth, Josephine looks around the town, all quiet and strange. She sees a rainbow over the bog. She had no idea there could be such colour in such places. Perhaps anywhere. She looks at the rainbow as the train sits, as a man loads his bicycle onto her carriage, and she drinks in the full spectrum of colours, thinks about all the strange mixes sitting beneath it. She looks at the bog, remembers the Heaney poem they did in a seminar a few weeks ago. What might be beneath all that mud and water. Bodies. Things salting. Things waiting. She has seen the dead come back once. It could happen again.

The train moves forward. She lies back, pulls out her phone, texts her Dad. 'I'm coming home, and I love you.' The rest can be worked out and spoken about. Talking, lots of it. That is the cure, she realises. You just must keep thinking and doing the things that emerge from the thinking. Otherwise, things judder to a halt, like a faltering train.

As Josephine goes inland, we must be pulled back. Like a wave we have come in, and like a wave the tide needs us always elsewhere. So, surrender to the backwash, leaving your salty remnants upon what you touched, spitting out those things inside of you that could not cling on anymore. And now we sit out in the middle of the darkened sea, deep down with the void, a story waiting to begin again, a wind waiting for whatever directs it to blow in whatever direction it is going to blow. And a great whale, with a small boy inside, both desperately pushing to come home.

ACKNOWLEDGEMENTS

Let me begin by thanking Dad, Mum, Chris and Sam: I can't express how much you have given me. Thank you also to every member of the Hubbard, Maidment, Wells and Williams families. This novel exists because I was awarded a scholarship to undertake a PhD in Creative Writing at Aberystwyth University. But it also would not have been possible without the support and kindness of some incredible colleagues. Thank you to Neal Alexander and Ann Matthews, my supervisors, as well as Naji Bakhti, Renato Sabbagh Bahia, Gavin Goodwin, Jamie Harris, Matthew Jarvis, Richard Margraff-Turley, Louise Marshall and Malte Urban.

I was lucky to join an extraordinary PhD cohort, including several writers I already admired. These people became wise consorts and excellent friends. They include Emma Butler-Way, Sophie Davies, Jennifer Dos Reis Dos Santos, Eluned Gramich, Amy Grandvoinet, Ed Garland, Sarah Reynolds, Sophie Squire and Joseph Thurgate.

This novel also would not have been possible without a number of resources: The Hugh Owen Library, the National Library of Wales, the Ceredigion Museum, the British Film Institute, *Born on a Perilous Rock* by W.J. Lewis, and the enigmatic *rdb notes* blog are some among many.

The character of Josephine was conceived in 2015, when my university flatmate, Frances-Mair Wells told me about the strangely isolating experience of working at the infamous Aberystwyth nightclub, Yoko's.

During my undergraduate degree, I made friends whose support and love has been invaluable: Heather Coombs, Vic and Emily Grant-Hill, Alex Grant, Jo Hooke, and Fraya Grattan.

During those years, I also became friends with two people who were probably my first two genuine creative colleagues, Rylan

Shafer and Joshua Nagle. Fellas, we have shared beers, cars, beds, books and ideas for almost a decade, now. I would not be a third of the writer I am without you.

Thank you to UCL's English department, particularly Philip Horne, Julia Jordan, Matthew Sperling and Xine Yao. Thank you, also, to my fellow students, particularly Declan Houten, Clara Irvine, Joseph Rodgers, and the members of the White Tiger Salon.

Returning to Aberystwyth for my PhD was one of the best decisions I ever made. Here, a number of friends supported this strange little book. These include Casper Drake, Chris Grattan, Cara Hannon, Molly Haywood, and anyone who read chapter nine and thought *I recognise* that place…

Thank you to anyone who read my work with attention and care. In particular, Dan Rhys Jones, Ivy Napp, Sarah Fletcher, Sam Quill and Sairah Ahsan. To T.R. Richmond, thank you for always believing in me, and for all your advice over the years. To Gareth James, thank you for showing faith, patience and grace, and some choice edits.

Thank you to the wonderful people at Seren Books, who've taken a leap of faith and made a dream come true in the process. And, finally, thank you to my editor, Martha O'Brien, whose friendship and forthrightness is always appreciated, both professionally and personally.

There are plenty of unseen heroes that help make any book. I've tried to mention as many of *Storm*'s as possible.

ABOUT THE AUTHOR

Alex Hubbard is a writer from London, living in Wales. He first came to Aberystwyth in 2015 and, like so many, fell in love with it. As a child, he was diagnosed with dyspraxia and struggled to learn to read. Once he worked it out, he quickly became passionate about stories, words and thinking about things which aren't real. Now, he is interested in how fiction can augment our shared senses of place and experience. If you also like the taste of evening air and the feeling that something unbelievable could happen, you might like his work. His creative work has appeared in *Nawr, Cerasus, The Forge, Abergavenny Small Press Literary Journal, Prole, Bandit Fiction*, and in the two anthologies by Think.Material Press, among others. He is currently writing a novel about rising sea levels and lost places.